Federation

Federation Trilogy Book Two

Tony Harmsworth

I dedicate this trilogy to Frank Hampson, whose artwork and storylines in the Eagle, inspired my lifelong interest in science fiction

Get Tony Harmsworth's Moonscape Novella FOR FREE

Sign up for the no-spam newsletter and get Moonscape and other exclusive content, all for free.

Details can be found at the end of FEDERATION & EARTH.

Copyrights and Thanks

Thanks to:
Mark Dawson, Wendy Harmsworth, and Melanie Underwood

Also, thanks to these VIP Beta Reader Club Members: Anne Marie Graham, Connie Moon, Mike Ramay, Nev Rawlins, Kevin Simington, Graham Temple

All rights reserved; no part of this publication may be reproduced or transmitted by any means, electronic, mechanical, photocopying or otherwise without the prior written permission of the author.

ISBN: 9781702747929

© A G Harmsworth 2019

Cover by Margaret Rainey

A G Harmsworth has asserted his moral rights.

Published by:
Harmsworth.net
Drumnadrochit
Inverness-shire
IV63 6XJ

1 Refresher

[Note for non-British readers – Tony writes using UK English spelling, punctuation, and grammar.]
[A word of caution or warning or whatever you wish to call it, from the author: – A small proportion of readers wrote critical reviews of the first book because, in their opinion, it criticised America and promoted communism or extreme socialism.
*[I suppose most of them will not read this second book in the trilogy, but I would like to remind readers that this is a **story**, a work of speculative science fiction.*
*[That an empire somewhere in the galaxy is able to make communism work, prevent all wars and rid their worlds of poverty and disease, does **not** mean that I would advocate it for use by humans in any country in the 21st Century.*
[I reiterate, the Federation Trilogy is a work of speculative science fiction, not a promotion of any particular political system. Enjoy it for what it is – a view into one possible future. Tony Harmsworth.]

*[There is a glossary at the back of the book or you can access it online here: **https://harmsworth.net/glossary.pdf**]*

Author Rummy Blin Breganin, a citizen of Daragnen, wrote his Federation Trilogy when he discovered that the Earth had been prohibited from all space flight and use of quantum technology, the key to interstellar travel.

His first book, written long after the events described in this second book, follows the story of Earth's first contact with the Federation.

Initially things seem to go well, but the Federation's economic system conflicted with that of Western Europe, the United States of America and many other countries. Its similarity to communism immediately caused suspicion and distrust.

The leaders of more than twenty countries were each taken to visit five Federation worlds, including one new member world and the capital of the Federation, Arlucian.

Gradually, President Spence of the USA began to be won over by all of the benefits of membership, but he realised that the Federation's economic system was going to be a hard sell to the wealthy minority who held much of the power in western democracies. They would have to forego their wealth in order to allow the general population to benefit.

The Federation began to make sense to him.

Its economic system relies upon automatons. Over several hundred thousand years, the manufacture of robots has been perfected. They can do anything and everything people could ever be asked to do. On Earth in the twenty-first century, we consider that a robot which can pick strawberries is the height of sophistication, but utility robots in the Federation can handle any task. Most are not designed to perform one function well, but to use their AI minds to work out how to do virtually anything. If a robot were asked to peel a grape, it would do so perfectly and then go on to prepare a seven-course gourmet meal or strip an engine and perform a complete mechanical rebuild.

Those same utility robots can also handle many other jobs from caring for paraplegics, handling all of their hygiene and other needs, to fetching and carrying in homes or industrial workplaces. A domestic robot could be asked to go and do the shopping. It would find out what was needed by examining the contents of the refrigerator, the store cupboards and freezer. Before it left it would even ask if anything special or unusual was required. Saying, 'Yes, get everything for a barbecue for eight people this Sunday, too,' would not result in a further string of questions. The robot would then get into the autonomous vehicle and go shopping.

Of course, some robots have more specialised functions. Medibots diagnose and treat all manner of medical problems and some are even more specialised to conduct surgery, from repairing cataracts to stenting blood vessels.

In an industrial or farming setting, robots would carry out all duties ever handled by people, from planting to dealing with cattle insemination programmes. If they ran into problems, they would ask for help – no, not from a person, but an overseer bot or monitoring system. During visits to worlds by leaders during the last book, some bots told the leaders they had not had contact with a living being in hundreds of years of manufacturing.

The upshot of the expertise of robots and other AI systems is that people no longer have anything to do. Profit from all the state-owned businesses goes into a pool and is distributed equally so that everyone shares in the wealth of nearly a quarter of a million worlds.

However, if people want to work they can do so and all are encouraged to work about ten per cent of their time. Inventors suddenly have the time to come up with new ideas and innovations and can get access to the equipment and machine shops or laboratories they might need. This means that, instead of having to develop it themselves, including all of the hassle of raising finance and running the business, they can hand over the idea to robots. They produce the items, keeping in production the successful products. They also keep stocks of more niche items which would never be profitable, but add to the life satisfaction of people. Inventors also receive small bonuses as reward for their ideas but it is never excessive, perhaps the value of another off-world holiday that year.

The system was of course seen by some as communism, a reviled system which reared its head on twentieth century Earth. It was so despised that many people were unable to get their heads around the fact that, in a world where the work was all done by automatons, it could actually work. In fact it was the obvious solution to the capitalist system which exploited people, often in other countries, to make others into billionaires. This saw wealthy countries ignoring poverty, starvation and disease in poorer countries; and consuming resources to the serious detriment of the general population and the environment.

In the Federation, the system resulted in everyone having a great standard of living, all receiving the same level of medical attention, living anywhere they wished on-world or off-world somewhere else in the galaxy. Poverty is non-existent in the Federation, but so is obscene wealth. Whether it be a person in a rural setting on Veroscando or the Federation president itself (a sexless budding creature), the income was the same. Volunteers could participate in the Federation rapid-reaction force to deal with natural disasters and unexpected outbreaks of disease, or they could volunteer as carers or write books, produce films and develop the arts. Anyone could do anything they wished to do which did not hurt others or their planets.

Eventually, President Spence achieved some progress with politicians and industrialists, but then there was an unexpected power grab by Vice President Slimbridge who had the president arrested for treason, claiming that he was about to hand over control of the United States to communist aliens.

The president suddenly found himself in prison, but the FBI soon realised that the charges were trumped up and helped him break out with the house minority and majority leaders, the main democratic candidate for president and several of the captains of industry who had been with the president at the time of the arrest and arrested as co-conspirators.

From the outskirts of Washington, they escaped in a Chinook helicopter to New York where they were going to claim diplomatic asylum in the UN complex. However, Vice President Slimbridge, with all the resources of the military, pursued them and had the helicopter shot down as it reached the UN building.

The UN had called a meeting to approve an application for Federation membership and Slimbridge intended to veto the vote. Unknown to him, President Spence and the other Chinook passengers had been rescued by the Federation from the helicopter an instant before it exploded. UN troops arrested Slimbridge under a warrant from the International Court of Justice in the Hague when he arrived for the debate.

Then, with Spence back in charge, the meeting was rearranged, and all the leaders of the world met at the UN HQ. In the meantime, the US military sprung Slimbridge and plotted against Spence.

On the day of the vote, Slimbridge had a small nuclear bomb exploded under the UN building killing all of the world leaders and the entire Federation diplomatic team. Virtually all of New York was destroyed in the explosion.

A new Federation ambassador was appointed and, after discussing the situation with the Federation Cabinet, it was decided to visit the UK prime minister. That chapter is included below and will bring you up to date.

2 Federation Deliberations

[Taken from a copy of Cabinet minutes, conditionally released early to me (Rummy Blin Breganin) by the Federation Cabinet Secretary when I told him it was research for my books. They are normally kept secret for fifty years. Because the following is taken from minutes, it is a considerable block of dialogue. I have removed almost all names and job titles to simplify it. RBB]

'We have to give Ambassador Trestogeen a concept policy,' said President Dimorathron to the fifteen members of the inner cabinet.

'These barbarians have killed an entire diplomatic team. Surely it's unprecedented?' said one of the group.

'Well… there was the case of Garrstend,' said another.

'That's delving deep into history,' said the president. 'That was more than two hundred years ago.'

'Did it get resolved?' asked another.

'Yes. They reapplied and complied the second time and there was no violence. At least, not like this,' said yet another.

'The group who carried out these murders must be punished.'

'How can we punish them without punishing their whole world?'

'Ha. They killed millions of their own kind to take this action. Surely something is wrong with the entire species!'

'The punishment must not physically hurt the people.'

'How can we do that? Not being members of the Federation will hurt almost everyone. There were thousands dying of starvation in a place called Sudan before this occurred. It won't get any better now.'

'Well, we can't continue membership discussions with such creatures.'

'Okay, colleagues, we are going to have to provide a punishment which their whole population will realise was caused by the rebels' violence,' said the president.

There were several calls of 'Agreed.'

'I'd still like to get some emergency aid into the famine regions,' said one.

'We can't put our own people in danger!' replied another.

'Right. How about we shut them off for a while? Isolate them?' asked the president.

'The way we did over Operiom?' asked another.

'Oh, yes. The plague planet,' said yet another.

'Well, yes,' said the president, 'but in that case we had teams of medics assisting them. It was more of an unfortunate quarantine.'

'Something along those lines.'

'Trouble is that the people who did this actually want isolation, so we're rewarding their actions.'

'That's a good point, but we have no choice really.'

'Let's ensure there is a way back for them – a way for them to contact us and start over.'

'Yes, that'll do it for me.'

'Okay. Isolation with a route to future membership?' asked the president.

'Yes, and leave a few spybots on the planet to keep an eye on changes within their political systems,' said the Cabinet Secretary.

'I'll inform Ambassador Trestogeen,' said the president.

'Is there no way we can drop emergency aid in the famine areas, Ye President?'

'I'll ask Ambassador Trestogeen to look into it. It should be possible to send in supplies on a drop and leave basis,' said the president.

«‹«O»›»

[Taken from Ambassador Trestogeen's files. RBB]

'Commander Wukkundi, you will be responsible for carrying out the plan. Is everything clear?'

'Yes, Ambassador, my FEU team can carry it out within a day or so, once you give the command. We'll also organise some freighters for provisions drops in the famine areas.'

'Okay. Do it.'

«‹«O»›»

[Taken from official FEU files and body-worn cameras. RBB]

Commander Ya Dustul Wukkundi, looked resplendent in her FEU uniform, her eight feelers each protruding from braided sleeves. She stood in front of her force of twenty-four volunteer operatives. The briefing had been long and detailed. Some of the Federation's largest freighters were already en route from Ecisfiip, fully loaded with provisions. Finally, the squad was ready to take action.

The stealth rapid-reaction vessel, Hidome, left the Ronoi's vicinity once the ambassador had come on board to monitor the Isolation Policy of the Federation. The Ronoi had been Ambassador Moroforon's flagship.

The Hidome changed orbit and was soon sitting alongside the International Space Station.

'Human Space Station, please respond,' said the commander.

The space station sat silently for several minutes, navigation and interior lights giving the only sign of its habitation.

'Ian Watson here, ISS commander. How can I help?' was the message which came through after twelve long minutes.

'They'll have been asking NASA what to do,' said the ambassador to the commander.

'Yol Watson, I am Commander Wukkundi of the Federation Enforcement Unit on board the Hidome. You are aware of the recent murders of our diplomatic team?'

'We are, but had no hand in it. We are a peaceful research facility only.'

'Nevertheless, my orders are to remove your space station from orbit. How long will it take for your crew to leave?'

There was a break of almost ten minutes.

'Yol Watson, please respond.'

The silence continued for another three minutes. 'Commander Wukkundi, the ISS is a non-partisan, international scientific research facility. It plays no part in the defence of the planet and has no political leaning,' said Ian Watson.

'How long will it take for you to leave the space station? Our orders are not subject to appeal.'

'To do so in an orderly manner would take about a week. An emergency evacuation would take a day,' said Ian Watson.

'You have forty-eight hours commencing now,' said the commander.

The Hidome dropped into a lower orbit and began destroying satellites. Detection beams located working and derelict equipment in orbit around the Earth.

What was called an "aconstik net" was released. It comprised an electronic network which held its shape as it moved through its retrograde orbit. Everything it encountered was slowed down enough to force it to drop out of orbit. The process would be complete and orbits of up to two hundred and forty miles cleared of satellites and old space junk within ninety minutes. The population was about to be treated to a stunning show of shooting stars.

Once that was complete, the Hidome raised its orbit to a geosynchronous location where a second net was deployed to destroy all satellites from three hundred miles to thirty thousand miles in altitude.

From that point, the commander began search and destroy tactics to locate larger satellites like the Hubble, Kepler, Tess, and others. By the time the Hidome returned to the ISS, all Earth and moon orbital satellites were destroyed, larger ones being flung sunwards for eventual burn up.

'ISS. Please confirm you have evacuated the space station,' said the commander.

There was no answer.

'Lieutenant, check the space station for signs of life,' said the commander.

'Yes, sir,' said the lieutenant, saluting and leaving the bridge.

A few minutes later he returned and advised that the only life signs were a container of bees.

'Bring the bee container aboard, check they are safely contained. Tell me when that's done.'

More waiting.

'Bee container on board, sir.'

'Captain, calculate the vector needed to have the ISS fall into an isolated section of ocean.'

'Done, sir.'

'Push it into that trajectory.'

'Done, sir.'

All of a sudden, the radio came to life, 'Attention Commander Wukkundi of the Hidome. This is Prime Minister Church of Great Britain. What are you doing? Our weather, communications and global positioning satellites are no longer responding.'

'Ambassador?' said the commander.

'Prime Minister Church, Ambassador Trestogeen here,' said the ambassador. 'All will become clear shortly.'

'We want to make it known that it was a small group of violent Federation-sceptic politicians and military men who caused the explosion. Most of the people of Earth were absolutely horrified,' said the prime minister.

'I will contact you in due course. Over and out,' said the ambassador.

From the bridge of the Hidome, they watched the International Space Station tumbling gracefully as it dropped out of orbit to meet its destiny in the Antarctic Ocean where any remnants which didn't burn up would be unlikely to encounter any shipping.

'Take us to Moonbase, captain,' said the commander.

The Hidome swung away from Earth and headed towards the pale disc in the distance. In a few hours it began procedures to hover above the human outpost.

'How many lifeforms, captain?' asked the commander.

'Ten humans and twelve chickens.'

'Beam the humans to reception room two and the chickens to the hold. Lieutenant, ensure the chickens are properly caged,' said the commander. 'Captain, as soon as they're aboard, explode a stamp bomb over Moonbase and destroy all other transmitting equipment on the surface. Once that's done, return us to Earth orbit.'

[A stamp bomb flattens anything underneath it. RBB]

«««0»»»

[Taken from Ambassador Trestogeen's office files and video. RBB]

The Hidome took up a position in orbit directly above London and the ambassador made a call to the British prime minister.

'Glad to hear from you, Ambassador Trestogeen. Can we talk about this situation?'

'We have some property to return to you and also wish to explain our position,' said the ambassador.

'Would you like me to call other heads of state to meet with you? There is also a new secretary general of the United Nations.'

'No. I will speak with you on the ground. Be sure there is someone to record the event. You will be expected to distribute the recording.'

'Are you intending to harm us? We know you have been destroying satellites and the ISS. Also, communication has been lost with Moonbase. The astronauts are not involved in the politics which caused this situation. We all feel dreadful about the explosion and will do all we can to put things right.'

'I will arrive in Horse Guards Parade at fifteen hours GMT. Be sure to have the area cleared. Thank you. Out!' the ambassador said.

«««O»»»

[Taken from Ambassador Trestogeen's office files and BBC video archives. RBB]

A grey mantle of cloud was releasing its relentless cargo of rain in bursts, varying between a light drizzle and a torrential downpour. Although well drained, Horse Guards Parade was accumulating a thin lake of water such that, during the heavier falls, the water bounced many inches back into the air as if trying to avoid potential disaster.

The prime minister stood with a heavily armed military squad. She and Britain's UN representative were protected by large umbrellas as the unrelenting rain did its best to drench them. Nearby, a BBC film crew was also cowering under a number of multicoloured parasols, more in keeping with the seaside in summer than a sombre political encounter taking place before the English winter had completed its miserable cycle. It was as if all the world's tears were falling in one cascade to grieve over the UN atrocity.

The rapid-reaction ship decloaked about two hundred metres above and descended at elevator speed to a location ten metres in front of the prime minister. Suddenly, no rain fell within thirty metres of the ship. A doorway opened.

The ambassador descended the floating stairway from ship to ground level, his fishlike appearance almost complementing the wetness of the day. Behind him were several armed FEU soldiers and Commander Wukkundi. They lined up opposite the prime minister's party as if to begin a macabre game of chess.

The atmosphere crackled for a moment and, to the left of the ambassador's party, a gust of wind materialised as a cargo of ten astronauts displaced the damp air which had been occupying the space. They looked around in surprise at their unexpected arrival back on Earth. One staggered at the unexpected increase in gravity. Almost simultaneously, a small compound of chickens filled the space to the ambassador's right and beside it appeared a table bearing something resembling an aquarium containing bees. Another table materialised beside the ambassador. It held a machine with monitor and keyboard.

The ambassador moved forward to the prime minister and one of his finlike limbs was offered to be shaken. Maureen Church looked at it, as if unsure what to do, then she took it and shook it gently. The ambassador bowed and moved back about a metre.

'I am Ambassador Yol Hareen Trestogeen. Behind me is Commander Wukkundi of the Federation Enforcement Unit.'

'I am pleased to meet you. I am Prime Minister Maureen Church. This is our UN envoy, Caroline Stoddart.'

'I have returned your astronauts from your moon, plus their chickens and a collection of bees which were left behind on the International Space Station. All life is precious to us, even that of the simple bee.'

'What can we do to put things right?' asked the prime minister, 'What compensation can we offer for the dreadful UN tragedy.'

'Prime Minister Church, do you know some wondrous technique whereby we can bring Slindo Merofort back to life and return him to his grieving wives and children, or Lyl Lindron to the person she was to marry in four weeks' time, or our Ambassador Moroforon who was on only her second assignment for the Federation? Her husband and family are distraught, as are the families of the crew who died. The community of Cluebians of whom Heldy Mistorn was a key member cannot come to terms with her loss. Perhaps you can advise me what words I should use to comfort the family of Councillor Churmbin who died with her unborn child and had been providing her time to the people of Earth for no reward other than the satisfaction of helping a neighbouring species find its way within the galactic community?'

'We are so sorry, Ambassador Trestogeen,' said the prime minister.

'Humankind seems to be proficient in offering apologies, but not really understanding the depth to which their actions have stooped. The group who took this action demonstrated very clearly what they felt about the lives of people, Earthly or Federation. Millions of your own people were killed and an area of the world was made uninhabitable for decades. We have been monitoring a radioactive cloud spreading eastwards and we can see US government forces assisting with the evacuation of even more millions of innocent people from their homes. No doubt they will say something like, "Sorry, but it was necessary!" to those who will live poorer lives because of their actions.

'Well, Prime Minister, sorry is totally inadequate, I'm afraid. The Federation president and his cabinet have decreed a punishment, the details of which I am here to provide to you.'

The ambassador handed over a document to the prime minister.

'This is a prohibition notice served upon your world for the murder of a Federation diplomatic team,' said the ambassador.

He opened his own copy and began to read:

FEDERATION PROHIBITION NOTICE

Owing to the actions of a rebel group on Earth in the Orion spur, which caused the murder of an entire Federation diplomatic team plus several million human beings, the president of the Federation and Cabinet have decreed the following action:

The planet, known as Earth, has demonstrated its unsuitability to enter the community of worlds which live in peace in this part of the galaxy. Isolation from space is the punishment.

1. All space exploration by Earth is prohibited.

2. All existing satellites and other space craft have been or will be destroyed by the Federation Enforcement Unit.

3. It is illegal for Federation citizens to land on Earth.

4. It is illegal for Federation citizens to contact Earth.

5. Any use of QE transmitters is prohibited, and such transmitters will be destroyed when detected.

There is one exception to item 5. A special QE transmitter is provided. It is set to a single frequency which can only contact Federation Members' Administration on Arlucian.

By Order of the Federation Cabinet 34/2/745816

Cabinet Secretary.

The ambassador closed the document.

'There are of course many pages of small print, but to summarise – your space-faring days are over. When you are ready to apply for membership in the future, you can contact us on the QE transmitter. Do not contact us unless you intend to join, all nations have agreed, and you have a single leader.

'Prime Minister, we're sorry – there's that word again – for all the human lives which will be shortened or be less pleasant than they would have been if membership had been completed. Your initial suspicions about us, particularly by the late President Spence are, in part, a cause. We should have deployed spybots to ensure action by the likes of this Slimbridge could have been detected and prevented, but Ambassador Moroforon decided that if you'd become aware of them, there could have been a paranoid adverse reaction. That was a regrettable and fatal mistake.'

'Ambassador,' said the prime minister, 'is there no other way of dealing with this. The heads of state at the UN were about to vote hugely in favour of joining. For that to be stopped by these evil individuals seems to be an overreaction. The wrong people are being punished. In fact, you are rewarding them. They are getting what they wanted. Isolation.'

'I will pass that comment on, but the situation in the United States of America today has not changed,' said the ambassador. 'Slimbridge is still in control and has crushed all opposition, even shutting down the media. Why have you not dealt with this? He and his ilk are those who are causing this prohibition, yet you allow them to continue to hold power, over a week after the event.'

'We are unable to take action, Yol Trestogeen,' said the prime minister. 'America has cut itself off from the rest of the world. They have threatened massive nuclear retaliation if they are attacked. There are enough nuclear missiles on all sides for the world to be destroyed.'

'There, in a nutshell, is Earth's problem,' said the ambassador. 'You must put your own house in order. Prove it by living peacefully, ridding your planet of weapons and using the funding saved to deal with famine and inequality. It should only take a decade and you can then reapply.'

'I don't know if we are capable of doing that without thermonuclear war overtaking us. Please don't abandon us in this way,' said the prime minister.

'I am but the messenger. Put your house in order. It is in your hands. Please advise the famine areas of your planet that some robot freighters will be delivering Federation aid over the coming days. Goodbye,' the ambassador said. He turned and entered the ship followed by the FEU squad and the door closed.

A few seconds later it lifted into the air, reached about one hundred metres and vanished.

The human party, with its puzzled astronauts and clucking hens, were, once again, standing in the rain. The prime minister and UN envoy dismissed the guard, refused any further press interviews, and entered the rear door of Number Ten, wearing expressions of devastation.

«««0»»»

[Taken from secret White House tapes, a practice reintroduced during the Trump regime. RBB]

In the Oval Office, the sound of jeers and chanting penetrated the usually adequate soundproofing. President John Slimbridge sat with General Braun, who had promised the protests would end.

'Any minute, sir,' said the general.

Both men rose from their seats and opened the door to the rose garden causing the crowd noises to grow in volume. General Braun looked at his watch.

Suddenly, volleys of shots rang out over the White House and the chanting turned into screaming. Within minutes the sound from the crowd was fading into the distance. A few more shots and peace reigned again at the White House.

'Thank you, General,' said the president, and the two men returned to the chesterfield to continue their discussions.

3 A Word From Me, Rummy Blin Breganin

The foregoing brings you up to date, but to really understand the overall story you need to read Federation. If you haven't done so, why not read it now… you'll be glad you did.

[You'll see various notes left by me throughout the trilogy. They are always in blue italics, but they may appear grey in some e-readers and paperbacks. This paragraph is an example.]

A little about me: My full name is Rummy Blin Breganin. I'm a male Daragnen and was born in 745,783 in the city of Glas.

I was schooled in Glas to age fourteen when I was invited to Dinbelay University. I left Dinbelay in 745,804 with multiple qualifications and five published works to my name.

My interest in the events which led to Earth's notorious attempt to join the Federation began after a visit to the Orion spur of the galaxy.

Now aged thirty-nine, some say my work is of galactic importance, particularly this recently updated account of Earth's interaction with the Federation. My three-volume work will provide you with a fascinating insight into a species which exhibits an extremely high level of intelligence yet failed to meet the Federation's membership criteria.

In addition to studying, writing, and historical research, I also enjoy shossball, boarding, sailing, and dimplert.

Today, I live in Dinbelay, where I'm a professor of modern history at the university. I have a wife and two teenage children.

Now, let me invite you into the chaotic world of planet Earth after the destruction of New York and the isolation of the United States of America. I will not apologise for the fragmented nature of my story. It is par for the course with such a multi-stranded tale.

The United States has decided to isolate itself. Other countries are left in the position whereby if they wish to continue to explore membership, they will have to resolve their relationship with the USA, which has made it very clear that any military invasion would be met by a massive nuclear retaliation.

May I remind you that although most of the trilogy is based on fact, diary entries, minutes and notes do not give a feel for actual situations. Copying out chunks of dry minutes or diary entries would not make interesting reading either so I have dramatised this version of my books to bring the story to life. If you want the dry, factual material, I have posted it on the Frame in Arlucian for academic reference.

RBB 36th Dorath 745822

4 London

[Taken from Mrs Church's diary. RBB]

'I can't believe they've just abandoned us,' said Lara Horvat, the new secretary general of the United Nations, as she sat at the long, polished, leather-inlaid table in the cabinet briefing room in Number Ten Downing Street.

'They're punishing the majority, when it was the tiny minority, who wanted to be isolated, who should be punished. Instead they are being rewarded for their evil deeds,' agreed the new British United Nations delegate, Caroline Stoddart. 'They'll be delighted that the Federation has severed diplomatic ties.'

'We are where we are,' said Prime Minister Church. 'Let's move on.'

'What is the situation over the building?' asked Lara.

'Our plan is to relocate all of the prisoners currently in both Swaleside and Elmley prisons. As soon as that is completed, the prisons will be demolished and construction can begin,' said the prime minister.

'What's the timescale for building work commencing?' asked Lara.

'About six weeks,' said the prime minister. 'The architects are modelling it on the original New York building. There are improvements, I believe, including more lifts and better fire and evacuation options. The A2500 road will be upgraded to dual carriageway through to the Sheppey crossing and both underground and overground rail links will be provided, terminating at a station within the UN complex itself. The rail links will connect with London, Gatwick Airport and Ashford, to tie in with Eurostar. It's a big project.'

'With improved communications, the Isle of Sheppey is perfect. I understand that we could be in the building by the middle of next year if there are no complications. I must say that it seems optimistic though.' said Lara.

'Yes, I'd be tempted to add at least six months to that, but they have promised to work night and day to finish it as soon as possible. The local population isn't enamoured with having such a huge building nearby, but there will be jobs at the UN and at the hotels which will inevitably be built to satisfy delegate accommodation. That should mitigate some of the ill will,' said the prime minister.

'Only the current area occupied by the prisons will become neutral territory, though,' said Caroline.

'That's fine,' said Lara. 'We're grateful that you are prepared to sign over part of your country to us.'

'Well, it is no big loss in the long term as we know Federation membership will come sooner or later and their outlook on property and national boundaries will take effect,' said Prime Minister Church.

'Ah, here's Malcolm,' said Maureen Church as the defence minister walked into the cabinet room.

'Sorry to be late,' said Malcolm Gorman. 'I was just getting the latest intelligence briefing from our man in Washington.'

'Any change?' asked Lara.

'Not really. Our man says that the White House shootings had an enormous effect. The military opened up with live ammunition and shot more than three hundred protesters. The rest ran off.'

'Three hundred!' said Caroline.

'Yes, although we cannot be certain. We're having to rely on unverifiable sources.'

'And they were doing no more than peacefully protesting,' said Lara.

'Our man says that he heard there were a few smaller protests elsewhere, but they broke up as soon as the military approached.'

'Once bitten…' said Caroline.

'So, it's as good as martial law,' said the prime minister. 'What's the media doing?'

'Slimbridge intends to run the country as a dictatorship,' said Lara.

'And our man says there are rumours that Congress is being "temporarily" shut down. The media is being kept muzzled and there was no reporting of the protesters being shot,' said Malcolm. 'We're still pumping media into the US and the large Internet companies are continually putting in workarounds. We don't know how long that will last, but Peter Stone, the search engine chief who was on President

Spence's membership team, is working out of Canada at the moment and spoiling every attempt to throttle the Internet.'

'They are trying to cut off the Internet? Can't they just cut the points of entry?' asked Caroline.

'Oh yes, they are certainly trying. It's not as easy as cutting the entry points though,' said Malcolm. 'The way we understand it, Stone is getting data into the country through ordinary telephone lines and he has some of his IT centres redistributing from there. Slimbridge can't really cut off the news coming in without pulling the plug on all telecommunications. Even then, someone with Stone's ingenuity would likely find a work-around.'

'It's difficult to see what we can do to help,' said the prime minister. 'It is fairly clear that any aggression towards Slimbridge could result in nuclear war. He's proven his ruthlessness by the use of the bomb in New York.'

'He's blaming it on anti-Federation terrorists and is claiming that he was still in jail when the New York explosion took place. It's a lie though. We can definitely place him in the White House an hour beforehand,' said Malcolm.

'What is frustrating is that we know that the Federation could put a stop to Slimbridge,' said Lara. 'They could scoop him out of the White House and let us deal with him, but they are expecting us to take that action somehow.'

'Presidents Yang of China and Olov of Russia fly in tomorrow and we'll see if there is any way we can progress things,' said Maureen Church.

'No President Ramseur?' asked Caroline.

'The French president is already here. We're having dinner tonight,' said the prime minister.

'I must get on with the agenda,' said Lara. 'It is kind of you to let us hold it in Downing Street.'

'Think nothing of it, Lara. Least we could do.'

'Is that the QE transmitter?' asked the secretary general, looking at the alien monitor and keyboard in the far corner of the cabinet briefing room.

'Yes,' said the defence secretary. 'You know, I wonder if we could call for help if the three presidents agree tomorrow. Maybe the Federation would do something if they knew how difficult our situation was.'

Lara walked over to the machine. It resembled a seventies' electric typewriter – bulky and heavy with a cast metal case. The qwerty keyboard was pretty standard, but there were twenty function keys on a raised section just to the right of the main keyboard. On the top, at the back, an eighteen-inch-square computer monitor sat lifeless.

'It would be an option,' said the prime minister, 'but Ambassador Trestogeen seemed to be quite firm on the fact that we must sort it out ourselves and only reapply for membership when we are unified under a single world leader.'

'Do you think he'd consider it if everywhere except the USA were unified?' asked Lara, returning to the table and taking her seat again.

'I don't see how we can do anything about Slimbridge and his government,' said Malcolm. 'The firepower of the USA is so overwhelming. Also, with Slimbridge in charge, who knows if he'll make a pre-emptive strike. He could lash out in any direction in his state of mind.'

'If he thinks an invasion is imminent?' asked Lara.

'Yes,' said Malcolm, 'or even if he feels threatened. A few missiles fired at the other powers would demonstrate that he'd stand for no attack from any of us. I still can't believe what he did to New York and someone capable of that is, frankly, capable of anything.

'I take it we're protected against a nuclear strike?' asked Caroline.

Malcolm replied, 'We have anti-missile missiles, but there really is little we could do. During the cold war we all relied on mutually assured destruction. I don't see how that would work with America as the aggressor. We'll see what the others say tomorrow.'

'I assume you have all of our forces on alert, Malcolm,' said the prime minister.

'Yes, of course, Prime Minister. We have four of our fleet of seven attack submarines in the mid-Atlantic and, as I speak, two more are on their way through the Suez Canal. Our four ballistic submarines are also in the North Atlantic. We have taken over control of the early warning stations from the US and they are on full alert for anything coming over the pole. I've had meetings with President Olov's people, and they're still on an official war footing, so remain on full alert too. We're relying on the Russians to tell us if they detect any launches at all. All the satellites being down doesn't help.'

'We don't want any accidents,' said Caroline quietly.

'Mistakes by the US are the only likely accidents, but, come to think of it, Slimbridge and his generals seem to have certain of the characteristics exhibited in *Doctor Strangelove*!'

'Malcolm!' said the prime minister sharply. 'I'd rather we didn't have any more of that sort of talk. Let's just retain our own rationale and seek out some sort of compromise.'

'Yes, sorry, Prime Minister,' said Malcolm, his voice betraying that he knew he'd overstepped the mark.

'Okay,' said the prime minister. 'We'll meet back here tomorrow and plan a course of action. I'll see if I can find out President Ramseur's feelings about it all tonight.'

«««0»»»

[From Drew Gambon's tapes and diary. RBB]

'We need a militia,' said Brad Gregg, a man in his fifties, rapidly greying, but who obviously kept fit. 'We can't just stand there and be shot in cold blood.' He rested his elbows on the desk and made a steeple with his fingers.

'I'm amazed the military followed orders,' said Rose Thorpe, a tracksuit-clad thirty-something, leaning against the wall. 'Surely they must know this can't be right. I mean, to be ordered to shoot unarmed citizens carrying out a lawful protest.'

'They followed orders. No answer to that,' said Brad, standing up and walking around the basement gymnasium.

'It didn't work in Nazi Germany!' said Rose.

'Oh, don't start comparing Slimbridge to Hitler…' said Brad.

'Well, why not?' said Drew, the swarthy man sitting on an exercise bike in the corner of the room. 'Hitler's holocaust was spread over years.

Slimbridge murdered nearly nine million people in the blink of an eye. Who's worse?'

'We need to come up with a strategy,' said Mike, a mid-twenty-year-old, built like a linebacker, resting his backside on a pool table and holding a rifle. 'I feel so helpless here with no particular objective and listening to you guys, who seem to be just as bemused as the rest of us. This is America, goddammit, how dare Slimbridge do this to our country?'

'A militia might be the answer. We could put together an armed militia,' said Drew. 'But we'd need to be prepared to shoot first or the National Guard will just massacre us.'

'This is ridiculous…' said Rose. 'Americans talking about killing Americans. Does the general population have the stomach for a civil war?'

A rugged looking man with a military air and in his late-sixties had been sitting quietly in the corner of the gym, listening carefully to what the others were saying. He stood up. Immediately, everyone paid attention. 'What I'm hearing here is certainly an uprising, but, as Mike and Brad said, we need to be organised.'

'Okay, General, how, where and when?' asked Rose.

Dick Beech, a retired four-star US army general, walked purposefully, but slowly across the room to Brad's desk. His charisma and natural authority meant that the others all watched him, waiting patiently for him to speak. No one would talk when "the general" was thinking, neither on the golf course, nor here, in this meeting which was contemplating the overthrow of the president of the United States.

He turned towards the others and perched himself on the front corner of Brad's desk. He still didn't speak. His golfing buddies had seen him do this before in the clubhouse. He had a certain way, which gave him the full attention of anyone within sight. No one saw his silence and stillness as an opportunity to speak.

'We're meeting in Brad's cellar,' he said. 'That won't do. There are five of us, that won't do either. If we're going to be effective, we need a figurehead. We need weapons, the militia Brad mentioned, and we need to link up with other likeminded groups.'

Drew put up his arm, as if in class. The general nodded, granting permission to speak.

'Mayne is certainly trying to marshal support if the black web's to be believed.'

'He's in hiding, though,' said Mike.

'He's also a Democrat,' said Rose.

'He's not in hiding, but he's keeping a low profile at a temporary office in Pittsburgh, last I heard. He left Boston in order to be more central,' said Drew.

'Hmm. While I never thought I'd support a Democrat, this goes beyond partisan politics,' said the general. The others nodded. 'Do we have any idea of the level of support he has?'

'Not really,' said Mike.

'How could we contact him?' asked the general.

'I think I could get through to him on the web,' said Drew.

'Do that and be sure to use burner phones for any telephone conversations,' said the general.

'Sorry,' said Rose, 'what's a burner phone?'

'A pre-paid phone which is disposed of after use. And for information, it is not just the card which needs destroying, you must destroy the phone too,' said Brad.

'Numbers,' said the general. 'What can we do to increase the size of our squad. If we're going to have any influence, there must be more than a handful of us.'

'Each of us could put out feelers,' said Drew. 'I know at least six who'd be supportive, including Harry West at the gun shop. He could be useful.'

'Okay.' The general nodded. 'Let's each of us find half a dozen who can be trusted, and we'll meet up again with them, here. If we're a group of thirty-plus, we'll have more to offer to a national organisation. Drew, you organise the meetings.'

'What about contacting Peter Stone? He's making waves against Slimbridge from Canada,' said Rose.

'How do we do that?' asked Brad.

'The web again,' said Mike. 'I'll get onto it when we leave here.'

'Security!' barked the general, stopping everyone in their tracks. 'Our most likely downfall would be to bring someone into our midst who then betrays us. Remember… as our number grows, the chance of traitors grows with it. Don't forget that there are people out there who believe Slimbridge's propaganda against the aliens.'

'Frankly, Dick,' said Brad, 'I don't give a shit about whether the aliens would be good or bad for us. What I do care about is some bastard murdering our president and taking over the country. Communism is also a worry as that's what the Federation system sounds like.'

'Sure does,' said Drew. 'Don't know how I'd feel about sharing wealth. I've worked hard for what I've got and I'm not going to give it up without a fight.'

'The trouble is,' said Rose, 'no one really explained the Federation system to us properly. Those question and answer sessions were pathetic. We need to really understand if we're going to make a fair decision.'

'It doesn't really matter which way we're thinking at the moment,' said Mike. 'We need to unseat Slimbridge first and then worry about the future.'

'Well, each to their own,' said the general, 'but we need a common cause if we're to succeed. Drew, will you find out what military weapons Harry could get for us?'

'What about money?' asked Drew.

'I'll look after funding,' said Rose. 'I don't mind putting in a few grand to get us started, but if Harry is on board, then he ought not to be making a profit out of this.'

'No, he wouldn't, but he still needs to buy in,' said Drew. 'I'll find out what sort of budget we'd need to get heavy duty weaponry.'

'That's very generous of you, Rose, thanks,' said the general. 'Drew, do your best to keep costs down. We need automatic weapons, handguns and grenades, if that's possible. Let's at least get our band equipped. Weapons for fifty people, say. Oh, and we'll need uniforms and gas masks et cetera.'

'Okay, Dick. I'll get onto it,' said Drew.

'Mike,' said the general, 'see if you can get me in touch with other groups plus Stone and Mayne. Find out about overseas help, too. Especially the Limeys. How would we go about contacting them? Damn it, I got on real well with Ken Hood. I don't know this new prime minister of theirs at all. So many good and wise men were lost to that nuke.'

5 UN

[Extracted from Lara Horvat's self-taken minutes. Again I apologise for the large amount of dialogue in this section. RBB]

'I call this summit to order,' said Lara Horvat, bringing down a gavel on the leather inlay of the table in the Downing Street cabinet briefing room.

Seated around the impressive slab of teak were Che Yang, president of China; Phillippe Ramseur, president of France; Maureen Church, prime minister of Britain; Marat Olov, president of Russia; Malcolm Gorman, the British defence minister; and Lara Horvat herself, the secretary general of the United Nations.

'I'd like to start by calling upon the British minister of defence, who has been gathering intelligence,' said Lara. Eyes turned towards Malcolm Gorman.

'Our man in Washington says that there is no change in the actions of Slimbridge. He has the US armed forces under his thumb via the joint chiefs. However, keeping his ear to the ground, our man says there are small pockets of resistance forming around the country. The trouble is that there are more than a few supporters of Slimbridge's xenophobic policies. Several opposition groups have been betrayed and the results have been disastrous.'

'How you mean, disastrous?' asked the Russian president.

'There've been a number of raids and several hundred arrests. One group of forty faced a firing squad. Our man says that is likely to be repeated with the others. We haven't been able to verify the numbers.'

'Does the man 'ave no shame?' asked the French president.

'Peter Stone, the Internet guru,' continued Malcolm Gorman, 'is still managing to frustrate all Slimbridge's attempts to shut down online communications. He's created a black web which can be accessed through any telephone line. It's text only, but now has thousands of ingress points in the US. They really can't stop it without shutting down all international communications.'

'Okay,' said President Yang. 'We must find a way forward, or forget the Federation and get back to running our own countries as best we can.'

'For the record,' said the secretary general, 'how do each of you feel about Federation membership? Prime Minister Church?'

'We recognise that membership has huge drawbacks for the wealthy, but it has so many benefits for the general population, that we feel we must support it. I'd like to visit other worlds, though. Ken Hood visited a number of Federation worlds and I know his initial scepticism, like President Spence's, was assuaged by the visits.'

'And is that the view of your cabinet?'

'Yes, it is.'

President Yang said, 'We are in favour. The super-rich will survive. Again, though, I rather annoyed with Federation for cutting us off from learning more about them.'

'Yes,' said President Olav. 'We most certain in favour, but fear that we need much help in controlling oligarchs.'

'La France is very much in favour, but 'ow can we argue for ze Federation when we 'aven't experienced it ourselves.' said President Ramseur.

'For such an ancient organisation, they don't seem to know much about self-promotion,' said the prime minister.

'No, good points all, and thank you,' said Secretary General Horvat. 'I believe our next move is for me to go and see President Slimbridge and see if there's any way of persuading him to change his stance.'

'Can't. Can't change stance. He's committed war crimes. Such person will never surrender,' said President Olav.

'I must try to convince him to, at least, communicate with us.'

'I, too, zink the task will be impossible, but, oui, you must try,' said President Ramseur.

'If you fail, Lara,' said the Chinese president, 'we need then attempt something military.'

'How you mean?' asked the Russian president.

'A covert force. Take out him and his government,' said President Yang.

'I agree,' said the minister of defence. 'Our man says that there is little real support for Slimbridge in the nation, despite the isolated cases of groups being betrayed. If he were gone, his support could vanish very quickly. It could solve all of our problems at a stroke.'

'Well, let's keep that option to ourselves for a while. I'll try official channels first,' said the secretary general.

'Also,' added the minister, 'the word "communism" is very emotive. I think it's one of the biggest problems in the USA. It conjures up a hatred which grew during the cold war. The trouble is that the Federation sounds like a communist organisation.'

'That's true,' said the prime minister. 'I wouldn't underestimate the feeling against the Federation. I did tell the cabinet under Ken Hood that there should be a much longer period of education and introduction. Ambassador Moroforon offered any number of additional exploratory trips to Federation worlds. The problem is that the politicians who went on those trips were so impressed they were almost immediately convinced.'

'Yes, same with President Ivanov. He returned talking about the Federation in glowing terms,' said President Olov.

'We should all have slowed things down. There did not need to be such a headlong rush. We mustn't make the same mistake if we get a second chance,' said the prime minister.

'Again, not being able to talk to the Federation about this is a real drawback,' said the secretary general.

'I have some information on Federation activity which might be of interest,' said the defence minister.

'Fire away, Malcolm,' said the prime minister.

'I've received communications from a number of observatories. They've been watching the build-up of a considerable fleet of what can only be Federation ships in orbit,' he said.

'Are they massing to strike America, do you think?' asked President Yang.

'Surely not. But there's no way of knowing,' said Malcolm. 'At the last count there were over ten ships. They're holding in an orbit about two hundred and fifty miles high. Some of the ships are rather large. I don't think we can do anything about them, anyway.'

'How large?' asked President Olov. 'When I flew out of Russia, I had a message to speak to a group of our astronomers. Probably the same information.'

'Many over a mile in length and have considerable girth. They'd be pretty obvious, even with only a good pair of binoculars,' said Malcolm.

'Amazing! What should we do?' asked Lara.

'Do not know,' said President Yang. 'I too been told astronomers seen things. Should have looked into it.'

'We can't do anything,' said Malcolm. 'We do have missiles capable of reaching that orbit. I assume China and Russia do also, but how would the Federation view such launches. I suspect they'd be swatted like flies.'

'We have spacecraft too,' said President Yang.

'We could launch a Soyuz,' said President Olov. 'It could only go and observe though.'

'We cannot attack them. It would be foolhardy,' said the prime minister, 'and I don't think there's much point going to visit them in orbit. That would achieve nothing.'

'I wonder if we should prepare a communique and use the QE transmitter to contact the Federation for assistance. What do you all think?' asked the secretary general.

'Oui, zat would seem a good move,' said President Ramseur.

Presidents Olov and Yang nodded in agreement.

'He was pretty explicit that we shouldn't use it until we'd got the whole world ready to join,' said the prime minister.

'But might never happen if don't get their help,' said President Yang.

'Look,' said Lara Horvat. 'Let me get my attempt at diplomacy with President Slimbridge underway and then we could consider contacting the Federation after we've seen his response. How does that sound?'

'Yes. Federation hardly likely attack us,' said President Yang.

'We are very vulnerable, are we not?' said President Olov.

'Oui, all our knowledge and technology is as nussing compared wiz zem,' said the French president.

There was general agreement to continue to observe until after Lara's visit to Washington.

'Right, other business,' said the secretary general, and the Security Council began discussions about North Korea and Israel who were potential stumbling blocks to any agreement.

«««o»»»

[From Jim Collins' iPad minutes. RBB]

Congressman Charles Mayne sat in a leather executive chair behind a contemporary desk in an anonymous looking hotel conference room in Pittsburgh. With him were some twenty smartly dressed senators and members of Congress. By the door, in military fatigues, were four soldiers bristling with arms.

'Thank you all for coming to this update,' he said in his characteristic Boston accent. 'I appreciate that you're all risking life and limb to be here.'

He surveyed the room and began his next sentence rather more forcefully, 'Fellow Americans, our country has been usurped by a tyrant. While I was no fan of Jack Spence's domestic policies, I appreciate that he was a properly elected president of our nation. John Slimbridge is nothing more than a powerful thug... a gang leader. He has no mandate for his actions – they are based on greed and selfishness. He's killed almost every leader of the world and can never be forgiven for his actions. He's a war criminal!

'I've been inundated, over the black web, by offers of support from small militias all over the country, many being led by ex-military men... the sort of men who could command armed forces. My problem is that I don't know how to make use of that support. How do we turn a ragtag number of armed squads into a coherent force which might be able to challenge Slimbridge?'

'We could assassinate him,' said a small man with a bald head in the front row.

'Is that a possibility?' asked Charles.

'I have a connection in the White House who would not be averse to spilling information about his movements,' said another suited individual.

'Morally, can we assassinate him?' asked Charles.

Calls of 'sure can', 'yes', and 'you'd better believe it', rang out from around the room.

'Kill the bastard!' was shouted by a woman on the left. Many looked around. They recognised her as Helen Bond, President Spence's sister.

'I'm sympathetic to your feelings, Helen, but we must ask ourselves if we'll be able to look each other in the eye if we stoop to Slimbridge's level,' said Charles.

'Charles, don't be concerned about that,' said the diminutive bald man. 'After we're successful, the Federation will take over and any charge which may be levelled at us would be quickly justified.'

'My brother was a good man,' said Helen Bond. 'He was vehemently opposed to the Federation initially, but I watched him learn about them, particularly after his return from Arlucian. He came to realise that the Federation would be good for the world, even if it upset the wealthy and influential.'

'I wish we had Federation help now. Their technology could solve this,' said Charles.

'My cousin in Denmark saw a news broadcast about a visit by the Federation ambassador in which he insisted the world must sort itself out before we contacted them again,' said one of the senators.

'Yes, I'd heard about that too,' said Charles.

'Charles, one of the militias which made contact is headed by General Beech,' said a man in the front row.

'What, Dick Beech?' asked Charles.

'Yes. Why not get him to lead the armed uprising?'

'Would he be the right man?' asked Charles.

'Very experienced. He was Jack Spence's main go-to man for military advice before he retired a year or so back.'

'So, he's a Republican,' said Charles with regret in his tone.

A man who'd been silent up to now, sitting next to Charles Mayne, said, 'That won't matter to him, Charles, he'll be as loyal to you as he was to Spence if it causes the overthrow of Slimbridge. The top military brass suppress their own personal political views.'

'Okay, Jim,' said Charles. 'Can someone make contact with him and ask him if he'd come to meet with me? Where are they based?'

'Florida,' someone called out.

Jim Collins said, 'We need to get something going before Slimbridge finds a way to shut down the black web. Our only advantage is that Peter Stone is orchestrating the protection of the web from outside the US.'

'I met him,' said Helen Bond. 'He was at the White House and Jack introduced me.'

'He escaped to Canada after Slimbridge began his crackdown on those who'd been on Federation familiarisation trips,' said Jim.

'Once we get something organised, it'd be good to involve him,' said the small bald-headed man.

'Yes, Burt, we'll do that,' said Charles. 'Everyone remember to keep quiet about this meeting. We'll never be sure who are secret Slimbridge supporters. His accusation that President Spence was handing over power to the aliens really struck home with some of the general public, and, sadly, many of them seem to have become a little paranoid about it. He also seems to have stirred up the extreme right. Take care everyone.'

«««0»»»

[Extracted from Captain Ya Istil Sperafin's log and communication records. RBB]

The Federation freighter Medorin descended towards a scorched area of land, dotted with scrubby patches of plants and trees struggling to survive during their battle with the lack of rainfall. A tented city, home to several thousand malnourished and almost starving men, women, and children, suddenly decamped its population to watch the enormous spaceship's descent. Dozens of volunteers from the various NGOs also turned their attention to the unexpected phenomenon.

The ship, over a mile long and the diameter of at least two football pitches, was now moving very slowly as it slid along its invisible glide path to the arid plain below.

A booming voice broke the silence which had fallen upon the mesmerised refugees. 'We are a Federation supply ship, packed with food, water and medical provisions. We are also carrying almost a thousand medibots to assist the human medical teams. Do not be afraid.

Our ship will hover a metre from the surface. Please stand clear to allow ramps to be extended.' It was repeated in several different languages broadly relevant to those within earshot.

Almost as one, thousands of the occupants of the city, disregarding the warnings, moved towards the landing spot, wanting to be among the first to get access to grain, rice and anything else on the ship. As they approached the vessel, they ran into a force field which held them back at a safe distance. People pushed against it and looked at their hands, trying to figure out what this invisible wall was made of. Some charged it, others put their shoulders against it. Nothing was able to penetrate.

The ship was mainly dark green, but with highlights of mint, emerald and sage. At the front, a glazed area allowed the occupants to see out and the people to see in. Many aliens of all different sizes, shapes and colours were looking down upon the canvas city, the population of which stared back at them in bewilderment. A fear began to grow, fear of the unknown. Some backed away.

A six-wheeled blue truck trundled down the first ramp and set off towards a tent which was clearly the hub of the NGOs. The vehicle contained two humanoid robots. This really frightened some of those trying to get through the force field. A few ran, more stood still, blankly staring at what appeared to be the cast of a Star Wars film, but the shapes of the robots made it very clear that these were not humans in costumes.

The almost deafening voice from the ship roared, 'NGOs, please go to the destination of the blue vehicle so that information can be provided about the supplies we are carrying. Others, please do not be afraid. We are here to help you. Soon, you will see large trucks exiting. Each contains hundreds of packages which contain a variety of foods and water. Please help yourselves and remember to take some for those who are less mobile.'

By this time, there were almost a hundred ramps on the city side of the freighter and a thousand trucks were making their way down and parking around all sides of the camp.

The smaller truck arrived at the NGO tent. The robots got out of the cab and waited for the volunteers to gather around while setting up a table before them.

The lead robot stood about two metres tall with a rectangular head the size of a microwave oven. Its torso, a metre in height, was roughly half a metre in diameter. Six arms projected, two just beneath a natural shoulder position, two directly in front of the robot and a further pair emerged from its back. Three sturdy legs, one on each side and a third slightly behind the others, gave it balance.

One of the robots picked up a package with its front, central arms, and emptied its contents onto the table. It spoke. 'Each of these packages holds about three days' supply of some green vegetables, some root vegetables, meat protein, fish protein, dairy protein and eggs in addition to three litres of water.'

The volunteers approached the table and examined the strange looking produce. It was like nothing seen on Earth. Purple, apple-sized tubers with yellow leaves lay beside carrot-length, currant red vegetables and warty potato-sized marigold objects. Eggs of various shapes, patterns, and colours sat in protective transparent boxes alongside blood red, sepia, white, lime and amethyst shrink-wrapped meats, fish and other proteins. Among all of these rested bizarre fruits of spectacular colours.

'All of this is safe for people to eat?' asked one of the volunteers who was dressed in medical scrubs.

'Everything is safe for human consumption. It is possible that there might be some allergic reactions, but they will be as rare as might be encountered from any earthly produce.'

The robot turned and cast an arm in the direction of the rear of the ship. 'You will see hundreds of transports parking to the rear of the ship. These are autonomous, solar-powered vehicles which have been esponged with English.'

'Esponged?' asked one of the volunteers.

'They understand English,' explained the robot. 'Esponging is an education technique. We are leaving them with you, and you can direct them to take you wherever you feel the need is greatest. On the other side of the ship we are unloading sufficient supplies to feed one hundred thousand people for one month. The packets contain a gas called thorbon. It is harmless but shuts down bacterial development even more effectively than freezing. Packets have a shelf life of many months, even these meats, fish and spurras. The transparent film used to cover the cardboard packets is made from a vegetable protein and decomposes quickly once opened. The thorbon inside only protects the cardboard and film until it is split or cut.'

'Wow,' said the same volunteer. 'That's ingenious. We've been battling single-use plastic for nearly a decade. Thank you so much. What are spurras?'

'A protein made from large numbers of microscopic aquatic invertebrates,' said the robot.

Four shorter, more spindly robots arrived in another vehicle and joined the first two behind the table.

'These,' said the main robot, indicating the new arrivals, 'are medibots. They have been esponged with human anatomy and we are providing them to operate under your direction. They are also esponged with English plus French and Sudanese Arabic. Use them as you will.'

An enormous tracked truck, a hundred metres long and twenty metres square pulled up behind the robots.

'This,' said the robot, pointing towards the truck, 'is full of medical supplies. Many are obvious. The medibots will be able to identify the drugs and their uses for you. Who is in charge here?'

'I suppose that I'm the leader of the biggest organisation operating here, the World Food Programme,' said a tall black man, dressed in contrasting brilliant white scrubs.

The robot handed the leader an envelope. 'This contains a four-digit number which will open the container and allow access to the medical supplies. Bringol, here, also knows the code and is fully conversant with everything we are providing.'

'What is your name?' asked Bringol.

'Albert. Albert Harrison.'

'I am pleased to meet you, Albert,' said Bringol.

Albert put out his hand towards Bringol, but the robot just looked at it. Suddenly the appendage came out and took Albert's hand in a gentle handshake.

'Sorry, Albert,' said the main robot, 'the medibots are not made fully conversant with all human customs. Now, I must continue to oversee the unloading of the supplies and then we will leave. The medibots and supply vehicles are yours to do with as you wish.'

'Are you serious. You're giving them to us?'

'Yes, they are yours and they are all solar powered.'

'Thank you, thank you. You cannot imagine how grateful we are.'

The two main robots hopped back into their vehicle and, within a minute had vanished up one of the loading ramps.

Sixteen supply ships visited some seventy areas of the Earth which had medical or famine problems. They didn't stay long. Within twenty-four hours they had all left, either into orbit or back to their home planets.

6 Washington

[From Lara Horvat's diary. RBB]

Lara Horvat arrived on an American Airlines flight into Dulles International Airport. There were only twenty people on board. Journeys to the USA had been discouraged by most countries once they had withdrawn their diplomatic staff.

President Slimbridge made no special arrangements to ease the secretary general's arrival. In fact, the opposite was the case. She had to clear customs like any other passenger. The scarcity of people wanting to enter the United States meant that there were no delays, but, nevertheless, she was singled out to have her luggage completely emptied and the final insult was a strip-search.

Not a little upset, she passed through into the arrivals area where she was greeted by Paula Wilson, her predecessor's biographer who had also become her unofficial assistant. It was that unofficial tag which had protected her from President Slimbridge's purge of United Nations' staff.

'Paula, how lovely to see you,' said the secretary general as the two women exchanged cheek to cheek greetings.

'Did you enjoy the flight? You took a long time to clear customs. Your plane arrived nearly two hours ago.'

'Well, you know. At least it was quiet, but airline food is still airline food. As regards customs, they took everything out of my cases, and had it strewn over four tables. When they finished, they threw it all back in any order.'

'Didn't you object, ma'am?'

'I think it was specially arranged for me. I was even strip-searched, including invasive examinations and a scan. I don't believe that I was just unlucky.'

'That's awful. I was expecting the president to provide an official welcome for you.'

'He did!' said the Lara sarcastically. 'I think he was trying to demonstrate his power and make me out to be insignificant. How are things this end? You must tell me how you've been getting on setting up somewhere to stay and offices.'

'I'd rather not talk here, ma'am.'

'No. Probably not.'

'What I can tell you is that I've rented a house in H Street which is fairly central. Your meeting is set for eleven tomorrow. I've got permission for the car to take you in, but it meant jumping through a number of hoops. Visitors coming on foot are less likely to be a threat.'

'What, he's worried about assassination?'

'Yes, ma'am. There have been threats, but they don't get aired on the main news media. When we get to the house, we can discuss the arrangements in detail.'

The secretary general quickly realised that Paula was concerned about being bugged and left her main questions until later.

The house was large by any domestic standard, almost a mansion. It was set back from the road and surrounded by metal railings with automatic gates protecting the large turning and parking area. The limousine Paula had rented for the United Nations pulled up to the front of the house and two casually dressed men arrived to open the doors and assist with the bags.

Once inside, Paula said, 'We're safe to talk now. The place has been swept for bugs.'

'Did you find any?'

'Yes, two in the sitting room and another two in the room we've equipped for conferences. We've left them in place and staff will carry out innocuous discussions in those rooms from time to time.'

'You're sure there are no others?'

'As sure as we can be. In the east wing there are four offices, including yours. Most of the domestic rooms are on the west side and upper floors.'

'Communications?'

'We have all the usual telephone lines, but you should take care what you say on the international line. They are probably all bugged, but certainly the international line.'

'Internet?'

'We have what passes as the Internet, a very restricted service, but we also have the black web coming into your office. I took the liberty of taking a spur off it for my office. Was that okay?'

'Yes, of course. So, the offices are clear of bugs as well as the upstairs areas?'

'As sure as we can be,' said Paula. 'Come this way, ma'am. There are some staff I'd like you to meet.' Lara couldn't fail to notice the wink Paula gave as she said the word "staff".

The two women moved through the entrance hallway and into a small dining room, where two men in jeans and sweatshirts were sitting on barstools beside a cocktail bar in the corner of the room.

As the women entered, they both stood up smartly.

Paula said, 'Madam Secretary General, might I introduce you to Democratic Leader Charles Mayne and his assistant, Jim Collins.'

'Your Excellency, welcome to Washington. Sorry we couldn't have met you more formally,' said Charles.

'Thank you, gentlemen. I hope you've not put yourselves in any danger, coming to meet me like this,' said Lara.

'We arrived as workmen with a plumber,' said Jim. 'We'll be okay if we don't stay too long.'

'Fill me in on the current situation,' said Lara, waving everybody to take a seat around the small oak dining table.

'It's quite amazing how quickly Slimbridge managed to gain control,' said Charles. 'Protests were put down by automatic weapon fire. The first, outside the White House, saw an unknown number of deaths but we think it was over seventy, and three times that number wounded to various degrees. It certainly cleared the streets.'

'Dreadful.'

'The second Washington demonstration was put down in exactly the same manner. Over two hundred protested but fled the moment they saw the troops. Still fifteen were killed. A protest in San Francisco ended the same way. Protesting today is done on the fly – a small number arrive with posters, banners or spray paint, put them up or scrawl slogans and disappear as quickly as they arrive.'

'How's the Slimbridge regime affecting the ordinary people?'

'Well, Your Excellency…'

The secretary general interrupted, 'Call me Lara, please.'

'I'm Charles and Jim answers to Jim or James.

'To answer your question, the ordinary people are not affected that much yet, but shortages are beginning to hurt. Coffee in particular, but also pineapples and bananas and the list is growing. We produce a huge amount of fruit ourselves, but it's always been topped up by imports. Now, nothing is coming in. It'll get worse. The US is self-sufficient in many things, but living standards will suffer. It's only been a month. Let's see where we are in another couple of months.'

'I see,' said Lara.

'Can I ask, why exactly are you here? What's the plan? What do you hope to achieve?'

'Firstly, let me say that the whole world is watching this situation. The Federation have prohibited any space flight and you must have noticed that all satellites have been destroyed.'

'Yes. You don't realise how much you rely on the global positioning system until you don't have it. I actually had to use a hard-copy map to direct Jim here.'

'Where are you based?'

'At the moment, I'm working out of an office in Pittsburgh. Boston had problems for me. I have to keep on the move.'

'We conducted a summit in London last week,' said the secretary general. 'Presidents Yang, Olov, and Ramseur and Prime Minister Church were all present. They are considering an attack by a small force to take out President Slimbridge and his main backers. I wanted to attempt diplomacy first.'

'They're actually thinking along those lines?'

'Yes, but there are also other ideas, like getting the Federation to engage with us and provide some assistance. President Slimbridge has made it very clear any invasion will result in a full nuclear response.'

'You see, none of us are receiving any of this news. He's locked down the media. You've a meeting organised with him?'

'Yes, tomorrow at eleven. I must try diplomacy although I don't expect to achieve much after my reception at the airport. I was strip-searched!'

'Really? My God! Well, Lara, I don't think you'll get far with diplomacy and if they're going to take out Slimbridge, they'll need to hit the joint chiefs simultaneously or they'll be quickly wiped out,' said Charles.

'We keep tabs on where they are,' added Jim.

'What are you doing to resist, Charles?'

'Ex-army chief, General Dick Beech, is paying me a visit later in the week and we're going to ask him to coordinate the militias,' said Charles.

'We heard some of them had been betrayed,' said Lara.

'Yes,' said Jim. 'The trouble is that anti-alien factions are everywhere. They're not a large proportion of the population, but they believe all Slimbridge's crap about an invasion, so are reporting anything they hear against the regime. The idiots think they're saving the country. It's our biggest problem. We're hoping Beech will have some workable solution.'

'Well, good luck with that, Jim, Charles,' said the secretary general.

'It is not the peoples' fault, of course, they are being swept along by Slimbridge's powerful rhetoric. They don't know what is true or false so take the fallback position that the president must be telling the truth. They believe him because it fits in with what they are hearing and seeing,' said Charles.

'Yes, we know how easily people can be deceived,' said Lara.

'Look, Lara, we're a danger to you and ourselves while we're here. It was great to meet you and had to be done, but we need to get away,' said Charles.

'Don't worry. I understand, and I now have the ability to report back some positives to the Security Council,' said Lara. 'You'll stay in regular touch?'

'Be sure of it,' said Charles.

'I'll tell the plumber we're ready to go,' said Jim, leaving the room.

The three stood and followed him through to the kitchen area, where they said their goodbyes. Charles Mayne and Jim Collins then left in the back of a somewhat battered grey van with "Ace Plumbers" printed on the side.

'Brave men,' said Lara.

'Indeed.'

'I'll show you around the offices and second floor,' said Paula and led the secretary general on a tour of the rest of the house.

'You know, Perfect Okafor, spoke very fondly of you, Paula.'

'That's good to hear. It was such an awful shock when the news finally got out about New York,' said Paula who broke down in tears. 'She was… such a… lovely person.'

'Yes. It is a tragedy. You will still write your book?'

Paula recovered her composure. 'Yes, when the time is right. I've spent the past four weeks putting it into some semblance of order. It kept my mind occupied. I lost a lifelong friend who was apartment-sitting while I was away and I know it's trivial, considering the loss of human life, but a very dear cat I'd had since I was at college died too,' Paula said, choking back tears.

'Are you happy to work for me?' asked the secretary general.

'Oh, yes. I'd love to.'

'Right. I'll let it be known that you are my personal assistant. That should offer you some protection.'

'I'm small fry,' Paula said. 'They won't be interested in me. I'll need to show proof of my position in order to travel internationally, though. This is your office, ma'am.'

Lara looked around the room and took in the view of the shrubs in the yard. 'Very nice.'

'Let me know if you need any extra furniture or anything.'

'This all looks fine. Desk, chair and that visitors' area is good too,' she said, walking over to a lounge suite at one side of the room. 'Okay. We'll get your credentials set up. For now, I want to unpack and get the creases out of my clothes. Then I'll come back down and get my thoughts in order for tomorrow's meeting with the president. I'd like you to come with me. Two pairs of eyes are better than one while we're in the White House.'

'Certainly, ma'am. Let me show you to your bedroom and the domestic areas,' said Paula, and the two women climbed the impressively wide staircase.

«««O»»»

[Mainly from Paula Wilson's recordings and Lara Horvat's cell phone recorder, but also the meeting with the president later extracted from clearer, secret White House tapes. RBB]

The secretary general was not expecting the media reception she received at the White House. The entrance was surrounded by television crews and journalists.

'Now what?' said Lara.

'I think he's pulling a fast one, ma'am,' said Paula.

'I was certainly not expecting a press conference. He must have an ulterior motive.'

The UN limousine slowed to a stop, causing the press to move to one side as Lara and Paula exited the vehicle. There was an immediate cascade of flash photography and shouted requests for comments on the reason for the visit.

All of a sudden, a hush fell over the media mob. President Slimbridge had emerged from the White House, smiling at and acknowledging individuals in the press pack. He marched purposefully over to the secretary general and shook her hand with a deliberately crushing grip. He guided her towards a lectern which sported the global icon which represented the United Nations. Beside it stood another bearing the seal of the president of the United States. They took their positions, the secretary general looking very short indeed behind the oversized lectern. She was much shorter than Perfect Okafor and wondered if this was another deliberate attempt by the president to intimidate her or diminish her importance.

President Slimbridge, full of smiles, began, 'It gives me great pleasure to welcome Secretary General Horvat, which clearly demonstrates that the United States is being welcomed back into the international community of nations after the dreadful terrorist attack upon the United Nations last month. Both the FBI and CIA are still trying to track down exactly who was responsible for planting the nuclear device under the UN building. We will find them, and they *will* suffer the full force of the law.

'Perhaps you would like to say a few words, Madam Secretary,' said the president, resting his hands on the sides of the lectern and turning towards Lara Horvat.

More flash photography took place and the television cameras swung around to zero in on her.

'Thank you, Mr President. I welcome the opportunity to discuss a range of issues with you today and that is the reason for my visit,' she said, immediately followed by a clamour of questions.

'No questions, sorry,' the president said to the press and to the secretary general, 'Right. Let's go inside.' The president turned away from the lecterns and returned to the entrance to the White House, followed by the secretary general.

They passed quickly through the lobby and into the Oval Office. The president's secretary took Paula Wilson to an anteroom and provided some coffee.

'Been in here before?' the president asked.

'Yes, once, for a meeting with Secretary General Okafor and President Spence,' the secretary general said brusquely, knowing the president wouldn't like the mention of his and her predecessors.

'Well, take a seat,' he said, planting himself behind his desk, leaning back in the chair and folding his arms defensively. 'Let's not beat around the bush. Why are you here? What do you want?'

'Mr President, thank you for seeing me at such short notice. Almost every country in the world wanted to join the Federation and the action of the, er, "terrorists" in New York has caused the Federation to ostracise us until such time as the world can speak with one voice. You've isolated the United States and I'm here to ascertain your position.'

'The Federation have shown their true colours then, abandoning you all. Their communist regime will never work for the USA. I can't imagine a time when we could vote in favour.'

'But, Mr President, you've been to Federation worlds and seen how well the system works for almost a quarter of a million civilisations. It's the fact that all manual labour is done by the automatons that allows the system to work. I agree it couldn't work in the old Soviet manner.'

'See,' he said, raising his voice, 'this is exactly the sort of bullshit which Spence swallowed, hook, line and sinker. The Federation only took us to worlds which they'd specially prepped to suit their needs. We never saw the worlds with shortages in shops and communist state-owned business regimes which forced them to work countless hours for a pittance.'

'There is no evidence whatsoever of any of that!' the secretary general said forcefully.

'You're being naïve, you're all being naïve. Have you been to their worlds?'

'No, but I hope to investigate several of them when the next opportunity arises.'

'Ha! The whole ploy was aimed at lulling us into a false sense of security and then to steal our best brains and technology.'

'Mr President! You cannot seriously believe that we have any technology which would advance the Federation. You've seen their robots, shuttles, farm and manufacturing machinery. What on earth would they want from us?'

'Exactly! That is exactly my point. They come here, all sweetness and light, to plough billions of dollars into our economies all on the basis that they are benevolent to all peoples. No one behaves like that, no one! It's a con!'

'I believe you are wrong. There are many humans who behave like that, volunteering to help other people. It is an admirable way of life.'

'Don't be ridiculous. Just because a few liberal do-gooders behave that way, does not mean that an entire empire can.'

'Okay, Mr President. Let's move on. We've heard about military shootings of people making peaceful protests. What's going on there?'

'They were organised by the same terrorists who blew up New York. We have done the world a service by tackling them. These weren't peaceful protesters; they were intent on disrupting the business of the United States of America and many were armed. Most were arrested. Unfortunately, some were shot by police defending themselves.'

'That is not what I've seen and heard. Also, most of the world's leaders believe it was you who was instrumental in blowing up the UN headquarters, not some never-before-heard-of terrorists.'

'That is patently ridiculous. I was actually in a police cell at the time. How was I meant to have orchestrated it?'

'Where did the weapon come from?'

'It was stolen from the military. The people responsible for taking the bomb have been dealt with. It was most unfortunate but nothing to do with me. I'm *insulted* that you might imagine I'd do such a thing.'

'Don't shoot the messenger, Mr President. I'm only telling you what other leaders are saying. Perhaps you can explain why you have refused diplomatic contact and isolated America. What are you trying to achieve through that?'

'Well, you can take a clear message back to my critics that I absolutely deny any involvement in the New York terrorist attack. We'll open the USA to the rest of the world when our ambassadors are invited back to their countries. It's *they* who expelled *our* embassy staff, *not* the other way around!'

The meeting continued for another thirty minutes before the president called a halt, saying he had other meetings to attend.

'Thank you for your time, Mr President,' the secretary general said, rising from her seat. 'I still do not understand your dislike of the Federation.'

'It's not the Federation per se, but their whole economic ethos.'

'Can we not spend some time talking about that to help me understand and report back to members?'

'No,' said the president. 'Anyways, I can't express the complexities as well as some others. Give me a moment… I'll get someone who can outline the reasoning behind our policies.'

The president pressed his intercom then picked up a handset. 'Matthew, can you see the secretary general. She's with me now and asking questions you're far better equipped to answer.'

He listened to the reply. Lara Horvat stood silently, doubtless wondering who "Matthew" was.

'Okay, she's leaving in a moment,' the president said, then turned to the secretary general and said, 'My economic advisor, Matthew Brown, will talk to you about the Federation's policies and ethos.'

'Thank you again for your time, Mr President,' she said.

'My pleasure, Your Excellency, but I must say that I am unhappy with your tone and attitude,' said the president, accompanying her through to his secretary's office.

'No more unhappy than I was being strip-searched at Dulles Airport on my arrival, Mr President,' she said, loud enough to be clearly heard by the secretary.

'Deirdre, the secretary general is meeting with Matthew. He'll be here shortly,' he said before returning to the Oval Office and shutting the door, somewhat more loudly than necessary.

'I'm sure Mr Brown will be here soon. Please take a seat,' said the secretary but, at that moment, a tall white man in his thirties with a buzz cut hairstyle and immaculate charcoal grey suit, marched into the office.

'Pleased to meet you, Your Excellency,' he said, offering his hand.

The secretary general shook it and thanked him for seeing her.

'Come this way,' he said. 'Would you like some coffee?'

'Yes, please, Mr Brown. I'd like my assistant to join us if we're going to listen to your views on the complicated structure of the Federation.'

'No problem. Deirdre, can you bring Her Excellency's assistant through to the small conference room?'

'Actually, she's already in there.'

'Right, fine,' Matthew Brown said as he guided Lara Horvat through the West Wing to a small conference room where Paula was sitting, reading her Kindle.

They all sat down at the main table and Matthew Brown asked one of the assistants to fetch coffee and biscuits for them.

He sat back in his seat, made a steeple of his hands, and asked, 'What would you like to know?'

The secretary general said, 'The Federation offers ordinary people the chance to live a better life than they do now, an end to war, poverty, famine, and disease. The rest of the world is finding it impossible to understand why the United States of America would not want to share in these benefits.'

Matthew Brown thought for a few moments, 'It is complex, but let me start by saying that the individuals may have a good life, but they have lost all opportunity for self-development. Without that, society will become static and stale. No proper rewards for innovation and invention.

'The Federation is communist. It requires total control and that'll stifle change. Vicissitudes will cease. With the state and automatons running everything, there'll be no inspiration to improve life. Geniuses will waste their talents looking after chickens or building model railroads. It's anathema to any ambitious, thinking person.

'The result will be that no one will have their own possessions and everyone will be forever dictated to by the "communist" state. Even their cultures and religions are being dictated.'

'Have you been to any of their worlds?' the secretary general asked.

'No, but I can visualise them. All I need to do is look at old film footage of the Soviet Union. We've seen it all before. It didn't work then, and it won't work now or at any time in the future. Large houses, taken from their owners and turned into tawdry apartment blocks. People corralled into grim concrete buildings.

'Also, stripping people of their jobs and only giving them a few hours a week in employment will drive them mad. My own father was a filling station assistant in his later working years. When he retired, he was completely lost and, after a few weeks, he asked for his old job back and worked there until he was in his late seventies. People want to feel useful. Make them feel useless and you destroy them.'

'Would you take the opportunity to discuss any of this with a Federation representative if the chance ever arose?'

'I'll argue the common sense of our viewpoint with anyone, Your Excellency.'

'And the famine in the world,' said the secretary general, 'the wars, the greed and selfishness we see with ninety-five per cent of the world's wealth being controlled by two per cent of the world's population. One person can be worth a hundred billion dollars, while a mother in

Myanmar is trying to feed her children on less than a dollar a day. You prefer that? For that's what we have today.'

'It's the wealthy who are the innovators, who create the jobs for other people so that they, too, can benefit from their innovations. Things are improving for the poor all the time. It trickles down from the wealthy. If people in other countries can't control their populations nor live within their means, that's not our responsibility. The United States, for decades, has handed out aid to underdeveloped countries as famine or disaster relief. Where do you think the money for that comes from? It comes from the fact that business and people generate wealth. You cannot be generous if you're living in poverty yourselves.'

Lara took a deep breath and said, 'Thank you for seeing us, Mr Brown, but we need to leave now. Your thoughts on the Federation are very useful and will be of interest to other UN delegates.'

'There is still a United Nations then?'

'Yes. A piece of land has been donated by Great Britain and construction of a new headquarters is underway to replace the building destroyed by the… er… *terrorists*.' The secretary general's emphasis on the word "terrorists" made it quite clear what she thought of that term.

Matthew Brown stood. 'Come this way, please, Your Excellency.'

Paula and Lara followed him through to the main reception area where he passed them over to an assistant. They were shown through to the entrance where the car was waiting.

All signs of the media were well and truly gone.

Once in the car, Lara asked, 'Did you record that?'

'Absolutely!'

'Type it up for me, please, Paula. Here's the recorder from my bag, too.'

7 Eskorav

[From Captain Ya Istil Sperafin's log. RBB]

The Eskorav and Medorin both hung in orbit above the swirls of an Atlantic hurricane, the vibrant colours of the land and sea almost hidden from sight except around the fringes of the storm and its attendant cloud masses. The freighter Medorin dwarfed the Eskorav. They both shared the green patchwork of colours which identified them as part of a Federation Enforcement fleet.

The Medorin had climbed out of the Sudanese gravity well, having shed its load of tens of thousands of tonnes of supplies to one of the Earth's most serious regions of famine. The Eskorav had been in orbit throughout, overseeing the enormous aid project being undertaken by the Federation. Prior to the aid beginning, there had been a fleet of supply ships surrounding and dwarfing the Eskorav. If anyone had cared to look at the right area of sky, they would have been eminently visible. Secrecy wasn't important to the Federation.

With the immediate aid programme complete, the two vessels were the only ships to remain in orbit and both skippers stood in the cockpit area of the Medorin, looking down upon the storm which was venting its fury upon the eastern Caribbean islands.

'This world does have interesting weather patterns,' said Ya Istil Sperafin, the skipper of the Eskorav, an egg-shaped mass of shimmering oyster coloured fluid which seemed to be held together by little more than surface tension.

'Yes, indeed,' said Yol Stirik Destrall, a huge powder blue gorilla-like creature, incongruously dressed in a neat, tight-fitting, green uniform.

'It's a severe tropical storm. They get them regularly,' said Ya Istil. 'No problems on the supply run?'

'All went fine,' said Yol Stirik. 'The other freighters have left, but we still have considerable supplies on board, and we'll be watching over the worst regions to see if the other nations make any effort to build upon our help.'

'Such a beautiful world,' said Ya Istil.

'Do you think they'll soon be invited into the Federation? Those people down there need help. Vast areas of the world are in poverty and other regions of the world are rich in financial terms as well as resources, although many of their resources seem to have been stolen from the poor.'

'You've been watching their television.'

'I have,' said Yol Stirik. 'They seem proud of their wealth and able to ignore the suffering of others. Their attitude towards poorer people, even those in their own economic areas, is lamentable. I heard a British politician saying that they should cut overseas development aid in order to put more aid into financing care for their own elderly, yet their elderly live in homes which are far and away more comfortable than the huts we have seen in, say, the north or the centre of Africa. They want to cut aid which is less than one per cent of their national wealth. Can such people ever be fit to join our community of nations?'

'Don't let it worry you, Stirik, it is out of our hands,' said Ya Istil. 'The ambassador will be here in a couple of days to assess progress. Other worlds soon adapt, and I guess the Federation believes Earth will change its ways too.'

'It just frustrates me. They are so cruel and uncaring as a species.'

'And violent,' said Ya Istil. 'Remember, they just blew up millions of their own people as a way of destroying our diplomatic team.'

'Yes. Shocking.'

'Have you seen the devastated area?'

'Not specifically. Is it noticeable?' said Yol Stirik.

'Very much so. We'll fly over it in a few minutes,' said Ya Istil, shaking herself and causing her body to ripple and shimmer and give the impression it might explode any second.

Yol Stirik watched with some apprehension. 'You okay?' he asked.

'Oh, yes. Just indigestion.' She turned back to the window. 'We're over central north America now. Keep watching.'

White cumulonimbus peppered the area south of the Great Lakes. Ya Istil was pleased to see that, far in the distance, the eastern seaboard of the continent was gradually entering the scene and was almost cloud free.

The stunning patchwork of cobalt and navy ocean crept over the curvature of the world, the darker areas partially concealed by scattered pristine white clouds casting their patterned shade.

The coast displayed a pallet of juniper and moss with caramel fields showing areas being cultivated. It was broken by grey and pewter plaids, indicating residential areas of towns and cities. As the ships neared the coastal conurbations, the checks resolved into city blocks and roads.

Further north, Long Island pointed its accusing finger into the Atlantic and, to its western end was a ragged circle of ash, dove, cinnamon and tawny destruction centred on the once home of the United Nations building which had been on the East River. Charcoal wisps of smoke were rising from some areas where fires were still smouldering after the nuclear explosion.

'That's it?' asked Yol Stirik.

Ya Istil gave her affirmative signal which involved a wave of beige liquid rising into view from the depths of her more pastel and grey normal body colour. 'Yes,' she said in Galactic Standard, in case the gorilla-like Stirik was unfamiliar with her species' visual language.

'There are still fires burning. I thought it happened a while ago.'

'Yes,' said Ya Istil. 'A month ago, but the areas of the city closest to the explosion are highly radioactive.'

'What's that greeny-brown rectangle?'

'They called it Central Park. The Ronoi was parked there.'

'And they got away all right?' asked Yol Stirik.

'Only just. The ship was quite badly damaged but managed to get into orbit. A number of people on board were injured, I narrowly escaped death.'

'You were on board?' asked Yol Stirik.

'I was first officer. Most of the deaths were the ambassadorial team there,' Ya Istil said, materialising a tendril to point at the location of the United Nations building, 'and crew who were sightseeing in the city.'

'Awful.'

'I'd better get back over to the Eskorav. I'll set up a lunch in a couple of days' time and invite your senior crew to come and meet ours. Perhaps you'll join the ambassador and me for dinner. Not sure of his plans yet.'

'That would be good,' said Yol Stirik.

Ya Istil created a few colours on one side of her body, showed them to a mobile device she carried, and promptly vanished.

«««0»»»

[From Jim Collins' records. RBB]

'What's the objective, Congressman Mayne?' asked Dick Beech after shaking hands with the Democrat Leader.

For security and secrecy reasons, the meeting was taking place in a hotel room in Pittsburgh. General Beech was accompanied by Mike Henderson and the congressman was with Jim Collins.

'I'm hoping you will provide the strategy, General,' said Charles Mayne. 'We think it is a priority to oust Slimbridge and the joint chiefs. They all seem to be in it together.'

'I won't be a party to swapping one dictatorship for another,' said the general.

'No. I wouldn't want that. As soon as we're in control, I'll call for a presidential election. You have my word.'

'I wouldn't take kindly to being let down, sir. I will hold you to that promise.'

'Please do,' said Charles. 'I'm an honourable American who supports the constitution.'

'Okay,' said the general. 'It will not be easy. The joint chiefs are well protected, as is the president.'

'Come up with a way. They must be removed from command,' said Charles, trying to exert some of his own authority into the meeting.

'What militia do you know of?'

'Jim here will liaise with you,' said Charles.

Jim said, 'We are in touch with fifteen groups spread around the country. Six of those are within fifty miles of Washington.'

'Right,' said the general. 'Colonel Mike Henderson here will be your liaison. He's my right-hand man and he'll keep in touch. He'll always know where I am.' He turned back to Charles Mayne. 'Sir, I'll need some time to work on this. I'll return when we have a strategy. I'm assuming you are making me your military chief.'

'Yes, I am. You come highly recommended and I'm told that you were an advisor to Jack Spence.'

'Yes, sir. I was his army chief until I retired two years ago. His death was a great blow to our country.'

'Indeed, it was,' said Charles.

'I'll need absolute control over the militia. From this point on I am their commanding officer. You will understand that you cannot interfere with the chain of command.'

'Of course, General, but I will need to know what is happening.'

'That won't always be possible. With covert operations, "need-to-know" is vital. You'll need to trust my judgement. You might not become aware of operations until they are completed.'

'As long as they follow the overall strategy.'

'They will.'

'How do you feel about the Federation, Congressman?'

'President Spence was very much against them, but then called in a number of bipartisan advisors and they all disappeared on a familiarisation trip. When Harry McBride, our presidential candidate, returned he was convinced it was the best thing since sliced bread. President Spence seemed to be of the same mind and the others who were with them. Not Slimbridge though, he seemed a very dour passenger. What about yourself, General?'

'Sceptical from what I've heard, but prepared to listen. It doesn't bother me as much as the fact that our president was murdered, and the country usurped. That is my objective in this, Congressman, overthrowing Slimbridge and his regime and seeing the proper election of a president.'

'We're more or less on the same wavelength then,' said Charles.

'More or less,' repeated the general. 'Where is Congressman McBride?'

'We don't know. We believe he might have been in New York. We haven't heard anything of or from him since.'

«‹‹0››»

[From Paula Wilson's notes about the post of secretary general. RBB]

The Department of Homeland Security made Lara Horvat's life very difficult over the application for one of the newly created exit visas for Paula Wilson. At last, she obtained one and it allowed Paula to leave the country with her. Lara had been worried that Paula might never be able to follow her if she hadn't waited to ensure it was properly authorised.

It was a miserable, wet and windy day when they entered the Dulles airport complex and things did not improve much after that.

'Why have you singled us out for searches,' asked Lara. 'You do realise we are diplomatic visitors and that I am the secretary general of the United Nations?'

'I'm sorry, madam,' said the rather embarrassed young man who was rifling through the contents of the suitcase. 'We were worried that you might be carrying important papers out of the country.'

'Nonsense!' Lara said, but could do nothing more than stand with Paula as three men pawed all of their clothes including make-up bags and Lara's soiled washing. The women insisted on repacking themselves.

With no time to spare, they passed through departures and boarded a United flight to Boston before transferring to a flight to Ottawa. There they had a layover before taking a second flight into London. There had been no direct flights into London since Britain had closed the American embassy.

'Dear God,' said Lara, 'that was ridiculous and obviously organised to cause us maximum inconvenience.

'I've never heard of such an invasion of privacy "looking for papers",' said Paula as they took their seats on the left of the aircraft.

'I hope we don't have the same treatment at Boston,' said Lara.

'Shouldn't do. We're through customs now, so should be okay.'

Soon their flight was approaching New York and the extent of the destruction hit home. All of those friends and colleagues who had been killed by President Slimbridge. Secretary General Horvat didn't believe, for a single moment, that terrorists were involved. Paula leaned across to look down at the devastation.

'My apartment was near the Bronx Zoo. Can't believe it's all gone. My God, there's still smoke coming from beside the East River, look!' Paula said, pointing at the graphite coloured cloud rising into the air over the location of the UN building.

'I was lucky,' said Lara. 'I was in Zimbabwe. My flight was delayed, or I'd have been arriving at Kennedy the morning of the bomb.'

'I was at my sister's wedding in Florida. That's what saved me, otherwise I'd have been in the UN building. I suppose it would have been instant. They'd have had no idea it had even happened.'

'No. The only saving grace. A single instant of incineration. Poor Perfect. So many gone. What a waste,' said the secretary general as Paula sat back in her seat. They'd lost so many friends and family.

They both enjoyed a sigh of relief when the plane crossed the Canadian border. There was a two hour layover in Ottawa before the flight to London Heathrow.

8 Sibernek

[Taken from notes kept by Dr Melanie Rogers. RBB]

Dr Ross marched through the double doors into the laboratory, looked around and ambled over to where Dr Rogers was lifting the leg of a mechanical man lying on its back on the bench.

'Where the devil did you get that?'

'Don't ask!' Dr Rogers replied, pushing down on the gold coloured knee to return the leg to the bench surface. 'Put it this way, a benefactor dropped it in. Apparently, it is a medical robot, one of many hundreds which have been left at famine sites by the Federation.'

'What? As part of the aid package they were mentioning on the news this morning?' Dr Ross asked as she lifted the robot's arm to examine the fingers. 'Amazing. So advanced. I suppose the benefactor was a government agent?'

The other woman just raised her eyebrows and continued to make notes. Dr Ross read them over her shoulder.

'I guess you called me to examine the brain?' asked Dr Ross.

'Yes. The Ministry of Defence has asked Sibernek to find out if it is possible to understand and duplicate it. Dr Barton asked me to call you and the gang of three from the chip lab. Paul won't be back from Ethiopia himself until Monday,' said Dr Rogers.

'Paul Barton's in Ethiopia!' said Dr Ross. 'Must be important if they've called him back.'

'He instigated the collection of this specimen.'

'Ah. All becomes clear. I suppose you want me to extract the chip or chips and get them to the gang of three to analyse them,' said Dr Ross.

'They'll be here shortly.'

At that moment three more people in white coats entered the lab. This was the famous gang of three who had invented the latest generation of Sibernek's chips. Jorg Bedan, a spotty, dark-haired scientist in a grubby white coat, who didn't look as if he was old enough to wear long trousers; Carol Swinford, a tall early-twenties blonde – the complete antithesis to Jorg – slim, impeccably dressed in what looked like a newly laundered coat, reflecting her immaculate grooming and hair; finally Jed

Coran, a more typical young professional who was actually wearing a tie of many shades of orange which complimented his shock of tousled locks.

'Oh, boy. We've got one!' said Jorg, rushing over to the prone gold and silver coloured figure. The others crowded in, too, and Dr Ross stood back to let them get a good look at the robot.

Dr Melanie Rogers admired their enthusiasm. These youngsters always made her feel ancient, even though she was still the right side of thirty and looked younger. She and Dr Gillian Ross had long been colleagues, moving from Intel to Sibernek together a few years earlier.

'How'd they get it?' asked Jed.

Dr Rogers replied, 'Apparently, Dr Barton asked one if he could examine him and when the robot said "yes", he was gobsmacked.'

'Is it deactivated?' asked Carol.

'Apparently. Dr Barton asked it to deactivate itself and it did,' said Dr Rogers. 'It's been like this ever since. A couple of warehousemen wheeled it in on a gurney a short while ago.'

'So, it could be hearing us?' said Carol.

'I've no idea,' said Dr Ross.

Jed said, 'Mr Medibot, are you hearing us?'

Everyone jumped when it replied, 'I am.'

'I had no idea,' said Dr Rogers.

'Interesting that it replied to being called Mr Medibot,' said Dr Ross.

'Mr Medibot,' said Jed, 'how did you know I was addressing you?'

The robot replied instantly, 'We are referred to as medibots. In addition, I could see the name tags on your jackets and knew I was the only unidentified person in the room. You do not need to add the honorific Mr.'

'Medibot, we were hoping to be able to dismantle you and find out exactly how you work,' said Dr Rogers. 'Would that be all right?'

The robot sat up on the bench, 'Yes. I have no problem with you examining me, but it might be best if I assist. It would be good if I were not damaged unintentionally during the process and some aspects might be better handled with questions.'

'I'd like to examine your central processing unit,' said Carol.

'In what way?' asked the medibot.

'I want to see the structure and how it might be manufactured.'

'My CPU comprises four chips. You can remove and examine them one at a time. If your intention is to reproduce them, I can advise how to do that without you needing to damage the chips.'

'That would be wonderful,' said Carol.

'We'd also like to see how your motors function. They are incredibly small, yet they are capable of moving your legs and arms,' said Dr Rogers.

'I can provide detailed instructions how to manufacture them and the systems which act as muscles,' said the bot.

'Would that not infringe patents or copyrights?' asked Dr Rogers.

There was a short silence before the medibot spoke. 'I understand. I had to look up the terms. There are no such things as patents or copyrights in the Federation. All technology is available to all.'

'Wow,' said Jed. 'Don't think that would go down too well with Sibernek's lawyers.'

'What about your software?' asked Dr Ross.

'By "software", do you mean my operating system?'

'Yes.'

'Operation systems vary depending upon the types of automaton. All contain protected instructions which can only be interpreted by our mind chips,' said the bot.

'What is a mind chip?' asked Jorg.

'It is the chip or section of a chip which permits us to think.'

'So, without that what effect would it have?' Jed asked.

'I could only fulfil functions which were included within the operation systems. Programmed is the word which most closely resembles them.'

'So, the mind chip is what makes you behave as if you are a living being?' said Jorg.

'Yes. Some would say it actually makes us living beings.'

'Whoa!' said Carol. 'You consider that you might be a living being?'

'Apart from my method of reproduction and bodily materials, I could be considered alive.'

The entire assembly stood still and tried to take stock of this revelation from the medibot. It believed it might be as alive as any human – or alien, for that matter.

Dr Rogers asked, 'Are all Federation robots potentially living beings by your definition?'

'It is not a definition, Dr Rogers. It is a problem of semantics really,' said the bot. 'In answer to your question, no. Robots with my type of mind are only those who need to perform functions which require conscious thought and the ability to understand previously never encountered situations. Like this one, in fact.'

'God! We can't dismantle you if you are alive,' said Dr Ross.

'As I say, Dr Ross, I am comfortable with my components being examined as long as they are not damaged. Also, if I work with you, much can be learned without any disassembly.'

'Do any of you ever think that the work you do is something you would rather not do? For instance, would you rather be reading a novel than helping to repair an injured creature's body?' asked Carol.

'No. My function is a priority. If there were no injured beings for me to treat, then I might either hibernate or do something interesting, like, as you say, reading a novel or an historical document, or even going sightseeing.'

None of those present missed the addition of "historical document" to the suggestion of a novel.

'What would sightseeing mean to you?' asked Jed.

'There is always knowledge to be gained by looking at things and places.'

'Does knowledge give you pleasure or what?' asked Carol.

'I don't know if I feel pleasure, but I do like to accumulate knowledge.'

'Interesting. How will this work?' asked Jed.

'I think we need to consider Medibot as one of the team, rather than as a specimen,' said Dr Rogers.

The interrogation continued.

«««o»»»

[From what I can ascertain, this is when Paula Wilson decided to make Lara Horvat's biography a second volume to the biography of Perfect Okafor, which was a work in progress. RBB]

Lara Horvat and Paula Wilson sat on a comfortable sofa in the secretary general's temporary office at the British Ministry of Defence. It was the first time they'd had a chance to talk confidentially about the White House meeting.

'What did you make of Brown?' asked Lara.

'He seemed nice enough, but I was surprised at his lack of understanding of the Federation's systems,' said Paula. 'When I was on the tour of Federation worlds with Perfect, it was quite clear that there was just as much innovation on their planets as there ever was on Earth. It wasn't suppressed at all in the way Brown imagines. In fact, there was more inventing and innovation going on *because* people had so much time to find new things to do and make.'

'Yes, he thinks the lack of incentives will erode the desire to innovate. I wish I could talk to one of the aliens about it.'

Almost as if the word "wish" had conjured up a genie, there was a muffled pop and Ambassador Trestogeen was standing near the desk, swaying back and forth to maintain his balance on his muscular tail.

'Ambassador!' said Lara as the two women jumped to their feet.

'Sorry, I apologise for my sudden unannounced arrival,' said the ambassador, looking at a flexible screen he held in one fin. 'I see the other lady is Paula Wilson, so you must be the new secretary general. We've not been introduced.'

'Yes, Ambassador,' said Paula. 'This is Secretary General Lara Horvat, but she does not speak Galactic Standard.' Paula interpreted for Lara.

'Oh, I apologise again,' the ambassador said in gurgly English.

'You weren't to know, Ambassador,' said Lara. 'Why are you here?'

'One of our bots let me know you'd changed locations and I wanted to fill you in with some interventions I'm making. You know about the relief supplies?'

'Yes. They've been well received. Thank you. Are we under constant surveillance by your bots? Where are they?' said Lara.

'We are monitoring certain key individuals. It saves time if I need to visit you. They are microscopic.'

'Hmm. Not sure I'm comfortable with that,' said Lara.

'We need to monitor to see how you are changing and adapting to life after the New York atrocity. We still have one freighter in orbit, but we're monitoring to see if your nations follow through on our help. All privacy safeguards are in place.'

'Please, sit,' said Lara, indicating the sofa. 'I didn't realise you were tracking us.'

'I will. Thank you. I know some people find my perpetual swaying unpleasant. The tracking is purely so I know where to find you. Ambassador Moroforon did not use surveillance bots and that was the reason we did not discover what President Slimbridge was doing in time to stop him.'

'That's an important revelation,' said Lara.

The atmosphere was a little strained so, to change the subject, Paula spoke up, 'Can I ask? Were you a water species and did intelligence arise before you left your oceans?'

'Yes, we had a considerable civilisation in our seas, long before we found ways to adapt to the land. We have membranes in our mouths and gullet which, as long as they are kept moist, allow us to breathe.'

'Would you like some water?' asked Lara.

'Yes, a beaker of water would be welcome.'

'Can you organise that, Paula, and coffee for us?'

'Don't alert anyone to my presence, Ya Horvat. I wish to keep my activities hidden.'

'No problem, Ambassador,' said Paula as she left the office, returning a minute later with a glass and jug of iced water, a coffee flask, some cups and a plate of assorted biscuits.

'Right, down to business,' said the ambassador. 'We've been watching for progress and, so far, have not seen much.

'The Americans are continuing their isolationist policies and we can see that they are threatening retaliation if anyone tries to intervene.

'We have provided considerable food and resources to poor areas of the world, but are not seeing any of the world's countries stepping up to build upon our support or improve the conditions of those who are not quite so poor.'

'The American situation,' said Lara, 'is very difficult. Their view of the Federation is that it is communist. I had a meeting with President Slimbridge and both Paula and I spent some time with his economic adviser, Matthew Brown. He explained some of his reasoning.'

'What were his points?' asked the ambassador.

'Paula…?' said Lara.

Paula pulled out her tablet and began to read, 'The individuals, may have a good life, but they have lost all opportunity for self-development. Without that, society will become static and stale. No proper rewards for innovation and invention.'

'Hmm,' said the ambassador. 'He is completely wrong. When the pressures of earning a living are removed from individuals and they are no longer forced to carry out particular jobs for others, it frees them up to invent, innovate and get great personal satisfaction from providing something new and good for society.' The ambassador materialised his secradarve and passed his fins over it, presumably making notes. 'Some innovation is created through necessity and we must admit that, with everyone having a good standard of living and all services provided at cost, innovation through necessity is an area which is less than effective. There are challenging games which fulfil that function to a degree and force people to come up with ideas in order to succeed. It is a fair point, though. What were his other criticisms?'

Paula swiped up her tablet and read, 'The Federation is communist. It requires total control and that will stifle change. Vicissitudes will cease. With the state and automatons running everything, there will be no inspiration to improve life. Geniuses will waste their talents looking after chickens or building model railroads. It is anathema to any thinking person.'

The ambassador thought for a minute. 'Yes, I suppose, strictly speaking, the Federation applies communist principles, but Mr Brown is immediately casting his mind back to your historical Union of Soviet Socialist Republics. Their system failed for many reasons and during its failure it did stifle change and dampen down inspiration. That would naturally create a situation where the talented people would lose any desire to innovate. Earth doesn't have the wherewithal to introduce an equal society. To do that you need willing robots who can carry out each and every function of a working human being without either monitoring or instructions. Either that or slaves.

'The bulk of the problems the old Soviet system created were caused by stagnated leadership, a fear of taking responsibility for anything new, corruption and some leaders who had taken so much power for themselves that no one dare speak against them. Propaganda swamped the USSR, killing not just ideas, but people too. Make a suggestion disliked by Stalin or Breshnev and you found yourself, not encouraged to improve your concept, but thrown into labour camps or worse. Any leader who cannot tolerate criticism is the same. In the Federation that cannot happen.'

'Yes, but that fear is natural,' said Lara. 'The Soviet Union is gone, and no one would want it to return. He mentioned that his own father… What was it he said, Paula?'

'My own father was a filling station assistant in his later working years. When he retired, he was completely lost and, after a few weeks, he returned to his old job and worked there until he was in his late seventies. People want to feel useful. Make them feel useless and you destroy them,' said Paula, laying her iPad on the table.

The ambassador continued, 'Going back to the USSR, they were unable to complete their project. They never could. It was impossible. Everything which is different about the Federation is missing from the Soviet Union. We have a willing workforce of automatons. They do anything people do not wish to tackle, freeing up the people to improve everything about their way of life. Corruption is prevented, power is no longer available to individuals who wish to be leaders. Income is shared as was the original Soviet intention, but they never had the wherewithal to carry it out. The Federation does. People can never be happy if they are threatened or coerced into work.'

'Yes, I see that,' said Lara. 'We are the converted. How do we persuade the likes of Brown and President Slimbridge?'

'Let me return to Mr Brown's point about his father,' said the ambassador. 'His father reached the beginnings of old age and suddenly had no purpose in life. It is something we deal with continually on worlds who have newly joined the Federation. There are detailed therapy plans which guide people out of their habit of working. The older the individuals are, the more difficult they find it to adapt and the more help has to be given to them. Mr Brown should visit one or two of our newer member worlds to see how it is dealt with. The most important factor is that no one – absolutely no one – is stopped from working if they really want to work. All they need to do is ask and they can do the job they really want to do. Some then continue for weeks or months or even years. There is no pressure to stop. The Federation does not force anyone to do anything unless they've committed a crime.

'I believe President Slimbridge was taken on a familiarisation trip?'

'Yes,' said Paula. 'He visited Arlucian, but,' she fussed with her tablet, 'he said to us, "This is exactly the sort of bullshit which Spence swallowed, hook, line and sinker. The Federation only took us to worlds which they'd specially prepped to suit their needs. We never saw the worlds with shortages in shops and communist state-owned business regimes which forced them to work countless hours for a pittance."'

The ambassador raised his glass and drank deeply from the iced water. 'I am horrified. We let the leaders choose which worlds they visited. Nothing was specially prepared except the meeting with President Dimorathron. Ambassador Moroforon even arranged visits to worlds which had newly joined, to show integration in progress. His accusation that there are hidden worlds with shortages and forced labour is ridiculous. That is only found on Earth!'

'Ambassador Trestogeen, we understand that,' said Lara, 'but we don't know how to convince those who believe President Slimbridge's disinformation. Can you help in any way?'

'I am not even meant to be here, Secretary Horvat.'

'It would be so good if you could talk to the Security Council. Please do so or, at the very least, let me tell them about your visit,' said Lara.

The ambassador stood, said a few words into a device on his fin, then said, 'I shall think on this situation,' and promptly vanished.

9 Militia

[From Drew Gambon's notes. RBB]

'Let's call this to order,' said Brad Gregg, bringing down a heavy glass paperweight onto the desk.

The group of five had swollen to more than twenty. Mixed ages, ethnicity and sex, although the majority were male and fifty-ish.

'Before we start, might I remind you that everything said in our meetings is secret. Speaking of our activities outside this room will endanger us all. Another group in Charleston was betrayed last week. They were taken away and nothing has been heard from them since. We believe they might have been summarily executed.'

'We don't know that for certain,' said General Dick Beech hurriedly. 'Let's not start jumping to conclusions.'

'Yes. Fair enough,' said Brad.

'Okay,' said the general, standing up and taking control of the meeting. 'You all know why you are here. We are setting up a militia. I have had a meeting with Congressman Charles Mayne, and he has appointed me his military advisor.

'I'll be travelling around the states, talking to small organised groups, like ours, and coordinating a plan. Brad is my assistant and Mike is now the leader of this cell. What he says goes.'

Mike Henderson stood and took a bow.

'Thank you, Mike,' said the general. 'Colonel Mike Henderson will be organising weapons and a location where you can meet safely. Brad's cellar will, in future, only be used when I need to hold meetings with cell leaders.

'What I do want to say to all of you is that we are embarking on a dangerous enterprise. Our country, which we all love, has been taken over by a power-crazy individual who has convinced himself that he is right in all matters. What we are doing is not because we are disaffected Republicans, or Democrats for that matter. We are taking action because our president was murdered by Slimbridge and we want to restore order and democracy. The general populace is not stupid, but people who are fed continual lies and alternative truths will be swayed by those arguments when there is no one putting an opposing point of view. Such people are a real danger to us, but they are not our enemies, it is a form of brainwashing and we need to rescue them.'

'Are you all with us?' shouted Brad.

'We are!' returned a chorus of voices as their owners began, uncharacteristically, banging on anything which would make a noise.

They quickly realised their rowdiness was not appropriate and, eventually, the din died down and the general continued. 'I am now handing over to the colonel. He speaks for me in all command matters.'

Mike lifted his muscular two-hundred-pound body out of the easy chair to the right of Brad's desk. The epitome of a fit American football linebacker, he strode confidently to take the ground in front of the assembly.

'You all know me. The people who we will be facing are disciplined, professional soldiers and police. If we are not from the same mould, people will die. Many of you… in fact, most of you are ex-military, but we all know how quickly we become soft and opinionated. I need to whip you into shape. This is not a game and any of you joining up with anything other than total determination to beat Slimbridge would be better not returning after this meeting. However, do tell me if that is the case. We will not hold anything against you. What we are about to undertake is not trivial and I need well trained soldiers who will follow orders. Do I make myself clear?'

There was a chorus of 'Yes, sir,' and several jumped to their feet and saluted.

'Right. We start tomorrow.

'We meet at nineteen hundred hours sharp at the Methodist church hall. Don't walk into that hall a minute after that time! Those of you who have uniforms, check if they still fit. Remove stripes or pips – no one brings any rank into the first session. I will appoint chains of command after I know your fitness and abilities. If you are wearing your uniform to the meeting, conceal it under coats. We don't want busybodies reporting a military gathering to the police. If any of you are challenged, you are attending a Gulf War reunion. Is that clear?'

'Sir,' came from the assembly.

'Is that not clear, Armstrong?'

'Yes, sir. Clear, sir.'

'Then next time answer before being asked!'

'Yes, sir,' the man said, colouring somewhat.

'Those of you with weapons. List them accurately together with ammunition. Don't bring the weapons, but do bring the list to the meeting. Be sure to check your weapons are serviceable. Major Drew Gambon will need those lists so that he can ensure we are all supplied. Major, how did Harry West react when you approached him?'

'Very well, sir. I have him researching what military weapons he can acquire. I'm seeing him again tomorrow morning. His son is here, sir. Show yourself, West.'

A young man stepped forward and saluted.

'At ease,' said Mike. 'Back to you, Brad.'

There was spontaneous applause and cheering.

'Meeting over!' screamed Brad above the cacophony, which gradually died down and was replaced by the hubbub of people discussing strategies and resources.

'Settle down, soldiers. This is not a Scouts' meeting!' shouted Mike.

'Anything else, sir?' asked Mike.

'No, that's fine, Colonel,' said the general.

«‹‹o››»

[Extracted from a private diary note appended to the United Nations minutes. RBB]

A magnificent buffet had been laid out on one side of a large meeting room at Number Ten Downing Street. The serving staff left, and Lara Horvat looked at the plates and dishes. The prime minister walked past the open door, saw the secretary general and came over to her.

'Everything okay, Lara?' she asked.

Taken a little by surprise at the sound of someone beside her, Lara turned to the prime minister. 'Oh, Maureen. Sorry. Didn't see you come in. Yes, everything's fine. It is so kind of you to offer this room and your catering staff for UN meetings.'

'Britain's pleasure, Lara.'

'Must admit, I'm tempted to sample one of these anchovy hors d'oeuvres,' Lara said and laughed as she popped one of the savoury nibbles. 'Delicious,' she said.

The prime minister also selected one and they ate the snacks like children who'd stumbled across the preparation of a wedding feast.

'Right,' said Lara. 'I must go and prepare my material for the meeting. See you back here at one o'clock. Do I need to lock the door to stop you snacking?'

They both laughed.

'No,' said the prime minister. 'I'll resist any further temptation until the others arrive!'

«««o»»»

[From White House tapes. RBB]

The Oval Office was silent despite the presence of the military leaders. Admiral Mann and Generals Burko and Braun, Matthew Brown and President Slimbridge were all seated in the easy chairs and chesterfield.

The president looked aghast at General Braun and broke the silence, 'You're having second thoughts?! It's a bit damn late to say you're rethinking.'

'Mr President,' said Admiral Mann, 'there is growing unrest in the country and while there is a hard core of supporters who believe the terrorist theory, the bulk of the population are hearing an increasing number of reports that it was us who blew up the United Nations building. We need to rethink.'

'And do what, exactly?' asked the president. 'Show weakness and suspicion becomes confirmation.'

'Sir,' said General Burko. 'We are getting intel on more and more armed groups and there are now rumours that they are coalescing under the command of General Dick Beech. That is a whole new ball game.'

'Dick Beech? You mean the retired general? Spence's man?'

'Yes, Mr President. We've heard that he is now having meetings with disaffected politicians from all sides,' said General Burko.

'So, you're all going soft on me now!' said the president. 'It was the three of you who encouraged me to take this course of action.'

'We're still backing you, Mr President,' said General Braun, 'but we all feel that the strategy needs to change or the Federationists will get organised and we could find ourselves in a full-blown civil war.'

'No,' said the president and bellowed into his intercom, 'Deirdre!'

The secretary opened the door and said, 'Yes, sir.'

'Matthew. Go with Deirdre and get the media contacts. I want to make a nationwide broadcast. Once you've organised that, find Madison and write me a speech to defuse these feelings of rebellion.'

'Yes, sir,' said Matthew, jumping to his feet and following Deirdre into the outer office.

'What are you planning, sir?' asked the admiral.

'Burko, where are you holding that group of rebels you captured in Charleston?'

'Still being held in Fort Jackson, sir.'

'How many of them?'

'Twenty-eight.'

'What sort of structure did they have?'

'Difficult to say, but six were quite high ranking military including three colonels, a major and two captains.'

'Current or retired?'

'All retired, sir.'

'This meeting is ended,' said the president. 'Burko, stay behind. I've a plan for the insurgents.'

«««0»»»

[Taken from Ambassador Trestogeen's office files and notes. RBB]

Hareen Trestogeen lounged on a padded sofa which matched his flatfish shape. He sipped from a large beaker of water and ran a sponge over his lips and gill area. Across the room a large window showed Earth; pale blue and white as it always looked from orbit in cloudy conditions. A cream and linen banded border showed the thin atmosphere which faded into the blackness of space. The captain of the Eskorav sat opposite him.

'Istil, I'm in a quandary,' said the ambassador.

'I realise that, Hareen. I told you it was unwise to go down,' the captain replied, her globular shape distorting and swirling with the colours of her own language. The ambassador would understand, but using Galactic Standard language ensured no meaning was lost in translation.

'They need help down there. Not just supplies for the poor areas, but help with a strategy to bring the country known as America back into the international fold.'

'I met both President Spence and then Vice President Slimbridge when I was first officer on the Ronoi.'

'Were you on board during the incident?'

'Yes, fortunately. Three of us had just returned from sightseeing in New York. We'd only been on board about ten minutes when the explosion rocked the ship. I was very lucky to survive.'

'I suppose your species tends to be rather fragile,' said the ambassador.

'Yes, Hareen. If I'd been thrown against anything with edges, I'd have certainly been punctured and died. When the main blast struck, I impacted a corridor wall. Painful, but nothing cut my membrane. Developed an enormous bruise, though,' said the captain as her internal organs came to the surface then retreated into her nebulous interior offering some sort of demonstration which was lost on the ambassador.

'What did you make of President Spence?'

'None of us liked him initially. He was full of suspicion of Federation planets, but by the time he returned with Vice President Slimbridge, he'd mellowed and become an actual advocate for membership.'

'Yes,' said the ambassador. 'I got the same feeling from Ambassador Moroforon's notes. What about Slimbridge?'

'Completely different. He seemed hard and uncompromising from what I saw of him on the way to and from Arlucian. Sceptical and distrusting would be good words.'

'Yes, I understand.'

'What are you thinking?' the captain said, flowing into a more upright-shaped balloon.

'I don't think I can persuade the cabinet to allow me to help Earth,' said the ambassador. 'So, I have to do it unofficially or not at all. How are the famine areas doing at the moment?'

'I had dinner with Yol Stirik yesterday. He says that all of the supply missions achieved their objectives. There are large amounts of resupply starting to go into North Africa from Europe and Russia. The Myanmar refugee camps are now being resupplied by the Chinese.'

'They've taken the principle of helping the poor on board, then? I wonder if that was, in part, owing to my dropping in on the secretary general.'

'Well, they always had helped less fortunate nations and regions,' said the captain. 'The problem is that none of them were doing enough in the past, even the Americans who have always supplied the majority of aid to poorer areas. Their aid has now stopped, of course.'

'The others, then, Britain, France, Russia and China, have learned from interaction with us and are trying to do more.'

'From what Yol Stirik says, yes. Very much so.'

The two creatures sat quietly, as if all that needed to be said had been said. Ya Istil Sperafin knew that she'd been called in to the ambassador to try to help him make a decision on intervention. It wasn't allowed and, if the cabinet discovered the truth, Yol Hareen Trestogeen would certainly be recalled and never invited to be an ambassador again. Istil knew which way she hoped Hareen would go, but would he? There were many hazards down that pathway.

'I think I'll have to investigate further,' said the ambassador. He looked at his secradarve. 'I'd like a cloaked shuttle to take me to London at the fourteenth hour please.'

'No problem, Ambassador. I'll see to it,' the captain said. 'You're going to intervene then?'

'Yes. I have to. As well as being the Federation's representative, I feel a connection with the people of Earth. They're so kind, but so foolish, almost in equal measure. Completely forsaking them strikes me as like deserting a drowning child.'

'It will not be seen like that on Arlucian.'

'I know. I'll find out whether or not we can work together and then make a decision,' said the ambassador.

'If you then fail to assist, it could have a worse effect than not helping in the first place,' said Ya Istil.

'I know, but still I must do my best. You'll organise the shuttle?' said the ambassador. 'You know I don't have very much time left?'

'What? Your spawning schedule?'

'Yes. I would dearly love to sort out this world's problems before the time comes.'

'I'll arrange the shuttle, Hareen,' said the captain, leaving the seat and floating out of the room on her personal hoverette.

10 Security Council

[Taken from Paula Wilson's minutes and Hareen Trestogeen's recordings. RBB]

President Marat Olov put an arm on Lara Horvat's shoulder, while holding a still replete plate of food in the other. 'A fine spread, Lara. Excellent,' he said.

The buffet had gone down well and Lara was pleased to see each of the leaders deep in conversation with each other. Perhaps that they were standing instead of formally seated at a table allowed them to be more relaxed with each other.

Caroline Stoddart, the British UN envoy was deep in conversation with President Che Yang, while President Phillipe Ramseur was in an animated discussion with Prime Minister Church and her defence minister, Malcolm Gorman.

Lara was pleased with the informality and walked over to Paula Wilson who was sitting on her own on the far side of the room.

'Okay?' asked the secretary general.

'Yes, ma'am. Just keeping out of the way.'

'They're all enjoying the informal nature of the lunch. I'm almost reluctant to break them away for the meeting,' Lara said and laughed.

'Ma'am, there is an interesting aura of cooperation in this room. Much better than the meetings your predecessor was trying to control prior to New York. Everything was so much more... fractious,' said Paula.

'Maybe we'll be able to all move forward together if we can solve the Slimbridge situation.'

Eventually, much later than planned, the plates emptied and were set aside.

'Ladies, gentlemen,' said Lara. 'Shall we retreat into the meeting room?'

'Indeed,' said Che Yang, refilling his orange drink from the jug and following some of the others as they moved through to the second briefing room, all still deep in conversation.

Lara waited until they were all seated. 'Let me call this meeting of the Security Council to order. Joining us today are British Defence Minister Malcolm Gorman, who you all know; Caroline Stoddart, the British UN envoy and Paula Wilson who was an assistant to my predecessor, and has decided to join my new team. Paula has visited half a dozen Federation worlds including Arlucian, so don't be tardy in picking her brains if you need to.'

The participants nodded to the co-opted attendees.

'Firstly,' said Lara, 'I wish to thank the British government for providing these meeting facilities within Number Ten and even more so for their kind provision of an area of land east of London for the new United Nations Headquarters. It has been planned and approved. Work should begin in a few weeks. Thanks also to those of you present and the twenty-two other countries who are collectively picking up the tab for the construction.

'Now, I'd like to call upon Malcolm Gorman for the latest intelligence from the USA.'

The British defence minister stood and walked to a position near the secretary general where he could be seen more easily by all of those in attendance.

'I bring no good news,' he said. 'We have reports of several, what they call "groups of insurgents", being executed. Three leaders of a group from Charleston were executed last night live on television. President Slimbridge then followed the execution with the following broadcast. I do apologise that the execution does appear at the beginning of this recording. I was going to remove it, but Prime Minister Church suggested I should show the whole episode, so consider yourselves warned.'

Malcolm Gorman pointed an IR device at the giant briefing-room television screen then sat down.

The film began with a title "Broadcast by President Slimbridge." A military detail marched into view from the left of the screen. Three soldiers broke away and took three prisoners with them. They were made to stand and face the front with a red-brick wall behind them. Nine other members of the detail were commanded by a colonel, standing to one side, to raise their weapons, take aim and fire. The prisoners, all dressed in white, were suddenly coloured in red as if they'd been splashed by paint. In dreadful slow motion they crumpled to the floor.

The scene changed to the White House, then the Oval Office and zoomed in upon a very serious President Slimbridge, immaculately dressed, facing the camera with his hands clasped together on the desktop before him.

'Citizens of the United States of America,' he said. 'It truly grieves me to have you witness the execution of previously faithful citizens who had become insurgents. They had been commanding a troop of more than one hundred persons and their objective was to overthrow your president. Their leader is Charles Mayne, a Democrat who desires the presidency for himself, but as an agent of the communist Federation.

'I wanted you to see what happens to traitors, and caution you that there are many more insurgency groups. Mayne's foot soldiers are being held in custody, but the crimes of the educated officers, two colonels and a captain, were beyond the mercy of our justice system. They were traitors.

'The Federation wants to take over the whole planet. They turned the heads of some leaders, fooling them into visiting many specially primed planets which were to show their political system in a good light. They were lying! They were only taken to planets to see staged presentations of people working together. It was all a lie! There are thousands of their planets where people are unable to scrape a living – where they live in concrete blocks of apartments, like the old Soviet Union – where there are shortages, disease and low life expectancy. All of this was hidden from view.

'I say to you, that if we became part of the Federation, at the moment of joining we would be overwhelmed by millions of robots who would force people to give up their property and begin a life of virtual slavery.

'My government, together with the chiefs of the armed forces, realised just in time what was about to be foisted upon the unsuspecting public.'

He unlinked his fingers and leaned forward towards the camera, adopting a more friendly demeanour and a quieter tone. 'It is a matter of great regret that we did not know that a group of anti-Federation terrorists were planning to destroy the United Nations building at the very moment when it contained all of the world's leaders and all of the Federation people too. If we'd known what they were planning, we might have been able to stop it and save New York City, but we didn't know. A simple veto from the USA could have stopped the plan to join the Federation at a stroke.'

He sat back in his chair. 'But we also know that the act of the terrorists stopped the Federation in its tracks, destroying the ringleaders and their worldly lackeys. Sadly, they also destroyed the innocent population of the city. That is, of course, the real tragedy… but it is always the innocent who suffer in totalitarian regimes.'

He paused again. 'I call on you now, everyone in this wonderful country of ours, the last bastion of freedom in the world, to keep alert. If you hear or see anything suspicious, let us know. Go to the local police or tell your local army base. The Federation has been wounded. They have retreated. We've seen nothing of them since New York, except their destruction of our space activities and weather satellites, of course.

'They destroyed Moonbase, destroyed the peaceful International Space Station, destroyed America's satellites which provided the GPS signals for navigation, destroyed our broadcasting satellites – this is coming to you via local relays. They even destroyed the fabulous Hubble telescope, the lunar orbiting platform, the satellites studying deep space and the sun. What will they do next?

'Citizens of the USA. We are in grave danger from the aliens, but also from their supporters on Earth, indeed, inside our own country. We must stay alert. The first year will be difficult as they are trying to stop international trade. If we can, with your help, survive this first year, then we will have broken the back of the crisis.'

During his last sentence, music began to play. Initially so quietly that it was almost impossible to identify it, but gradually the famous anthem grew in intensity. The *Star Spangled Banner* was soon in full swing. Superimposed flags, blowing in the wind, materialised behind the president as he stood and placed his hand firmly over his heart. Throughout the country, many citizens followed suit. Many others must have been sickened by the executions.

The anthem came to an end and the scene returned to an exterior view of the White House before fading to black.

'What threatened punishment could have made these soldiers obey such orders?' asked the prime minister.

'Is 'e mad?' asked President Ramseur.

'It would seem so,' said President Yang.

'Is there more, Malcolm?' asked the prime minister.

'It is full of lies, of course, and not just his speech. The group of insurgents was thirty strong, not a hundred. We don't think Charles Mayne was actually commanding them. However, that is where there is some better news.

'We know from communications which have reached us through Peter Stone in Canada, that there is now a properly organised militia being formed. It will be supporting Charles Mayne and is being commanded by General Beech, who was once President Spence's head of the joint chiefs.'

'Yes. Met him a few times,' said President Olov.

'It will take time,' continued Malcolm, 'but at least we know it will be well organised. Less good news is that we hear that Slimbridge's broadcast has been well received. It was, of course, aimed at the gullible.'

The prime minister said, 'Unfortunately, when people have no other point of reference, they can be easily sucked along on a wave of distorted national pride. In decades to come, they will wonder how they allowed it to happen.'

Malcolm Gorman returned to his seat and Lara Horvat took over the chair.

'I have some good news too,' she said.

All eyes turned back to her.

'Paula and I had a visitor the other day. He asked me not to tell anyone, but as I report to those of you in this room, I think I have a duty to be honest about it.'

The level of interest of the others tangibly rose.

'Ambassador Trestogeen materialised in my room in the office you are loaning me at the Ministry of Defence.'

There was considerable shock and sounds of 'really?' in the room.

'What he say?' asked President Yang.

'He asked about my White House meeting. No one will be surprised to hear that it went badly. President Slimbridge passed me on to a Matthew Brown who told us his views on Federation politics. It was all dreadfully distorted and, of course, the president himself denied any involvement in the New York debacle.'

'Well, 'e would,' said President Ramseur.

Paula handed out transcripts of the meetings with Slimbridge and Brown.

'I put all they had said to me,' the secretary general continued, 'to the ambassador and he was horrified at the distortion of the truth.

'I told him we needed help and he left, saying he was going to "think on it", but I've heard nothing since.'

At that moment there was a pop and increase in air pressure. Lara and Paula recognised the sound and feeling instantly – Ambassador Yol Hareen Trestogeen was standing, or rather swaying, beside the giant television. 'Good afternoon,' he said in his less than perfect esponged gurgling English. 'One of our bots told me you were all in one place, so I hope you don't mind the intrusion.'

11 Operations

[Taken from Brad Gregg's memoirs. RBB]

When all is said and done, the success of any operation comes down to good intel and subsequent good planning. General Dick Beech was an exceptional strategist. Today, the White House would find out just how good he was.

Six unremarkable passenger carrying vans, portraying a number of bus operator names, turned into a suburban street and continued in file. It could have been a day out, a trip to the theatre or a sports event, but closer examination showed that the windows were rather darker than the normal glass found in these vehicles. They had all been adapted so that it was impossible to see the interiors from either the sidewalk or any passing vehicles. If you had been able to see through the windows, you'd have found that each bus contained between twelve and fifteen men and women, kitted out in camouflage fatigues with weapons on their laps. Some, the less experienced, fiddled with their guns, checking and double-checking the magazines, firing mechanisms or, in some cases, the safeties.

City Tours, the front vehicle, passed the last of the houses of the township and, three hundred yards later, pulled into a rest stop on the right of the road, the dappled sunshine running across the livery and windows. The other five vans continued onwards, keeping well within speed limits. The last thing they wanted was to be pulled over by an inquisitive patrolman.

The interior of City Tours, if it could have been seen, would have shown that it had nothing to do with learning about the local city. It was bristling with communications equipment. General Beech, Brad Gregg and a couple of others sat silently. They were waiting patiently, the air conditioning keeping the van's interior bearable, but not cool. The radio sprang to life and a short message was heard, directing police officers to a disturbance at a filling station on the highway to the north. The officers replied that they were on their way. The message was of no interest to Beech. It would only be of interest if it was something on this eastern side of the city. Now that they were beyond the city limits, any disturbance which could possibly bring the police their way would be even less likely.

'Couple of minutes,' said Brad and the general nodded.

In the driver's seat, another of the group was continually scanning her wing mirrors in case any inquisitive individual decided to find out why there was a tour bus sitting in this particular rest stop. No one approached. The closest houses were at least three hundred yards behind them. A farmhouse was on the left, about half a mile ahead of them and the target home nearly two miles ahead on the right.

'B to F in position,' a voice said over the radio.

'They're in position,' said the general.

'Six limos of various sizes, two motorbikes and one air force jeep outside the house. Two armed soldiers in the driveway, looking bored. F out.'

'B to E turned and ready,' said another voice.

'Clear the approach,' said the general.

'Ready to snipe,' said one of the militia from coach F over the radio.

'Go for that!' the colonel's voice was heard on the same channel.

The general listened intently. Mike was a good man. If anyone could pull this off, it was him.

Three men with rifles burrowed their way through the hedge and scrub trees until they had a good view of the soldiers leaning against the three-bar stock fence shielding the driveway. Two positioned themselves in the grass and wildflowers the other side of the hedge, lay on the ground and adjusted their rifles and telescopic sights. The third soldier crouched behind them with binoculars. The guards were approximately a hundred metres away along the drive. An easy shot with a sniper's rifle, but these weapons were adapted to use poison darts, so not as accurate.

'I'd still prefer a bullet. I don't like this,' whispered one man to the other.

'Just don't miss.' said the crouching man. 'Ready?'

'Ready,' said one.

'Ready,' said the other.

'On the word fire. Three. Two. One. Fire!'

Both men squeezed their triggers simultaneously. The weapons gave a loud crack. Not as loud as a normal gunshot, but certainly loud enough to be heard at the target's range.

All three watched. One man crumpled to the ground instantly. The second looked down at his jacket and tried to knock something off himself.

Within three seconds there was a second crack which caused the soldier to look towards the bushes. He had just unclipped his radio and was about to sound the alarm, when he too collapsed in a heap.

'Snipe done,' reported the third man. 'House quiet. No one outside.'

'Go, go, go!' came the general's voice.

The four coaches turned into the driveway and accelerated towards the house.

'B to E on the drive,' reported the third man, then he turned to his snipers and said, 'Quick, back to the vehicle.'

The men were soon back in coach F, which reversed rapidly up the driveway, stopping by the two collapsed soldiers. Five men were out of the coach and pulling the soldiers on board. They then waited, effectively blocking the driveway. Near the house, the other four vehicles were decanting fifty armed militia behind a barn, about forty yards from the house.

«««0»»»

[Sorry. I had no records to work from regarding the party, but assume it was something like this. I had Brad Gregg's notes and memoirs to assist me with the assault. RBB]

'Happy Birthday to you!'

'Happy Birthday dear Julia,' the voices sang.

'Happy Birthday to you!'

Surrounded by cheers and clapping, a ten-year-old girl blew out the candles.

'Make a wish,' her grandfather said.

'I did, I…'

'No, don't tell us or it won't come true,' called her mother quickly to stop the child revealing her innermost desires.

Everyone laughed.

All of a sudden there was a crash. The armoured front door held.

'Down, down, down!' shouted a captain in the hallway. 'Edwards, Dredge, here quickly. We're under attack.' He looked towards General Braun. The general nodded and ran through the kitchen towards the panic room.

A second huge crash still failed to get through the door.

The children and family were all prone on the living room floor.

Captain Tomkins shouted through to them. 'Stay down and keep still. Don't move and keep quiet!'

This time the door gave way. Edwards and Dredge immediately opened fire through the opening. There were some cries and shouts. Gunfire came the other way and the two men fell to the ground. The children and some of the adults in the living room began to scream and cry.

The captain had positioned himself on the next floor where he had a clear shot of the hallway through the timbered landing and bannisters.

Another volley of shots came through the doorway and the captain saw two, then four, then eight men enter and look into each of the ground floor rooms. Two more entered and he decided to take action. He began sweeping his automatic weapon fire from side to side into the hall area. Six men fell instantly, then his fire was returned. He retreated along the upper landing.

Four more men entered. 'Where's Braun?' asked Colonel Mike Henderson.

'Don't know, sir. One man upstairs.'

Mike dashed through to the lounge and satisfied himself that the general was not among those on the floor.

'Get that man upstairs!' said Mike and, into the radio. 'Twenty men in here at the double to search, and beware, we have one remaining rogue on the first floor.'

Mike turned towards the kitchen area, waited for some of the squad to enter the building and called four of them over. 'The bomb shelter is in the cellar. Four of you with me.'

Mike and his team made their way through the kitchen, then a utility room where there was a strong door. Mike pulled on the handle. It was locked. 'This is it, pass me the bullhorn,' he said.

Mike turned on the device and held it against the door. 'General Braun. The house is in our possession. If you give yourself up now, then your family will not be harmed.'

They allowed five minutes and when there was no sound from the shelter, Mike spoke again into the bullhorn, 'General Braun. You must surrender. If you do not open this door within five minutes, we will shoot one of the civilians who was at your granddaughter's party. Five minutes. Not a second more.'

'Get me the name of some adult from in there. A woman about thirty would be best,' said Mike and one of his team dashed off through to the lounge area.

He was back within a minute. 'Madelaine Ash – about thirty-five.'

Mike flipped on the megaphone, 'General Braun. You have two minutes thirty seconds before we shoot Madelaine Ash through both knees. Come out now,' he said into the bullhorn. 'Is Janet nearby?' he asked the team.

'Guarding the party guests.'

'Go fetch her,' Mike said and then, into the bullhorn, 'Two minutes.'

'One minute,' he said into the bullhorn.

The original soldier returned with a young woman also in militia uniform.

'You able to do a convincing scream?' asked Mike.

'I'll have a go, sir.'

'Right. David, when I say fire, I want you to fire your weapon into that pile of washing. Janet, you scream as if you've been shot through the knee. Then a second shot David, and a second scream. Make it good, Janet.'

Mike turned on the bullhorn. 'Ten – nine – eight – last chance, General – six – five – I mean it – three – two – one – fire!'

The shot rang out and Janet made a valiant attempt at a scream and crying out, then she shouted, 'No, no!' David fired again and she released another agonising scream.

'One more minute, General, and the next shot will be between her eyes. Come out now, unarmed and she'll be rushed to a hospital. No one else will be harmed and you will be taken into custody. We have no intention of killing you. Come out now!'

A few seconds passed and then the sound of bolts being drawn came from the door.

'Be ready,' said Mike and two men aimed their rifles at the door.

The door opened and General Braun emerged with his hands raised. 'You won't get away with this?' he said.

'Search him, Hugh.'

The soldier made the general raise his arms and patted him down thoroughly. After a minute, Hugh said, 'He's clean.'

'I don't know who you are, but rest assured we will hunt you down for this,' said the general.

'Okay, get him out of here and clear the grounds now,' said Mike. He shouted after them, 'And let him see Mrs Ash so he knows we didn't harm her.'

Within ten minutes all the guests' cell phones had been removed and the house evacuated of militia. The coaches sped down the driveway and left in different directions, all taking separate routes once they got to the highway.

In the rest stop, General Beech was given confirmation of the success of the exercise. Four cars arrived a minute later and the important staff headed away, leaving just a couple of militia in the bus to make their own escape and to hide the communications vehicle.

«««0»»»

[From White House tapes. RBB]

'What do you mean, he's been kidnapped? How the blazing hell could that happen?' shouted President Slimbridge, thumping the antique desk to punctuate his words. A teacup rattled in its saucer.

'I'm sorry, sir,' said the one-star General Perkins. 'He was protected by a force of five. Four Marines and an air force captain. Two vanished with him. The captain and one of the other Marines were killed and the other is now under treatment. No civilians were harmed, and our men killed one of theirs although it is believed another two were wounded. It was a very well executed plan.'

'I want to know how it was done. Detail. By lunchtime, General.'

'Sir, who should stand in for him?'

'I don't know. Who's the most senior army general?'

'Winston Delve, sir, but he's in Hawaii which is why I'm here.'

'Get him back, then. Today! I want all the military chiefs here this evening. Can you get him back by then?'

'Yes, sir.'

'Right. Get out of my sight and be sure I have the report by midday, General!'

'Yes, sir.'

The general left the room rather more hurriedly than he might have ordinarily and the president walked to the French windows, opening them and stepping outside where he stood in the walkway, watching rain cascading into the White House garden.

He turned and re-entered his office. The soldier in the walkway closed the door after him. He couldn't have failed to have heard the string of profanity the president uttered as he walked to his desk. He sat, seething with anger.

'Deirdre! Coffee!' he shouted, then said more quietly, 'and make it strong.'

12 Pittsburgh

[From Jim Collins' notes and digital recordings. RBB]

Barbara Lemsford stood stock-still behind her desk. One of the three soldiers stood facing her, legs apart, pointing his automatic rifle at her chest. The other two pushed open the doors off the main office and satisfied themselves there was no one in the suite.

The ranking officer, a captain, approached her and stood far too close, invading her space. She shuffled back, pushing the chair behind her. He raised his pistol and pushed the barrel up against her throat. She was shaking all over and now sweat was forming beads on her brow. She couldn't believe she was being treated like this by an American soldier – with all the finesse of the German SS from the Second World War. The gun barrel was hurting the soft tissue under her throat.

'Where is Congressman Mayne?' the man barked straight into her face. She could smell garlic on his breath.

'I don't know. He said he had a meeting,' Barbara said with a trembling voice and on the verge of tears. 'Please remove the gun.'

The captain stood back, kept the gun pointed at her and surveyed the desk. He grabbed a large desk diary from the pile of papers on the right. He flicked through the pages until he found today's date. 'Why's there nothing in here?' He threw it down on the desk noisily.

'He called in and said he had a meeting. He didn't tell me when or where.'

'Does he do that often, then?'

'Not often, but it isn't unusual,' she said looking down at the pistol.

'Where do you think he might be?'

'I've no idea.'

The captain lowered his pistol and turned to leave. 'Come on,' he said. 'We're out of here.'

«««o»»»

[From Jim Collins' notes and digital recordings. RBB]

'It's on the news now,' said Jim, pointing up at the television above the counter of the diner opposite Charles Mayne's Pittsburgh office.

'Can you turn that up, Maisie?'

The anchor came onto the screen, 'We are now hearing that there is an arrest warrant out for Charles Mayne. The charge is insurgency.' A portrait of Charles came onto the monitor then it showed several sequences of him touring factories and meeting the mayor and others.

Another man sitting with Jim and Charles was looking up and down the street. They were all relieved when they saw the soldiers exit the office and drive east. Another car, with two smartly dressed men in the front seats, sat watching the office. Perhaps Secret Service or FBI.

'We need to get you away from here, Charles,' said Jim quietly.

'I want to know if Barbara is all right first,' he said.

'Burt, call the office. Just see if it gets answered. Say nothing,' said Jim to the small bald-headed man who was sitting opposite them

Burt Kass set the phone to hands-free and dialled. It rang four times and was answered, 'This is the office of Congressman Mayne. How may I direct your call?'

'She's there. She answered okay,' said Jim. 'Now let's get away while we still can.'

'Give me your phone, Burt,' said Charles.

He looked at the unfamiliar screen, found the keypad and dialled a number.

It seemed to take an age to be answered, 'Hello.'

'Helen. It's Charles. No, no, I'm fine, but I daren't turn my phone on. Can you give Barbara a ring at the office and make sure she's okay? We know she's answering, but I want to know she hasn't been harmed.'

Helen Bond was obviously saying a few words and then Charles finished the call.

The three men finished their coffee, Charles keeping his face turned from the street, and then Burt's cell phone rang. He looked at the caller's number and handed it straight to Charles.

'Yes? –You're sure? – Good. Helen, clear this number out of your phone's memory, please. – Yes. – Better safe than sorry. – I will. Goodbye.'

'Where's your car, Burt?' Jim asked.

'In the lot behind the Fine Wine store.'

'Collect it and then wait at the end of the alleyway behind the diner. We'll watch for you turning out of Fine Wine before we move. Don't hurry. Just stroll along the street. Don't look at the men in the car.'

'Okay,' Burt said and nonchalantly rose from his seat, put on his Fedora and made his way out of the diner and along the street to the Fine Wine and Good Spirits store.

A couple of minutes later, his grey Dodge Durango appeared at the Fine Wine junction. It waited for a break in the traffic and turned onto the main road, immediately indicating right and disappearing down a side street.

'Keep looking at the ground, Charles. Follow me closely,' said Jim. 'Maisie, you've not seen us, okay?'

'Say, who are you guys?' she said and laughed.

Jim and Charles made their way behind the diner counter, through the kitchen and out of the rear door. Jim checked both directions. There was no one in the alley. He waited until he saw the Durango arrive at the end, then they both walked hurriedly towards it and got into the rear seats, as the glass in the back of the vehicle was heavily tinted.

'Okay, Burt. Drive. Head south. Stop at the first phone shop you see. We need some pre-paid cell phones. They'll be tracking Charles' and probably mine as well. How much cash have you got on you, Charles?' said Jim as he checked the contents of his own wallet. 'We won't be able to use plastic.'

'Hey, can they track us with the satellites all down?' asked Charles.

'Yes. Different system. Phones register with their closest cell tower.'

About an hour later, in the town of Somerset, they pulled into a Giant Eagle store. Charles stayed in the back of the car. He was too well known. Jim and Burt headed into the store.

'You got credit on your plastic, Burt?'

'Yes, no problem.'

'Good, we'll keep the cash for the time being. They won't be trying to track you.'

'No, wouldn't have thought so. What do you want?'

'Go get some snacks, bottled water, Hershey bars to keep us going. It's a long drive to Jacksonville, where I think Dick Beech is currently. I'll get the phones and come find you.'

'Sure thing, Jim,' Burt said and hurried off to the snacky aisles.

13 Surprise

[Taken from Paula Wilson's minutes and Hareen Trestogeen's recordings. RBB]

Several of those present jumped in fright as the giant flatfish in a sparkling cape materialised before them in the middle of their Security Council meeting.

'Ambassador. Welcome,' said Lara, who was first to regain her composure.

'Yes, welcome to London again,' said Prime Minister Church.

'We were just discussing you,' said Lara.

'I have decided to provide a little more help to you. However, you must be aware that I am actually breaking diplomatic protocol, as the Federation Cabinet has stipulated that no one should contact you at this time.'

'You most welcome,' said President Yang. 'These meetings confidential. We will not be talking of your visit.'

'Our problems are enormous. Some we can deal with, but others seem insurmountable,' said Lara.

'Frankly,' said President Olov, 'we do not know how to deal with America. We're all trying to build upon your aid in famine areas, but we can do little more.'

'Ambassador,' said Maureen Church. 'We are learning more about the factions which do not want us to join the Federation and their reasons. We cannot run roughshod over their opinions. They believe that the Federation would be bad for Earth. Free will and freedom of speech is more important than helping the many. Work is a right, not just a way of creating a living. Workers socialise as well as make things. They create worthwhile environments for people to enjoy. These are the views of many in the United States particularly, often the more insular groups who rarely travel abroad and are set in their ways.'

'Zere is also a serious attitude zat ze Federation, it is a communist regime and you are 'iding planets vere zere is virtual slave labour and shortages of consumer goods,' said President Ramseur.

'Please sit,' said Lara.

'These seats are not comfortable. It is not important,' said the ambassador.

Paula quickly left the room and two men entered with a sofa.

'Peter, Barry, do not discuss the ambassador's presence. Not with anyone. Government secret,' the prime minister said very seriously.

They both confirmed they wouldn't and left.

My staff all know about secrecy, but we usually brief them if something unusual is happening and your presence could not be more unexpected,' said Maureen to the ambassador. 'So, I thought I'd better emphasise the need for confidentiality.'

'I understand,' said the ambassador who took a reclining position on the sofa. Paula provided him with a jug and glass of water.

'The attitude of the American citizens,' said Lara, 'is probably borne out of decades of fighting communism and communist states. In fact, they even consider socialism to be as bad.'

'It is very difficult for us to dispel such viewpoints,' said the ambassador. 'The only way is to take these people and let them loose on our worlds. They would soon find that there is no coercion in the Federation. However, that may not have come over clearly under Ambassador Moroforon.'

'May I speak?' asked Paula.

'Please do,' said President Yang.

'I was with Secretary General Okafor and Ambassador Moroforon and many of her team when we toured Federation worlds. The system came over very well, but it is human nature to be suspicious of anything which challenges your current thinking,' said Paula.

'So,' Prime Minister Church continued, 'if your view is that the Federation is communist, nothing you see will change your mind and, if you feel strongly anti-communist, you are likely to think that things are being hidden from you. It is classic conspiracy paranoia.'

'But how do we deal with it?' asked President Olov.

'Ambassador. My name is Malcolm Gorman and one solution does come to mind.'

'Fire away, Malcolm,' said the prime minister.

All eyes turned to the defence secretary. 'Would it be possible for the rest of the world to join the Federation and leave the United States as an independent nation. They could trade with other countries, but would not be compelled to adopt any of the economic systems. Frankly, North Korea operate like that right now. Could it be a way out of the impasse?'

The ambassador adjusted his seating position and drank from his glass of water. 'What you are suggesting would be unprecedented.'

'But if it solves ze problem?' said President Ramseur.

'It would mean that they continue to run their economy as they do now. They would be isolated from our technology. I cannot envisage such a relationship,' said the ambassador.

'Why not?' asked Presidents Olov and Yang almost simultaneously.

'What about travelling to other worlds? Would we allow that?'

'Well, Yol Ambassador, it might let them realise what they are missing,' said Prime Minister Church.

'This is so radical, I will need to take some time to think it through, but thank you Mr Gorman. You have opened up an interesting new idea,' said the ambassador. 'Goodbye,' he said and vanished from the room. A gentle pop announced the vacuum being filled.

'Oh. I had other questions,' said President Olov.

'Me too,' said the prime minister. 'The next time we encounter the ambassador, we must let him know that we have a string of questions.'

'Oui, zat was most unsatisfactory,' said President Ramseur.

'Thinking about Mr Gorman's idea, how would it work for the rest of us?' asked the secretary general.

There seemed a better humour in the room all of a sudden, as if the back of the situation had been broken. Knowing the Federation were available, even if only occasionally, provided relief to everybody.

'There'd need be strict borders,' said Che.

'And some sort of exchange rate between ze afed and ze dollar,' said Phillippe.

'There could be a rush of people wanting to leave the USA to enter Federation territory. We'd need an immigration system,' said Marat Olov.

'I don't think the Federation would worry about that, actually. In fact, I think they would welcome it,' said Lara.

'And there could be some wanting to go the other way,' said Maureen.

'Would that be likely?' asked Che. 'If life is so good in the Federation, why would people want to give that up to live in the USA?'

'People wanting to keep their personal fortunes. Our oligarchs for instance,' said Marat.

'I wonder what the Federation's view of that would be?' asked Malcolm. 'Would they be able to take their wealth with them?'

'Might not bother Federation,' said Che. 'They so enormous, small leak in economic system in one of a quarter of a million planets hardly cause run on the afed. It be like us being concerned about economic status of single apartment block in Beijing.'

They all laughed. Che continued, 'Have to transfer personal wealth from afeds to dollars. What would dollar be worth? A few oligarchs buying dollars would have interesting effect on dollar value.'

'I don't see how zat would work,' said Philippe.

'But the Federation don't seem to like to ban anything, do they? Surely, they'd want to allow people to leave, if the USA would have them,' said Lara.

'I can certainly see why Yol Trestogeen wants to take his time considering the possibility. Good thinking, Malcolm,' said Maureen.

They talked on late into the afternoon and the conversation remained just as lively at the UN dinner that evening.

«««O»»»

[Taken from notes kept by Dr Melanie Rogers. RBB]

'I can see the structure easy enough,' said Carol Swinford, 'but these printed circuits are finer than anything we are capable of producing.'

'Yes,' said Dr Rogers. 'Medibot, we use EUV, extreme ultraviolet light, to produce our most advanced chips. You are obviously using something even finer. What's the process?'

'Let me examine some of yours,' said the robot.

Jorg scurried off and returned with a glass container holding a number of unencapsulated chips. 'Here,' he said, handing over the dish.

The medibot lifted the dish to his eye and they watched as the lens structure moved back and forth in the eye socket.

'You have a built-in microscope?' asked Brian Talbot, the chief executive of Sibernek. He'd come down to see what progress had been made.

'Yes, Brian,' said the robot. 'We need them for microsurgery.' It continued to move the glass dish from side to side and then flipped over some of the chips and examined the other sides.

'What process has been used to make your chip?' asked Dr Rogers, tapping the microscope she was examining.

'I see how you have used EUV to etch the silicon,' said the robot. 'It is only the scale which is letting you down. These chips have circuits around fourteen nanometres wide. Ours are much smaller.'

'What does that mean?' asked Brian.

'Fourteen nanometres is getting close to atomic dimensions,' said Jed. 'We thought we were close to the limit.'

'And the Federation chips are how much smaller?' Brian asked.

'It is the circuits rather than the chip itself. At least a factor of fifty. Even our electron microscope has difficulty showing the pattern,' replied Jed.

'So, Medibot, how's it done?' asked Dr Rogers again.

'Not easy to answer,' said the robot. 'I can see the circuitry, but cannot figure out the manufacturing method. I've never had to examine something so small before. I think you will need to speak to the manufacturing plant themselves.'

'And where is that?' asked Brian.

'On Opwispitt. It is the third planet circling Estrangel.'

'I thought you said you could help us make this,' said Brian.

'I believed I could, but now I see that I can't. However, you can make them using your EUV system, but they will be larger and not as fast. It will still be a huge improvement over what you are currently producing… if this is a good example,' the robot said, laying the dish of chips on the nearest bench.

'Let me know if you get any further. I'm returning to my office,' said Brian Talbot impatiently.

Dr Ross passed Brian Talbot in the doorway and got short shrift. She came over to the others.

'What's eating him?' she asked as she laid a globe shaped device, smaller than a tennis ball, on the bench.

'Oh, he's just annoyed we've been unable to make progress on the chips,' said Dr Rogers and explained what the medibot had said.

'That's the motor, Medibot,' said Dr Ross, pointing at the globe-shaped object.

The medibot picked it up and examined it. 'Very good. It looks as effective as mine. Let me try it.'

The scientists watched as the robot disassembled his shoulder, allowing the arm to hang loose while two of his other arms attached his original shoulder motor to his bicep area with some tape. He then picked up the globe and positioned it into the vacant spot, soldering some temporary connections into place and slotting the arm and collar bone connecting shafts into place. He performed a number of functions with his arm, shoulder and hand on that limb.

'Very good,' said the medibot. 'I can feel the difference. It doesn't move quite as easily, but certainly does the job. I'm impressed.'

'Excellent,' said Dr Ross. 'We're on the right track with the motors then?'

The robot handed her the joint and refitted his original. 'Yes,' it said.

'What causes it to feel different?' asked Jorg, keen to reach perfection.

'Materials,' said the robot. 'The main ball component in our joints is made from an alloy which needs no lubrication. I don't know its exact composition, but that is the only reason your joint is not as good as my original.'

'Okay,' said Dr Rogers. 'At least we know we're making progress, despite disappointing the boss.

'It really annoys me,' protested Jed, 'the way Talbot breezes into technical meetings, stirs everyone up, destroys chains of thought and then disappears as if he's had some major influence on our deliberations, when all he's done is cause distraction and confusion.'

'He's the boss and has earned that right,' said Jorg.

'With respect,' said Medibot, 'that is one of the disadvantages of having people in charge of manufacturing processes.'

'Wow!' said Dr Rogers. 'That is quite profound.'

'Not really,' said Medibot. 'Our production managers are fully conversant with everything the sub-robots are doing and making, including the latest technology. A living person who is trying to perform that function, quickly discovers that he is overwhelmed by innovations and can no longer keep up with the technological developments and so becomes a less effective manager as time goes by.'

'That is so true,' said Carol.

'Okay. Let's move on to those schematics,' said Dr Ross. 'I'll feel a lot happier when we've managed to construct something close to your sophistication, Medibot.'

14 On the Road

[From Jim Collins' notes and digital recordings. RBB]

I can't remember having to drive so far. Usually we flew if we were travelling interstate. We stopped at a motel in Gaston, just south of Columbia and sent Burt to get some fast food. We didn't dare eat out. Charles was too recognisable. At the motel, I checked us in. Then, as soon as the owner lost interest, Charles pulled a coat over his head and walked to the chalet. Fortunately there was a light drizzle, so it didn't look out of the ordinary.

Nine hours we'd been driving and it was incredibly nerve-wracking, as our names were on the news bulletins every hour and half hour. It seemed there was a real hue and cry for us.

Each time we saw a police patrol vehicle, we both made sure to turn up our collars and look away. At one point, a patrol car followed us for over thirty miles. We felt sure he knew who we were. All of a sudden, his sirens and flashing lights came on. He accelerated rapidly and passed us. We all expected him to pull in and force us onto the shoulder. We held our breath, but he didn't stop and was soon disappearing from view ahead of us while Burt maintained an unflinching fifty-five miles per hour.

The chalet had two bedrooms and Burt offered to sleep on the couch. We showered to freshen up while Burt was out. Then we used a burner phone to contact Jan, my wife. She agreed to get Carol Mayne to pack up some clothes for Charles and she'd make up a case for me. One of Charles' aides, William, would then collect the cases. He was ex-CIA and would throw off any tail before driving south to meet us in Jacksonville. Either that or he'd arrange some other method which wouldn't be tracked.

'How often can we use each phone, Jim?' asked Charles.

'Just once, then we need to switch it off and remove the battery,' I said.

'Can't we just replace SIM cards?'

'No. The moment a SIM card is in a switched-on phone, the handset's serial number is transmitted to the nearest cell tower. If you change sims, the same number is transmitted, so in effect it is the handset which is being tracked.'

'So we'll have to junk the handset after each call?'

'Yes, but only if it is to a number which is likely to be of interest. We can call a hotel or garage, but not our wives or the office. Those will need a new handset each time.'

'How many did you get?'

'Twenty. That'll do us for now,' I said.

Charles watched for Burt and, once he'd arrived with the food, we were able to unwind a little.

'Pass the ketchup,' I said, and Charles tossed over a couple of packets.

We worked our way through a KFC bucket of chicken pieces, and three Big Macs with fries. There is something comforting about fast food when you're under stress.

'When's the news on this channel?' asked Charles.

'Any minute,' I replied.

'How are we going to contact Beech?'

'William has one of our numbers and will find a way to get it to Beech to call us.'

'I suppose they're using burners too?' said Charles.

'For sure. Burt, we've got clothes coming for us but what're you going to do? I didn't dare ask Jan to contact Miriam, as anyone monitoring her would have made a connection between you and us,' I said.

'No headache. There's a store down the road. I'll pop in first thing and get some shirts and underwear. Can get things for you guys too.'

'Yes,' Charles said. 'Get me a couple of T-shirts and some underwear. Maybe a hooded top too.' He wrote sizes on a piece of motel paper. I did the same.

'Another four cheap handsets, too, Burt. Different makes if possible,' I said.

'Sure thing,' said Burt.

Once we'd killed the food and a couple of beers each, we turned in for the night. The place was comfortable, but would we sleep? Fugitives in our own country!

«‹«o»›»

[From Brad Gregg's notes. RBB]

'Inside,' said Mike Henderson roughly as he pushed General Braun through the door to the den.

The prisoner looked around the place in which, it was fairly obvious, he was going to be incarcerated.

'I suggest you give up this crazy rebellion,' the general said. 'If you give up, you'll be treated fairly. If you resist or continue your action, you will end up dead.'

'We're not interested in your threats, General.'

One of the militia carried in some bottled water, sandwiches and some fruit, putting it down on a coffee table beside a small couch. Against the other wall was a single bed with chests of drawers on each side. A bucket stood on the floor. A couple of paperbacks and a toilet roll sat on a small coffee table and a towel hung over a small washbasin against the opposite wall.

Mike slammed the door and pulled across a heavy steel bar which would stop the door opening.

'Who's doing this?' shouted the general from inside the room.

'You'll find out when we're ready to tell you!' Mike shouted back and walked up the stairs from the cellar area. Fifteen of the militia men were standing in the living room.

'At ease, men,' said Mike.

'Excuse us, Colonel!' said one of the two women Marines.

'Sorry, Martine.'

She laughed and most took seats or sat on the floor.

'Find a news channel, Joe,' said Mike.

A soldier turned on the television and started working his way through the channels. Eventually CNN announced itself to the watchers.

'Reports have been received that Charles Mayne, Democratic hopeful, has been accused of insurrection and there is a reward of fifty thousand dollars for information leading to his capture,' said the announcer as video sequences showed the congressman. 'Also, James Collins is being sought for the same offence.' A still image appeared of Charles' chief aide.

The next sentence certainly worried Mike. The anchor said, 'It is believed that Charles Mayne has recruited retired general, Dick Beech who is also wanted for actual insurgency and conspiracy to commit treason. Anyone who knows the whereabouts of any of these individuals who support the alien invasion, should report it or any other information to the police or call this hotline,' he said as a freephone number appeared on the screen.

The scene cut to the White House Press Briefing Room, where the spokeswoman was seen walking into the room and standing behind the lectern.

'Sinister forces are at play in the nation. Militia groups have been observed moving around the country, although, mostly, they are trying to conceal themselves which makes tracking them difficult. We believe they are being supported by the aliens. If you see anything suspicious, people in military garb doing anything unusual, then please do not hesitate to call the number on the screen now or report it to any police station.'

The news channel had added a short section of video to accompany the last part of the report. It was an old sequence of film showing a tentacled creature with the Clueb, Heldy Mistorn, exiting a town hall with a couple of human soldiers alongside them. It had obviously been extracted from a television report of one of the information meetings prior to the New York explosion.

'The administration wants to make it perfectly clear that anyone withholding information about the insurgents will be considered to be one of their number and will be prosecuted under the same treason laws. Don't turn a blind eye to anything suspicious! Report it immediately. If they are innocent, you'll have done no harm. If they are insurgents, you will have been a great help to the United States.' She closed her folder and immediately left the briefing room without taking questions.

'That doesn't sound good,' I said.

'No,' agreed Mike.

At that moment there was a sharp bang on the front door. All of the Marines leapt to their feet and were ready for any imminent attack.

The first knock was followed by another two, a single and then three.

'It's the general,' said Mike.

Two Marines went to the door while three others remained concealed, ready to shoot any unwelcome incomer. I looked through the spyhole and said, 'It's him.'

The visitors quickly entered the property and the door was hastily closed.

'Hi, Brad,' said General Beech. 'Excellent house you've chosen.'

'Yes. The long driveway means comings and goings can't easily be seen and we're well outside Jacksonville.'

'Where's the guard?' asked the general.

'Just arrived, was about to set it up,' said Mike, arriving from the kitchen with two militia in civilian clothes. 'Right, you two. Down to the entrance and call us on the walkie-talkie if anything, anything at all, spooks you. Remember, it's the FBI and Secret Service we're hiding from, in addition to the police. If you see a fifteen-year-old girl delivering leaflets for the county fair, we want to know about it. Okay?'

There were two smart, truncated 'yessirs' in response.

'Careful now,' said the general. 'Keep your guard up, but remain concealed. Find a couple of shovels and make it look as if you're doing some ditching or something if anyone passes by.'

'Yes, sir,' they both said, pulling smart salutes at the same time.

'Any chance of some coffee?' the general asked. 'Mike, Brad. Meet Jack Spence's White House chief of staff, Bob Nixon.'

Introductions and handshaking took place and they all moved through to the living room where coffee was soon prepared for all.

'You have him all right?' asked the general.

'Yes, sir,' said Mike. 'There's a cellar here and we have him locked in the den.'

'Any windows or access to the outside?'

'No, sir, just a couple of air bricks below ceiling height.'

'How're you guarding him?'

'Door is securely locked with an iron bar across the outside.'

'No soldiers?'

'No, sir.'

'Put someone outside the door. You need to listen for any noises,' said the general.

'Ah, we've covered that, sir. We're monitoring him with a baby alarm,' said Mike.

'Add a guard anyway.'

'Yes, sir,' said Mike, immediately detailing three Marines to stand eight-hour guard duty each.

With coffee finished, the general asked me to call everyone not on specific guard duty to come through to the living room. In three minutes the entire squad was present.

'Good morning, men… and women,' the general said, then indicated Bob Nixon. 'This gentleman is Robert Nixon who was the White House chief of staff for Jack Spence. He has spent quite a lot of time with the aliens and was with the president on his week-long visit to Federation worlds. I've asked him to tell you a little about what he saw so that you have a better knowledge of the Federation's activities.

'Most of you already know that joining or not joining the Federation is secondary to me. The reason I am leading this uprising in Charles Mayne's name is because Slimbridge and his generals murdered our president as well as hundreds of world leaders and most of the population of Manhattan. He is an evil usurper and must be brought down. However, we can provide you with better first-hand information from someone we trust who was in favour of joining the Federation, then it will help you understand why Slimbridge decided to carry out his assassination in such an extreme way.

'Bob, the floor is yours,' said General Beech, taking a seat at the back with the others.

Bob Nixon, an undistinguished looking man in his late fifties with a bald head and dark sideburns, probably dyed, stood up to his full five feet ten inches and walked around to the front of the room.

'Gentlemen and ladies, whatever your politics, I thank you for being among this creditable force trying to overthrow Vice President Slimbridge. Sorry, I still can't bring myself to call him the president.

'I was fortunate enough to have returned to the White House on the morning before the atrocity in New York. When I realised what was happening, I fled the building, but not before I saw the joint chiefs and the vice president entering the Oval Office. Slimbridge claims he was still in jail when the explosion occurred. It is one of, and not the first, of his string of lies since he claimed office. Slimbridge was most certainly in control when the atrocity took place.'

Bob took a step or two backwards and leaned on the stone fireplace. He was obviously upset. 'When Jack Spence... died, I lost... not just a president, but a good... no, my best friend.'

He wiped his eyes, 'I'd known Jack Spence since college when he first mangled me on the football field. I was a not particularly good wide-receiver and he was a linebacker, He put me in hospital and, that evening, he came to visit me. It began a friendship which lasted... well... the rest of his life.

'You probably don't know, but I was writing his biography. I have spent the last few weeks completing it and I intend to publish at the earliest opportunity.'

He stopped speaking, looking around the room at vague points near the ceiling and the carpet and the closed curtains. He was struggling to compose himself.

'Sorry. Sorry. This is the first time I've spoken about it to anyone other than family,' he said, dabbing his eyes.

He pulled himself up into a smart stance, put away his handkerchief and began to speak in a more forceful manner. 'When the Federation arrived in New York, Ambassador Moroforon addressed the UN and I can tell you that she did not impress Jack. The Federation has all the hallmarks of communism. Their system strips the wealthy of their assets and distributes the wealth among the entire population of each of the worlds. Their robots are capable of stopping war, terrorism and civil unrest. They told us they could stop the drug trade "at a stroke" and robot police would prevent crime.

'Robot police? Think about that. It sounds like a nightmare and that is how both Jack and I saw it. A totalitarian force of mechanical beings running our way of life. But then Jack went off with the Federation and visited a number of worlds. Three were established Federation planets. One was a new member, still in transition, and the final worlds were Arlucian's moon and then the planet itself – the centre of government for the Federation, which, incidentally, comprises nearly a quarter of a million civilised planets.'

Bob saw a barstool in the corner of the room. 'Pass that stool over to me, please.' It was passed hand to hand. Bob positioned it beside the fireplace and perched himself on it, looking around at his audience.

'I watched Jack change. It would be fair to say that, initially, he had a distinct dislike of everything the Federation stood for but, by the time he'd got back from Arlucian, he had begun to change his tune. We both became convinced that the Federation could only be a force for good.'

He pulled a small tablet from his jacket pocket and waved it at Dick Beech, 'Don't panic, Dick. It's not connected to a phone network, so can't be traced,'

He swiped the screen a few times then began to read, 'Against the Federation: the wealthy and successful lose their vast fortunes as do the enormous companies; nationalisation on a global scale; you cannot benefit from things you invent or improve; all work is done by fleets of robots; even management is by robots; innovation would be stamped out, or so it seemed.

'But what of the benefits: no one will ever need to work again unless they wish to; everyone earns the same income, from the person who was once a chief executive, right down to one of those starving babies which charities show us in Africa. Famine is a thing of the past, almost every disease is conquered, anyone can live anywhere they wish, but huge mansions will vanish, making way for homes for the many.

'Even more important, war is ended, as is persecution, abuse and discrimination. I think it was the vanquishing of war which was most influential upon Jack.'

'Let me tell you of some of these worlds he visited,' he said and so began a talk which lasted the best part of an hour. Everyone in his audience was enthralled.

«««o»»»

[From Jim Collins' notes and digital recordings. RBB]

I suppose we were all refreshed from the night in the motel at Gaston and we were soon back on Highway 26, heading southeast. Burt had managed to buy us a couple of hooded sweatshirts so that we could hide our faces if we needed to.

Charles and I were still all over the television and radio news. We'd definitely have to be prepared to conceal ourselves.

'I think we should get off twenty-six and use smaller roads,' said Burt. 'You two'll be too easy to spot. Need to get rid of this Pittsburgh registered car too.'

We pulled off towards Orangeburg. Burt left us beside one of the lakes on the northern approach and we sat quietly on a bench, watching some fishermen who were far enough away to be unable to recognise Charles.

Burt took more than two hours buying overnight bags for our clothes and then trading in the car for an anonymous looking Ford. Our communication burner rang.

'Yes,' I said.

'Five minutes,' said Burt and we ended the call. We'd decided to be cautious even if one of our burners was calling another. No lengthy conversations and phones were turned off immediately they were no longer needed.

Charles and I ambled back to where Burt had dropped us and, as we reached the road, the used Ford pulled up beside us. Burt had done well; dark tinted glass in the rear section. We drove for another few miles until we found a quiet junction with no nearby homes. Here we turned and headed back towards Orangeburg.

'No problems with the car?' Charles asked.

'Nah. The guy couldn't wait to make the sale. He wouldn't let me have the documents until he receives mine from me. Made the deal even more costly. You owe me whatever loss I make when all this is over, Congressman.'

'Least of our problems,' said Charles quietly. We both sat well back in our seats as we travelled through Orangeburg and found our way back to Route 26.

Once again, we were cruising at fifty-five and trying to mind our own business. Twenty minutes later we reached the 95 intersection and headed south.

'Still think we should get off the highway,' said Burt.

'Don't know,' I said. 'Travelling on smaller roads leaves us more likely to be seen by local police. What d'you think, Charles?'

'The longer we stay on the highway, the faster we'll reach Jacksonville.'

One of the burner phones rang. 'Yes,' I said.

'Dick,' the voice said.

'Yes.'

'Zoo. There are three parking lots. Two small, sandwiching a large one.'

'Got that.'

'Park in southernmost small parking lot. Trunk open. Bag on hood. Make?'

'Ford Edge, grey.'

'Five today possible?'

'No.'

'Midday tomorrow?'

'Yes,' I said, and the connection was cut. I switched off that burner and removed the battery.

'Why tomorrow?' Burt asked.

'Could still be four hours,' I said.

'Should do that easily by five.'

'Would rather we were fresh.'

"'Kay.'

The car progressed at fifty-five almost due south.

«««O»»»

[From Brad Gregg's notes. RBB]

'I think I'd go mad if I had nothing to do,' said one of the militia.

'We spoke to many people about it,' said Bob Nixon. 'On the transition world, Jack said that there were many people who found it difficult to adapt, but they were found useful work to do that kept them in contact with others so that there was no loneliness or isolation. The Federation doesn't want to force you to stop doing something you enjoy. They actively encourage it to help during transition. The main pursuit of those who were finding it difficult was in actually helping others. It became a social pursuit. Many took up art, gardening, woodwork, crafts and hobbies.'

'And everyone gets the same income, including babies, you say?' asked another.

'That's right,' confirmed Bob.

'I've got four kids, my wife and my mother-in-law. Does that mean we'd have seven times the income coming in?'

'Absolutely, and they reckon it'd be about fifty k, so your household would have three hundred and fifty thousand a year to live on,' said Bob with a flourish.

'That's massive! Why should Frank have all of that when my wife and I would only have a hundred thousand?' said another.

'What do you do now?' asked Bob.

'Soldier, private.'

'What do you and your wife earn, combined?'

'I'm on about thirty k and Julie earns thirty-two.'

'So, your total of sixty-two thousand is nearly forty thousand short of what you'd get from the Federation system, but, and here's a game changer, there are no property taxes and food is extremely cheap. Your hundred thousand is actually worth a whole lot more,' said Bob.

'Right... but I could stay a soldier?'

'There is a Federation rapid-reaction force which you can volunteer to join, so no problem,' said Bob.

'It all sounds too good to be true,' said another soldier.

'That's what Jack thought until he studied the nitty-gritty.'

'And you're sure there aren't planets which operate like the old Soviet Union or where there's a slave trade?' asked a sergeant.

'Absolutely. Jack and the other leaders chose which planets they went to and there wasn't a whisper of discontent on any of the worlds Jack visited.'

'So, who loses?' asked the man called Frank.

'All the billionaires and all the megabillion corporations will vanish over a few years. The huge corporations will be producing their profit to share with everyone and all the billionaires will have a few years to adjust.'

'That'll piss off the tech billionaires for sure!' someone said, and everyone laughed.

«««O»»»

[From Jim Collins' notes and digital recordings. RBB]

The radio kept us informed with its half-hourly news broadcasts. 'The fugitive ex-general Dick Beech is still being sought. He was last known to be in Florida. The FBI say that there was a sighting of Charles Mayne in South Carolina and he is believed to be heading to meet up with Dick Beech. If anyone sees either of these individuals who are wanted for treason and insurrection, contact any police force.'

'That's not good, Charles,' I said.

'No. Burt, get us off ninety-five at the next junction. Too risky to stay on the freeway now.'

'Will do. Damn, we just missed one, but there's signs for another a couple of miles ahead,' said Burt. 'Brunswick. We can get off there.'

'Traffic jam ahead,' I said.

We slowed to a crawl as we joined the queuing vehicles. Now it was stop-start and much of the time was stop.

'We definitely wouldn't have made Jacksonville by five with this hold-up,' said Burt. 'Looks like an accident. I can see police lights ahead.'

The traffic continued to crawl along but, as we could see traffic management, we hoped we'd not be too long getting through the delay.

'Jim, Charles, problem!' said Burt.

'What?' we asked in unison.

'I don't think it's an accident. It looks like a roadblock. Cars are being checked. We're in trouble,' said Burt, indicating left and pulling into the middle lane when one of the cars behind felt amenable. Next he moved into the outside lane.

'What're you doing, Burt?' asked Jim.

'There is a break in the central barrier about fifty yards ahead. I'm going to cut through.'

I looked at the traffic on the other side of the highway. It wasn't too busy, but pulling through into faster traffic would be hazardous. If we caused a problem, there'd be horns sounding and the police would realise we had something to hide. I guessed there was no alternative.

The traffic continued at a crawl and we were now just a couple of car lengths from the break in the barriers. I estimated that the roadblock and police were only about a hundred yards ahead.

'They might not see us if you're quick, Burt,' said Charles. 'They're concentrating on seeing who's in the cars. If you can get through and out of the way of any traffic, we might not be noticed.'

One car length remained. Burt pulled as far over to the right of the outer lane as he could without letting anyone come through on the outside.

'Fucking van is making it impossible to see the fast lane on the other side,' said Burt.

I could see his problem. When he turned, he'd be side on for just a second and would have to go quickly or he'd draw attention to us.

I watched him slowing his crawl and preparing to cut through.

'Hold tight,' he said, and the car swivelled.

I saw him look right at the oncoming traffic and then he shot across the highway and into the middle lane. A car in the outer lane blasted us with his horn, but we were past him and accelerating northwards. Charles and I looked out of the rear and saw a couple of police staring in our direction. The question was, did they see what we'd done, or would they assume it was a couple of rubberneckers getting in each other's way as they came past the roadblock?

Burt was quickly doing fifty-five and keeping out of the way of other traffic. The Brunswick off-ramp was less than a mile ahead.

'Shit!' Charles said. 'Flashers coming up behind rapidly.'

Burt floored it and the Ford leapt along. Soon we were doing ninety and he hit the off-ramp at speed, tyres squealing as we took the shallow bend, but there was an intersection right in front of us. We all looked left as Burt slammed on the brakes and cut through traffic into the fast lane of another split roadway. I caught sight of a sign which said, "Golden Isles Parkway".

'The cops have got delayed by a truck,' shouted Charles.

We rapidly approached another junction. There was stationary traffic for red lights. Burt cut onto the central grassed area where we bounced and hit concrete near the junction. There was a sickening crunch from beneath the vehicle, but we were still moving and Burt steered us through the intersection and accelerated down a side street, throwing us violently sideways as he swung into a Holiday Inn parking lot, drove us round the hotel as if on a race track and out the far side, turning into more hotel parking lots.

One was packed with vehicles. Burt found a space which was concealed from view, cut the engine and we all sat, panting, looking around for the police.

Five minutes, ten minutes, fifteen minutes passed. No sign of any pursuit.

'Go get us three rooms, Burt. We'll lie low,' said Charles.

We watched Burt leave the car and stand up straight as if stretching after a long drive, but also looking in all directions for any sign of the patrol car. Once he was sure we were all in the clear, he walked back out of the busy parking lot and across to the Holiday Inn.

When he returned, thirty minutes later, we were very much relieved. We both pulled up our hooded tops and grabbed our bags.

'Take everything,' said Burt. 'I've got us a rental car. Look out for the oil on the off side.'

I picked up the map, the bag of used phones and our snacks bag. I stepped over a pool of oil, spreading from underneath the vehicle. Must have cracked the sump. We followed Burt into the Holiday Inn, sighing with relief when we reached our rooms without anyone paying us any noticeable attention.

Later, we ordered a Panera meal which Burt collected for us. After eating we got an early night and tried not to allow our precarious situation to keep us awake. We were only a couple of hours from Jacksonville zoo. Hopefully Dick Beech had some security to offer.

15 Orbit

[Taken from Ambassador Trestogeen's office files and notes. RBB]

'Has it ever been done before?' asked Ya Istil, resting in her specially shaped seat in the captain's office off the Eskorav's bridge. The room held a kidney-shaped desk made from some iridescent material which gave the impression it was forever moving, like swirling multi-pastel-coloured clouds. Some papers were scattered randomly and her secradarve floated, motionless, to her right. Was it in contact with the ephemeral surface or hovering just above it? Impossible to say. Behind her, an oblong window revealed deep space, taking in part of the violent central area of the Milky Way galaxy.

'Admitting part of a planet? No, I don't think so. I have an assistant on Pestoch looking through records for me as we speak,' said the ambassador, standing and looking down through the viewing window at the cause of all his troubles. North America was passing beneath them.

'How would it work?'

'Simply, the entire planet would become part of the Federation with the exception of that single country. They could continue as before.' He returned to the couch.

'What would happen with imports and exports?'

'Well,' said the ambassador, 'that is only the first of the headaches. I can't imagine the rest of the world needing to import anything from America when there is the whole Federation to deal with, but I can imagine America wanting to continue to import all of the produce they have always obtained from other countries – tropical fruit, vegetables and so on.'

'Are they capable of being self-sufficient?'

'Yes, I think so. There would be certain items they can't grow, but with careful management of resources it would be possible.'

'Why can't they import from the Federation part of the world?' asked Istil.

'How would they pay? If they have no afeds, they'd only be able to pay with dollars and they would be of no use to the Federation.'

'But couldn't they take them, knowing that Federation goods flowing into America would soon make them realise what they are missing by not being members.'

'What? Just take their dollars and consider it a cost of bringing Earth into the empire?'

'Yes. America would be watching the rest of the world very carefully to see how the Federation system worked. The ordinary people will soon be queuing to leave the country, surely?'

'That may be so, but it would leave America with only the idealists and the rich,' said the ambassador.

'Exactly!' said the captain, the contents of her body colourfully adding to his point. 'But who is going to do the menial jobs – the farming, the cleaning, the carpenters, bricklayers, plumbers? Those are the people who would likely be first to leave. There'd be no point being rich, but having to work tirelessly to maintain their own homes and sources of power, food and repairs.'

'Yes. I see what you're getting at. You think there would be a collapse of their internal markets and they'd soon be wanting to join the Federation?'

'It could happen. That is why you'd need to be careful what they could buy from the Federation. If they were able to buy robots for instance, Hareen, then they might be able to live in luxury.'

The ambassador materialised his secradarve and made some notes. 'I need some statisticians to analyse the probabilities.'

'Are you sure the Federation wouldn't want to import American products?' said Ya Istil as her secradarve took on some informative colours.

'I don't think so,' said the ambassador.

'Well, I'm looking here at the exports of the USA and there seem to be a lot of their items which could still be in demand.'

'What sort of things?'

'Bourbon whiskey for a start,' said Ya Istil and laughed, which was a colourful experience for anyone watching.

'Yes, I've heard of that,' said the ambassador making more notes for his secradarve. 'I'll find out more. I need to go away and think about this quietly.'

'Take your time. I'll never tire of the Earth's weather patterns.'

'Yes. Beautiful,' said the ambassador, heaving himself off the couch and leaving through one of the two doors in the office wall.

An hour later, the ambassador called the captain on the intercom. He'd made his decision and said to Ya Istil Sperafin, 'Take me to Arlucian, please.'

'Will do. It'll take about four or five hours. I'll let you know exactly how long later.' The captain rose from her seat and exited the office through the second door onto the bridge of the Eskorav. 'Yol Derodin, set course for Arlucian!'

«««o»»»

[From Jim Collins' notes and digital recordings. RBB]

Of course, the incident on 95 was on the morning news, but with embellishments – 'The fugitives, Charles Mayne and two assistants, were almost apprehended at a roadblock on Interstate ninety-five yesterday afternoon. They set off at high speed, opening fire at anyone who got in their way.'

The television showed distressed people arriving at an emergency room.

'One family was run off the road and both the young children were killed. Another car was riddled with gunfire, killing the mother and her elderly aunt.'

Anonymous images accompanied the invented incidents.

'My God,' said Charles, blood pressure rising.

'They are believed to be in the Brunswick area and anyone who sees three men acting suspiciously should contact the police.' An image of me appeared on the screen. 'In addition to Charles Mayne, James Collins is one of the three, plus an unknown third individual.

'When last seen, they were driving a grey Ford Edge, but they are likely to have switched vehicles.'

'None of this is good,' I said. 'They'll have been speaking to car rental places in the area. They might even know which car Burt has rented.'

'Only one way to find out,' said Burt. I'm going out for a drive. Expect me back in about an hour. If I'm not here by nine, you're on your own.'

'Okay, Burt. Take care,' said Charles.

'We need to talk to Beech,' I said.

'If we're not at the zoo at midday he'll no doubt call, but what worries me is that we're putting him in danger too. Maybe we should just go into hiding,' said Charles.

'Not a chance. Charles, you are the figurehead. People will rally around you.'

'What, a murderer and on the run from the authorities for treason?' the congressman said and flopped down, exasperated, into the easy chair in the hotel room.

'They'll soon realise it isn't true when we start to mobilise our resources. Don't get depressed, Charles. We need you at your most vibrant and charming.'

'I suppose.'

«««O»»»

[From Brad Gregg's notes. RBB]

'I think we'd better talk to Braun,' said Dick Beech to Bob, Brad and Mike.

'Right. Where? We can go down to the den or I could bring him up here,' said Mike.

'No, let's go down,' said the general.

'Dean, Geoff. Go down to the two on duty and open up for us. Get rid of his slops and check he's not made any weapons for himself. And watch out for any tricks. Look sharp now,' said Mike.

'What are you intending to ask him?' asked Brad.

'I don't know. Let's just see what he has to say for himself,' said the general.

A couple of minutes later, one of the soldiers returned and said it was all clear. The general's party followed him back to the den. The door now stood open and General Braun was sitting in an easy chair on the far side of the room. His feet, inside shoelace-less brogues, rested on the bare concrete floor of the den.

'Ha,' he said, 'the traitor Beech!'

'Hi, Walt. Let's not start with insults. Are you well?'

'I'll be better when I see our roles reversed.'

'Not going to happen, Walt. We'd like to know why you have taken part in Slimbridge's coup. You know darned well that Jack wasn't a traitor.'

'I know no such thing, Dick. He was about to hand over power to aliens who would have enslaved us all.'

Bob spoke, 'You know that is not true. I organised and accompanied you and the joint chiefs to see Federation worlds together. Where was the slavery?'

'Ha, we saw two worlds. How many are enslaved elsewhere to provide the luxury they were enjoying?'

'That is paranoid thinking,' said Bob. 'There were six groups of leaders who visited a total of thirty-six planets, plus the capital. Why was there not a single whisper of foul play?'

'Good organisation. Look how our publicity has turned you into hunted traitors. The Federation just did that in reverse.'

'I'm wasting my time,' said Bob.

General Beech took over, 'Walt, I am disappointed in you. In fact, I am horrified with what you have done. You have killed millions in the New York atrocity.'

'That was terrorists!'

'Don't give me that crap. We know it was done by Slimbridge with your help. I wasn't finished, though. You killed dozens outside the White House.'

'Not true. That was media exaggeration.'

'Nonsense. We know people who had friends or relations killed there and in other peaceful demonstrations. What about your blatant execution of the three soldiers the other night before Slimbridge's lying address to the nation?'

'Those are the only three who've died. We had to keep order and they were traitors.'

'As are we according to you. Just look at what Slimbridge has done to our country! It's frightening. He, with your help, is turning our wonderful country into a police state. You should be ashamed to be helping him.'

General Braun sat silently.

'Well, you're helping him no longer!' said the general forcefully. 'The International Criminal Court will deal with you when this is all over.'

'Fuck off!' was his response.

General Beech turned to Mike and said, 'Lock him up again. We're wasting our time here.' They all left the den.

As they climbed the stairs from the basement, the general said, quietly, 'Find somewhere else to keep him, away from here.'

'Yes, sir.'

«««O»»»

[From Jim Collins' notes and digital recordings. RBB]

Charles and I breathed sighs of relief when the room door opened and Burt walked in with pancakes, bacon, eggs and sausages in takeaway trays. We all tucked into a much-needed breakfast.

'Surprised me when the original room was empty,' said Burt. 'Thought the worst.'

'Sorry,' I said. 'Thought it was sensible to switch rooms while we waited.'

'No problems?' asked Charles.

'No. I drove in several directions and even got back on to ninety-five for a few miles. Nothing at all. The roadblock was no longer there.'

'They'd have realised we wouldn't get caught after having seen the first one,' I said.

With breakfast finished, we packed our overnight bags and followed Burt down to the car park. Charles and I hid our faces from any cameras we noticed as well as other people.

'I'll stay in the lobby. You two go on. Now they've got alerts out for three men, we'd better only move around in twos,' I said. Burt told me how to find the car and the two of them left the hotel. A few minutes later we were heading towards Jacksonville along smaller, coastal roads running near or parallel to I-95. Getting over the creek was a problem as we left Brunswick. If there had been a roadblock there, we'd have been in real trouble.

Driving past Kings Bay Base saw us keeping our heads down, but a little further on, Burt parked up and walked into another car hire firm. Thirty minutes later we were in an Acadia SUV heading south again. We all felt a little safer in the bigger vehicle and it gave us off-road possibilities too.

'At last,' said Charles as Burt turned into the Jacksonville zoo.

The three large car parks were easy to find, and we had no problem parking in the third, smaller area. It was eleven thirty. Half an hour to wait.

As midday approached, Burt opened the trunk wide and put his overnight bag on the lid, then rummaged through it, removing various items and then neatly folding and replacing them.

The burner rang. 'That's not a Ford.'

'Had to switch,' said Charles.

'Get out, walk around the vehicle and get back in.'

Charles followed the instructions then closed the door.

'Okay. Sit tight. Be ready to transfer vehicles. Turn off all cell phones and other communication devices,' the voice said and broke the connection.

'Charles, Jim. It might be better if I headed back to Pittsburgh now,' said Burt.

'Okay. Take care,' I said.

'You have all the burner numbers?' asked Charles.

'Yes.'

'Okay, Burt. Thanks for all the help,' said Charles. 'It won't be forgotten and we'll sort out the cash with you as soon as we can.'

'Don't worry over that just now.'

A blue minivan, labelled, DOLPHIN TOURS, pulled up alongside us and the sliding door opened. A man in camouflage uniform waved us in. Charles and I hurriedly transferred vehicles, the door was slammed and, in no time, it turned and was away, almost before we'd got seated. Out of the rear window, I saw Burt closing the trunk and getting back into the rented SUV.

'Where are we going?' asked Charles.

'Somewhere safe,' said the soldier.

We sat back and strapped ourselves in. The man was most uncommunicative and we gave up trying to make conversation. We did notice that he made dozens of different manoeuvres including turning into cul-de-sacs and dead ends. Probably satisfied that we weren't being followed, he turned southeast, and we headed towards the Florida coast.

«««o»»»

[From Brad Gregg's and Jim Collins' notes and recordings. RBB]

Grangewood was one of those large, millionaire's houses on the Ponte Vedra coast just south of Jacksonville. The approach was over a quarter of a mile of wooded driveway and the building could not be overlooked from anywhere except the Atlantic Ocean. The house itself was built in the Italian style with large airy rooms and the exterior had been washed with honey and cream, plus contrasting rusty orange on selected walls. Large French windows opened out onto patios on the ocean side of the property.

The minibus made its way up the driveway and stopped at a barrier manned by two militiamen. Our driver identified himself and we proceeded to the large parking and turning area at the back of the house. Another van was parked to one side. The yellow and green livery announced that it was CAWTE PRIVATE TOURS. Three other cars were parked nearby. Through some shrubs to the side of the property, I could see two hefty jeeps with camouflage paintwork.

'Okay,' said the guard in the rear with us, 'we're here.' He jumped up and slid the main door backwards on its runners.

Charles was first out and was greeted by General Beech who first saluted, then hugged the congressman. I got the same warm welcome and soldiers carried our bags into the house.

'You had a bad time?' asked the general as he guided us through to the eat-in kitchen where he grasped a coffee pot, offering it to the two of us. Real coffee, not the hotel variety. We sat around the breakfast bar and told the general of the events of our journey.

'We were worried about you after the U-turn on ninety-five. You were lucky to give them the slip,' said the general.

'Yes. If it hadn't been for a truck getting in the way of the patrol car on the off-ramp, he'd certainly have caught us,' I said.

Bob Nixon, short and balding, entered the room. I didn't know him, but Charles was quickly on his feet and warmly greeting the ex-White House chief of staff. 'Bob, how lovely to see you. Thought you'd been in New York.'

'Was lucky, Congressman, I'd returned to the White House and then vamoosed the moment I realised what Slimbridge was up to.'

'Come and join us, Bob,' said the general. 'Coffee?'

Bob nodded and we continued to talk around the breakfast bar.

'So, what's the plan, General?' asked Charles.

'Well, Congressman, this evening I'm holding a strategy meeting with all the important players that we've been able to get here. Peter Stone will also be on a phone link. What I suggest is that the two of you settle into your rooms and then come down to the living room, through there,' he said indicating a passage from the kitchen, 'and we'll see where we are going from here.'

'I take it you've got Braun somewhere?' I asked.

'Better than that,' said the general. 'We've also got Buck Burko, so the pressure is growing on Slimbridge. We did have Braun here, but moved him and they're both being kept elsewhere now.'

'Excellent,' said Charles.

'So, freshen up then make yourselves at home. Early dinner at six. Can I suggest you work out what you are going to say at the meeting, Congressman? Something upbeat and positive if possible.'

'Certainly, General,' said Charles.

'Eric!' the general shouted and a soldier entered the room. 'Show the congressman and his assistant to their rooms.'

The upper floor was home to numerous bedrooms. Charles was given one with an ocean view. Mine was equally luxurious but overlooking the vehicle parking area and the camouflaged jeeps. After unpacking, Charles wanted some time to marshal his thoughts before the meeting, while I strolled into the garden and enjoyed sitting in a pleasant glade surrounded by subtropical shrubs. I thought it would be a good idea to try to relax.

16 Seat of Government

[From Ambassador Trestogeen's files. RBB]

Pestoch, the ambassador's home world was located in the same star system as Arlucian. The ambassador took the opportunity to spend the best part of a day in the sea beside his home. Pestochians needed to keep their bodies moist and it was a delight for him to live totally submerged whenever he got the opportunity. Usually, for Hareen, this meant in a freshwater environment on-board ship but, for this one afternoon and evening, he could enjoy the saline solution of his home oceans. This could be the last time before the spawning.

Clumsy and distracting when they stood on land, in the water they were completely different creatures, able to move quickly and gracefully, their scales luminous and vibrant, outshining their colours when on land. They had a surprising turn of speed and were not averse to consuming other fish on the fly.

The next morning, the Eskorav made the short hop from Pestoch to the capital planet of the Federation, Arlucian. From the spaceport, Hareen had plenty of time to get to the council chambers for his meeting with the president and cabinet. Direct materialisation in the council building was prohibited, so he used a taxi service.

The streets of Oridin, Arlucian's capital city, were the usual chaos, but autonomous vehicles, able to communicate with each other, made easy work of the congestion until the final approach to the General Council building, the seat of government. Millions of tourists visited the council each year, plus an equal number wanting to visit their councillors to make points about life or the needs of their own worlds.

Hareen found it easier to use a hoverseat to move about within the complex rather than walking. Although Pestochians were familiar with walking, their balance not only left them short of energy after long walks, but also distressed anyone who saw them walking. The swaying motion could be quite disturbing to some other creatures.

Hareen entered the enormous, vaulted reception complex and robots at the main desk quickly located Yol Debert Indafark, the newly elected head of Earth's section of the Orion Spur of the galactic arm. He had replaced Ya Prold Churmbin who had been killed in the New York atrocity. The two creatures headed to a reserved meeting room off the main concourse, which was heaving with, literally, thousands of different species of creatures from Federation planets.

'You've managed to get a meeting with the president,' said Yol Debert, a short, stocky being with a large waistline, reminiscent of Tweedle Dee or Tweedle Dum. The illusion was quickly shattered because Yol Debert's skin was gherkin green and contained a chlorophyll symbiote. He was covered in protrusions similar to hydra, each containing hundreds of sensory receptors and capable of releasing chemicals. When his species was meeting others, they had to hang a red chain around their necks to indicate that they were poisonous to the touch. A simple handshake could be fatal to some species. Lovemaking with each other, however, some researchers have claimed, is the most sensuous experience of any intelligent creature, often lasting for days on end and requiring extended recuperation.

'Yes, Debert. The meeting is for three of us. My deputy, Yol Terend Stograther will be joining us too. I hope you'll support my idea. So, firstly, I'd like to put the plan to you. It would be good if you were prepared to go along with it, as I don't think a partial membership of the Federation has ever been attempted before. It would give me a better chance of getting it through.'

'Right, Hareen. Fire away. You know that President Dimorathron's term of office ends in a few weeks. He'll find it difficult to endorse anything radical,' he said, settling back into an orange half-globe seat, rather unpleasantly clashing with his skin colour.

'Yes. My own time is even more limited.'

'Sorry?'

'I have had five regenerative spawnings, so my time is running out. I could be gone before the new president is in place and, anyway, they always take months to settle into the post.'

'Okay, let me know what you have in mind. I didn't know your personal situation.'

'Cannot be helped,' said the ambassador sadly. 'The lifecycle of my species, but it certainly gives me an incentive to get this resolved.'

«««O»»»

[From News Media and Admiral Mann's memoirs. RBB]

It was a major undertaking now whenever President Slimbridge decided to travel outside Washington, which had become a virtual police state with armed men and armoured vehicles on every corner.

Travelling to a rally in Baltimore was hardly any distance, but the president was becoming increasingly worried about the scale of the opposition to his presidency. This particular rally was made up of several thousand specially selected supporters of the president's position. The idea was to record the rally for television and overseas broadcasts and to use anonymous videoed sequences to illustrate support in the future.

Matthew Brown had organised it well, so that there were over twenty independent camera teams giving different views and aspects to the crowd, the speech and the cheering.

It hadn't been difficult to select the audience. The country was polarising. Anyone with hard right political views seemed to be against the aliens and the religious right had been encouraged to tack itself onto the belief that the Federation was an atheist as well as a communist regime. This wasn't in fact so. The Federation supported all peaceful religions and only intervened if they were violent towards others. Many humans, however, couldn't give a reason why they disliked the Federation. This was simply the natural xenophobic reaction experienced by some when encountering the unknown. A certain proportion of a population always reacted badly, whether owing to upbringing or some inbuilt fear like that of spiders or snakes. The rally, it seemed, would be made up of all of these fringe groups, but Matthew had added extreme xenophobes and racists to the audience. Fringe views then seemed to be being adopted by the mainstream. The majority simply believed their country was a takeover target and they were determined to resist at all costs, without any real understanding of how great that cost might be or even whether there was a cost at all. It was a natural progression caused by hearing only one side of an argument being promoted.

Matthew checked out the security arrangements with Mayor Lymington, but he'd already been around the field with Admiral Mann to ensure he could keep an eye on the new general who had taken over one of the joint chiefs' roles. It should be impossible for the rally to be approached or for unrest to be stirred up during the event.

'So, Mr Mayor. You will present your short speech as agreed, then introduce the president using the exact terms we discussed,' said Matthew.

'Don't worry, Mr Brown,' said the mayor. 'I'm a supporter. I think John Slimbridge saved us from being invaded and taken over by communists. Can't understand what Spence was doing, getting so involved with creatures from other worlds. How will the president arrive?'

'We're keeping the arrangements strictly on a need-to-know basis. Let's just say that the baseball diamond behind the stage is to be kept clear.'

'Right, okay.'

'Now, you're sure about your speech? No deviation,' said Matthew.

'Don't be concerned. You can rely on me.'

'Good. The president needs to know who his friends really are.'

«««0»»»

[From Brad Gregg's and Jim Collins' notes and recordings. RBB]

General Dick Beech stood at the front of an assembly of some thirty key figures. To his right, a television monitor showed the billionaire software guru, Peter Stone, who had been instrumental in keeping the Internet coming into the United States and ensuring some news from the outside world found its way into ordinary homes. A video camera mounted on a tripod recorded the meeting so that it could be sent to other groups.

The general banged a heavy glass paperweight onto the top of a nearby table. 'Congressman, ladies, gentlemen, marines,' he began. 'It gives me great pleasure to call this first meeting of the FREE AMERICA organisation to order.'

The room fell into silence, the audience eager to hear what the general had to say.

'Until now we've been a loose assembly of militia, spread across the country. Tonight, we take this to a whole new level, but firstly I'd like to welcome our leader, Congressman Charles Mayne,' said the general, stepping to one side and the assembly applauded as the congressman walked over to take centre stage.

'Thank you all for the support you are giving the cause,' said Charles Mayne in his slow, deliberate, Boston accent. 'I appreciate that you are all risking your lives by even being here. That will never be forgotten.' He paused for effect.

'Firstly, I want to assure everyone that, although I have ambitions to be president of the United States, this is not the way I would want to achieve it. You have my word, all of you, that when we have unseated Slimbridge, my presidency will be brief and, within six months, there will be a full election for a new leader. You, hearing me here today are the guarantee that this will happen,' he said seriously, then he pulled himself to his full height, clasped his hands together and began the meat of his address.

'We are not going to form full strength armies to overthrow the tyrant. That might have been the way to proceed in the eighteen-sixties, but today, with sophisticated weapons and tackling a madman who is even likely to use tactical nukes, a full scale civil war is out of the question. Too many good people would be killed or maimed.' Again, he paused.

'Instead, FREE AMERICA will become a thorn in the administration's side. We will adopt the tactics of the Scot, William Wallace, rather than the massed armies of our nineteenth century civil war.' Another pause.

'Have you ever attended a barbecue in the late summer, only to discover a nest of flying ants or yellow jackets has awoken just in time for the festivities. We all know what happens. Grown men run around swatting the air and totally failing to strike a single one. The insects, however, have spoiled the party and may not have even bitten or stung anyone. It is the fear which spoils the party. We intend to use similar tactics to spoil Slimbridge's party!'

'Now, I'm going to hand back to General Beech who was also President Spence's senior general prior to his retirement just over a year ago. The general is still fully in the swing of modern military thinking. He is the man who will help us free America.' The congressman stopped talking, reached his hand towards the general and shouted, 'FREE AMERICA!'

It echoed back to him and the general grabbed and shook his hand as calls of 'Free America' continued to ring out. It is amazing how loud fewer than forty people can be. Charles Mayne took his seat and General Beech, now wearing his jacket with six strips of multicoloured medal ribbons, pulled over a barstool and sat casually to address the leaders of his army.

'Yellow jackets, wasps, hornets, no see ums, flying ants – all good analogies. We are going to bite or sting Slimbridge and his administration from every quarter. We already have Generals Braun and Burko in custody at a secret location. Have you noticed how neither capture has made the news?

'As I speak, a Slimbridge rally is beginning in Baltimore. It is a staged rally and everyone there will have been vetted to ensure that they are a Slimbridge or anti-alien supporter. It is exactly the sort of target, the Free America organisations would be likely to select. What this means is that they will be putting a lot of resources into ensuring nothing goes wrong. We already know that there are armoured vehicles camped out near the venue and there is word that two battalions were on the move towards Baltimore this morning.

'Huge resources and planning are being put into stopping any attack by Free America. But, you know what…?' the general paused and looked around the faces which were hanging upon his every word. 'We will strike them anyway and will do so in a manner that they will have prepared for, but is known to be the simplest to evade when professionals are involved. You will see the results live on TV in,' the general looked at his watch. 'In about thirty minutes.'

The general gave time for the information to sink in.

'We are planning many similar events, and this is what makes the insect analogy so good. The more they prepare for us to strike, the more innovative we shall be and the more they will have to prepare for our next move. Our actions will drive them mad.'

Charles stood and joined the general at the front of the audience. He said, 'We intend for them to be wasting so much time on trying to stop Free America attacks that will rarely happen, that they will be running themselves ragged. This is also where Peter Stone comes in.' The congressman pointed at the computer monitor standing on a desk in the corner of the room. He pointed an infrared control to raise the sound level.

'Good evening, everyone,' Peter Stone said. 'I am glad to be able to join you, even if it is only via the black net.

'I have a network of Free America supporters who will be leaking information about the "attacks" which are being planned. They will always fail to provide the necessary detailed information to stop them and, of course, most will not even happen. The ones that do will be sufficiently accurate to ensure they are taken seriously, but be so misleading that the general's men will be able to carry them out with little personal danger.

'Almost half of the US population is now listening to our news programme, The Voice of Free America, which we transmit through the black web from Canada. It will never refer to the fake events, but when a real event takes place, like tonight, we'll be sure to give them maximum coverage and inflate their seriousness.'

The billionaire continued, 'The overall strategy will increase the paranoia of Slimbridge and his key advisors, while giving the whole United States the impression that Free America is far larger and better organised than we actually are – no offence intended, Dick. The effect of paranoia on the enemy should never be underestimated.'

'Now,' said Charles Mayne, checking his watch, 'let's see what President John Slimbridge is saying at his Baltimore rally. Thanks for joining us, Peter. We know you need to get away now as you will shortly have a lot to occupy you.'

The image of Peter Stone disappeared from the monitor and the channel changed to the image of Slimbridge speaking to his massed supporters.

17 Arlucian

[From Ambassador Trestogeen's files. I apologise for such a large chunk of dialogue. RBB]

Yol Debert Indafark led Ambassador Yol Hareen Trestogeen and his deputy, Yol Terend Stograther through the chaos of the council reception area, where myriad aliens from some of the two hundred and fifty thousand Federation worlds carried out their council duties or looked around curiously as tourist visitors to the seat of government of the empire.

They approached a double door where an FEU guard in uniform stood. He, she or it was not a species which Hareen recognised. His, her or its plum purple skin contrasted with the juniper green of the tunic and the multicoloured feathers of the ceremonial helmet. Probably specially selected for size, he, she or it stood nearly three metres tall and was muscular with it. All four arms gently cosseted a weapon which undoubtedly could cause severe damage to life or property.

Beside him, her or it sat a slender male figure who was difficult to see in detail. He kept fading in and out of existence. This was a person from Terotone and they had mindreading and mind control abilities. They could also ease pain, grief and depression in other creatures. They were oft encountered and both Hareen and Debert were familiar with them. The Terotonian stood and briefly touched each of the visitors with his large, but slender, eight-fingered hands.

He spoke to the guard. 'These are Councillor Yol Debert Indafark, Ambassador Yol Hareen Trestogeen and Deputy Ambassador Yol Terend Stograther. They have a meeting in fifteen minutes with the cabinet.'

The guard said, 'Welcome. You may pass.' He, she or it stood to one side, a three-fingered hand waved at a switch in the wall panel and the double doors opened inwards revealing a lushly carpeted corridor. They had passed security.

The end of the short corridor opened out into a plush reception area manned by a robot which bore all the similarities of a Daragnen, down to the shortness and the head which was almost part of the torso. The resemblance was so close that Hareen concluded that Daragnens must like anthropomorphising their automatons.

'Please take a seat,' it said and pressed an intercom button. 'Gerady, the cabinet meeting at four is in reception.'

'Acknowledged,' a tinny voice was heard to say through the communication system.

None of the visitors had ever had an audience within the actual cabinet room of the president. Everything here was new to them.

A slight aroma of ginger pervaded the reception area, complementing its butterscotch carpet and buttermilk walls. Giant micro-thin screens filled almost every inch of space, and a continual progression of live images entertained the visitors. Each vista, lasting about a minute, was from a different Federation planet. Some showed preserved ancient buildings from pre-Federation days others, scenes of countryside with bizarrely coloured crops or trees. A variety of coloured atmospheres and moody, dusky scenes with giant worlds hanging in alien skies meant there was always something wonderful to watch.

'Excuse me,' said Debert, 'is every Federation world represented in these moving murals?'

The robot replied, 'There are twelve screens each portraying more than twenty thousand images so most worlds will certainly appear sooner or later.'

They watched a camera panning over a stunning seascape and it was followed by a smog of moss green which almost hid the few buildings looming in the background. Another scene showed a painfully scorched desert and it was followed by one of pewter glaciers and oppressive slate coloured clouds, transmitting rapid shards of lightning in every direction. It was quickly gone and a pastoral scene showed giant robot cultivators in fields of cornflower blue crops.

Hareen was almost disappointed when a large, elaborately carved door opened and a Clueb flew into the room. These coal black flying cherubs had the special talent of remembering everything which was ever said in their presence or seen by them. They liked nothing more than filling their minds with facts, figures, faces and situations. Cluebs habitual nosiness had created an enjoyable niche for them. Important individuals, like the president and some of the senior councillors, invited Cluebs to act as assistants and there was never a shortage of volunteers.

'I'm Ya Gerady, President Dimorathron's assistant. Please come this way,' she said and flew at walking speed ahead of Debert, Terend and Hareen through the door into the cabinet room, her wings a blur of transparent gossamer. Once inside, she shot through the air and sat on a perch behind the right side of the president's tank.

The room was grand; the central table constructed from polished rock, full of small aquatic fossils from some extreme otherworld past, forever frozen in this seat of immense power, which ruled with a velvet-gloved, benevolent hand. Around the table sat ten of the Federation's most senior ministers. They were all well known by most people and were made up from a spread of councillors who rotated their roles every two to four years. The variety of aliens was remarkable in its diversity.

Also in the room, the vice president sat at one end of the table. She was a Purrs, a large blue apelike creature. At the other end of the table was the president. A strange spectacle, it was a budding creature, hence the honorific Ye. It lived permanently submerged in a silver tank which stood about one point five metres high and a third of a metre in diameter. The top was a transparent dome filled with a yam-coloured liquid. The president had a fluid shape like the body of an octopus. Its most prominent features were its two sunken eyes. The tank had many controls and dials and, from the centre of the front, a tentacle in a semi-transparent sheath waved the visitors into the room.

It pressed a button and said, 'Come in, Debert, Hareen and Terend. Take a seat. It is so pleasant to see you and Gerady tells me that you have a concept which is going to lighten our dreadfully boring cabinet meeting.'

It laughed at itself fluidly and one or two of the others also made sounds of amusement.

'Ye President, it is an honour to actually meet you after our many conversations by ultrawave,' said Hareen.

'I retire soon, Hareen and, I must say, I will be sad to miss the antics of the planet Earth which it has been our pleasure and pain to share,' the president said and laughed again.

Hareen knew not to take the president's lightheartedness too seriously as he had been told the creature possessed an uncompromising facet too.

The president continued, 'So, what news of this planet Earth? I met some of the people not long ago and Gerady was telling me that I had an appointment coming up with President Spence of the United States of America, but I understand he died with the diplomatic team in the atomic explosion in that city – what was it called?'

'New York,' said Hareen.

'Yes, New York, that's the place. A shame. They all seemed nice people. Sad, and they're all dead now except that, what did she call herself – an ordinary citizen – Gerady tells me that she was the only survivor.

'Sorry, Ye President. I don't know to whom you refer,' said Hareen.

'Gerady?'

'Paula Wilson,' said the black cherub.

'Ah, yes,' said Hareen. 'I met her not long ago.'

'Yes, we understand you have been, shall I say, rather elastic with some of the conditions of the Earth prohibition,' said the vice president.

'I have, but I needed to understand better the nature of the problem,' said Hareen guiltily.

'Ha ha, not so serious, please. We understand, but now you wish to empty the rulebook into the nearest nova. Is that right?' said the president.

'Perhaps.'

'Okay. Let the serious business begin,' said the president.

Hareen materialised his secradarve and had it display a Mercator projection map of the Earth, showing all of the nations of the world in deliberately contrasting, but not too solid, colours. The large screen was on the opposite side of the room. The cabinet members on that side swivelled in their seats to see.

'This colourful map is Earth, split into its two hundred independent nations. The blue areas represent oceans, seas and lakes. The nations each govern themselves as if they were individual planets, although some like this bloc,' the secradarve highlighted the countries of the European Union, 'have loose associations.'

The map darkened so that the oceans and seas remained a lapis blue, the land masses all became pine green except for the rose-pink territories and mainland of the United States. 'The largest area, which you are seeing flashing is the bulk of the USA,' said Hareen.

'That is another very large area at the north west,' said a cabinet member.

'Ah, yes, but it is not as large as it appears because of the Mercator projection. It is called Alaska and is sparsely populated. The other small rose coloured areas include the islands of Hawaii and Puerto Rico, and are territories controlled by the main USA.'

'Yes, continue,' said the president.

'I believe it might be possible to allow the USA to remain completely independent of the Federation while the rest of the planet joins,' said Hareen.

'And what about each of the smaller territories and that larger one in the north east?' asked another cabinet member.

'They should be given a choice. Stay with the USA or join the rest of the world in the Federation.'

'How do you feel about this, Debert? Is it practical?' asked the vice president.

'As long as there are strict borders, it could be achieved,' said Yol Debert, 'but I'd rather the north east area, Alaska, and the islands were part of the Federation as they could become very isolated. They might want to use their polluting transport methods to travel to and from them and that would not be acceptable as we bring the planet's environment back to acceptable levels.'

'Why can't they use shuttles?' asked another cabinet member.

'We're not intending the separate nation to have access to Federation technology,' said Terend.

'Ha, to let them know the rest of the world is getting benefits they are missing out on,' said the president and chuckled.

'In part, yes, Ye President,' said Hareen.

'Presumably,' said the vice president, 'there would be some interaction with the Federation sectors and that would mean some complex rules, similar to those we have with the loosely associated planets.'

'There's news this week that Cafi is joining after a referendum,' said a fourth cabinet member.

'Excellent,' said the president with a chuckle. 'We'll all be a little poorer for a while. Detail, Hareen, what would happen with produce and currency?'

'Debert, Terend and I have been through the economics with some advisors. It is believed that very little produce would move from the United States to the rest of the world. Anything they currently produce could certainly be acquired from the Federation territories. There are exceptions. Speciality goods like certain alcoholic beverages and spirits, speciality foods and so on. They could be purchased in border shops or online. Items exported in larger quantities, if that happened at all, could be distributed by us to their point of delivery. Their trucks will certainly not be allowed over the border for more than a few months.'

'What's wrong with their trucks?' asked the vice president.

'Pollution again. They use internal combustion engines. We'd make an exception for electric trucks, but they are few and far between,' said Terend.

'Ho ho,' said the president, 'They could set up an historic transport amusement park.'

Hareen continued, 'Their other exports would likely be tourism. People would want to visit the United States in quite large numbers to see attractions such as your suggested ancient transport exhibits, museums, the Grand Canyon, national parks and so on.'

'This is where currency becomes a problem,' said Yol Debert. 'How many afeds would people need to buy dollars. There would need to be an exchange rate.'

'And what will they do with the afeds they receive for goods and from visitors?' asked the president.

'If the currency trading were only undertaken by the USA government, then afeds could buy any produce they wanted from the Federation,' said Yol Debert.

'Could they buy our technology? I'd be happier if it were only consumables they could purchase. You said you didn't want them using shuttles,' said a cabinet member.

'Yes,' said Hareen, 'we think it would be a bad idea for them to be able to buy robots because they might use those robots to keep themselves in luxury, encouraging the manual workers to leave for Federation territory.'

'What about tourism the other way? If they have afeds, surely they could enter the Federation territories and go anywhere. They could even fly here. Do we want that?' asked the vice president.

The president said, 'I'd have thought we'd have wanted as many of them as possible to visit territories on the Earth and other planets. Anyone who sees how good life is in the Federation can only return home with glowing reports of what their friends and relations are missing.'

'That's what Yol Debert, Yol Terend and I thought, Ye President,' said Hareen.

'*See?* I can't imagine how this cabinet will survive without me,' the president said and laughed out loud.

'Ha ha,' said one of the other cabinet members, 'without doubt they will not be so much fun!'

'Well, Hareen?' asked the president.

'We do think it will be good for the Earth and will eventually change them as they learn more about the economic system. Especially the ordinary citizens,' said Hareen.

'Yes, like, what's her name?'

'Paula Wilson,' said Gerady.

'Yes, that's her,' said the president.

'There is a complication,' said Hareen.

'What, only one?' asked the vice president, laughing again.

'The president of the United States of America is the man who deliberately killed all of the Earth's leaders, our first diplomatic team and several million of their own citizens. He will be escaping justice,' said Hareen. 'Secondly, there is a resistance group called Free America who want to overthrow President Slimbridge, and they will be rather annoyed if the country is isolated because we are not willing to tackle Slimbridge ourselves.'

'I see,' said the president more soberly. 'If you are leaving them as independent, that has to mean you can't interfere.'

'That's what we were thinking,' said Debert.

'What do we think? Show of hands, please. Yes?' said the president.

Eight hands or feelers or tentacles reached into the air plus the vice president's.

'No?'

No one moved.

So,' the president said, 'you two are abstaining. Why?'

'I am prepared to wait and see,' said one.

'I almost voted no, but decided it would be an interesting experiment to observe,' said the other.

'Okay, Hareen and Debert. You have permission to explore the possibilities. I'll have my office appoint a couple of economists and a lawyer to assist,' said the president.

'We'll also need permission for more interaction with the people,' said Hareen.

'Granted,' said the president. 'Thank you for asking this time! Anything else?'

'Not right now, Ye President,' said Hareen.

'Meeting over then,' said the president.

As Hareen and Debert turned to leave, the president called after them, 'I will no longer be holding office when this gets underway. Hareen, please keep me personally advised how it all goes… if you live to tell the tale!' He laughed as the three visitors stood beside the door.

'Unfortunately,' said Hareen, 'I will probably have gone before you depart, Ye President. I've had my last regenerative spawning.'

'Oh dear, Hareen. That is sad to hear. I didn't know when I made my thoughtless comment about you living to tell the tale. I will miss you. Terend, will you undertake to keep me in the picture after I've retired?'

'Certainly, Ye President,' said the deputy ambassador.

'Now go! We have much boring business to discuss,' said the president loudly and then broke into laughter. 'And a fond goodbye to you, Hareen. I'll miss you and your interesting intrusions.'

'Thank you, Ye President. Enjoy your retirement.'

«««0»»»

[From digital recordings and several files and biographies. RBB]

The atmosphere at the showground was full of anticipation, as was always the case when a presidential address was about to take place. Police in pairs circulated among the audience, occasionally stopping to speak to people and more rarely asking to see inside small bags or mini-backpacks. Less obvious were the individuals from the FBI, meandering unobtrusively throughout the crowd, listening and watching for anything which might result in a potential disturbance. Finally, the Secret Service operatives, noticed by no one, invisibly patrolled the entire assembly.

The roar of the engines of Marine One, the president's helicopter, passed over the ground, lights blazing through the late afternoon daylight.

It touched down on the baseball diamond behind the stage and the powerful engines fell silent. No one could see the helicopter here, but they knew that President Slimbridge had arrived and proceedings were about to begin. The anticipation of the crowd was palpable.

The mayor of Baltimore climbed the six stairs to the stage and approached the lectern, attracting cheers and generous applause. He waved the sound down, but it took at least a minute before he was able to be heard. He cleared his throat, looked at his notes for the speech, which had been written for him by Matthew Brown, and began to address the crowd.

His enthusiastically supportive speech received thunderous applause. He turned to the right. From behind a curtain, President Slimbridge walked onto the stage to the most raucous support. Again, more than a minute elapsed before the mayor was able to welcome the president. The two men shook hands and hugged each other, the president raising an arm to acknowledge the support from the showground.

After even more hugging, handshaking and waving by both men towards the supporters, the president took his position behind the seal of office. Numerous camera crews and photographers made their way among the crowds, filming thumbs-up, smiling faces, cheering voices and adoring leaps into the air. This was exactly what President Slimbridge needed to boost his popularity. Fortunately, only he and a few of his closest advisors knew how low his esteem had fallen.

'Hello, Baltimore!' he shouted and was immediately drowned out by the cheering crowd. It was almost a minute before it calmed down enough to allow the president to continue.

'Thank you so much, Baltimore.' Another explosion of applause stopped him in his tracks.

'Please, please settle down,' he said and walked back and forth on the stage waving for them to settle and listen.

Of course, that just fired off another bout of adoration. Eventually, it tailed off and the president returned to the microphone, delighted that Matthew's strategy had worked so well.

'Citizens of the United States. Thank you for inviting me to speak to you here tonight. I know how you've been fed misleading stories by the nation's enemies and today I want to put the record straight.'

At that instant, eight gunshots rang out over the assembly. In seconds, Secret Service agents dived onto the president, slamming him down onto the stage, while another rushed on from off-stage and threw a shrapnel-proof mesh over the men on the floor.

In the audience, people screamed and dived for the ground. Others looked for the exits, while the army entered the park and began to search among the crowd for whoever had fired the shots.

While they searched, eyes concentrating on the people and the seating areas, no one was looking upwards.

Four relatively small drones rapidly arrived from different directions, hovered at about a hundred metres above the crowd and exploded.

But this was no high explosive designed to maim and injure; this was more like a muffled sonic boom. Thousands of tiny FREE AMERICA leaflets, just a few inches long and one wide were thrown outwards and upwards. The explosive sound caused everyone to look upwards. At that moment, projected downwards by the force of the blast, fifty gallons of pea-green indelible dye sprayed everyone in the showground. There was barely a face in the crowd which was not showing luminous evidence that FREE AMERICA had struck.

It was all seen on television. As expected, the broadcast was quickly shut off, but not before the green faces had been seen by the entire nation.

'And so,' said General Beech to the much smaller audience in the Ponte Vedra mansion, 'Free America has indelibly stamped its intentions upon the country. The hornet has caused its havoc! We stung him good!'

18 Sibernek Laboratory

[Taken from notes kept by Dr Melanie Rogers. RBB]

The research scientists at Sibernek were enjoying a coffee break. Paul Barton, head of research, had returned from Ethiopia and his arrival meant that there was now a buffer between the team and the CEO, Brian Talbot, who always emitted such negative vibes.

Melanie, Gillian, Jorg, Carol and Jed sat with Medibot at a large table in the research department's canteen.

Paul stood behind the medibot, holding a tennis ball. 'You think it's ready?' he asked.

'It works well,' said Melanie. 'Has performed nominally in every scenario.'

'What do you think, Medibot?' Paul asked.

'Most functions are good, but the tennis ball test will be interesting to observe,' it said.

'Right,' said Gillian Ross. 'Let's drink up and get back to the lab to put it through its paces.'

In the laboratory, a mechanical man, very similar in size and shape to the medibot, stood on one side of the room next to a workbench.

'Hi, Sib,' said Paul as they all entered. 'Have you missed us?'

'No, Dr Barton, I have not missed you,' said Sib. 'I am not capable of such an emotion.'

'What have you been doing while we were away?'

'Nothing of great import, Dr Barton. I have practiced some of the problems you gave me to solve.'

'Have you improved your responses?'

'I have answered all of the problems within the time specified, Dr Barton.'

All of a sudden, Paul Barton threw the tennis ball at Sib and shouted, 'Catch!'

The ball flew through the air and rebounded off Sib's chest an instant before one of its hands intercepted the trajectory. Sib responded by running forward and grabbing the ball on its second bounce.

'Not bad, Sib,' said Paul.

'Not as good as Medibot,' said Jed.

'No,' said Paul.

'The comparison is not relevant really,' said Medibot. 'Sib's chips, being that much larger, are proportionately slower. However, Sib's compensation for his failure was excellent.'

'You caught four, thrown at you simultaneously,' said Carol.

'Yes, but the same test for Sib would have him miss each of the four balls by a similar margin. What you have produced is remarkable and you have not produced Sib to play ball games. His problem-solving and interaction capabilities in unexpected situations are excellent.'

'That is true, but we were hoping to have reproduced your abilities,' said Gillian Ross.

'Have you observed Sib's projectile throwing?' asked Medibot.

'No. Sib, can you…'

'Stop!' said Medibot. 'Let me.'

Medibot crossed the room to the opposite side from where Sib was standing. It put an arm out to one side and opened its hand. 'Sib,' it said, 'throw the tennis ball into my hand.'

Sib raised its hand and threw. The ball sailed through the air in a graceful arc and hit the centre of the medibot's hand, which closed around it.

'You see how well you have built Sib,' said Medibot. 'Sib has no practical experience with projectile trajectories, yet almost instantly calculated force, trajectory and distance so as to cause the ball to strike the palm of my hand.'

'I see,' said Paul. 'Pretty damn good, really.'

'It is the chip size which limits processing speed, and this is also why Sib cannot "think" in the way I do and carry out normal conversations. You treat me as a person and Sib as a machine. You did not invite Sib to join us for the coffee break earlier,' said Medibot.

'Yes, a valid point,' said Paul Barton. 'However, I think we're ready to convince Mr Talbot to put Sib into production. He'll be extremely useful in defusing concerns over AI.'

«««0»»»
[From White House tapes. RBB]

Grim faced and clenching his fists, President John Silvester Slimbridge was staring at the five men who sat in his visitors chairs.

Admiral Mann, General Delve, the replacement for General Burko, General Alexander, General Braun's replacement, Piers Andwell, head of the Secret Service, and Matthew Brown all stared back at him. Matthew's face was covered in green dye as was the left of General Alexander's.

'How could you let this happen?' asked the president. 'You say you actually received a warning too.'

'Yes, but it was non-specific,' said the admiral. 'We thought the shots were it.'

'And they were blanks?'

'Yes, Mr President, fired remotely by rifles hidden inside drainpipes. We didn't know that at the time and the Secret Service protected you well,' said General Alexander.

'I didn't get stained because I had four men on top of me,' said the president. 'Look at Matthew's face. It's ridiculous. How long before it washes off?'

'Not good, sir,' said Matthew Brown. 'It could be more than ten days. I'm using peroxide to try to speed up matters.'

'And thousands of my supporters are the same,' said the president.

'Yes, Mr President,' said the admiral. 'And there's worse news. Free America radio is telling people to put green make-up on their foreheads or cheeks to show their support.'

'What are you doing about this radio station?' asked the president. 'Why can't you shut it down, or broadcast interference or something?'

'The problem, Mr President,' said Piers Andwell, the Secret Service chief, 'is that it is coming down the telephone lines. We can't stop it without shutting down all telephone communication. We can't block it or mask it with interference because the incoming frequency constantly changes.'

'And this is Peter Stone's handiwork?'

'Yes, sir, and it's coming from Canada,' said Piers. 'He's a pretty clever individual and has all the resources of his company behind him.'

'Can't we shut down his revenue stream?' asked the president.

'We've already done that, sir, but his business is global,' said Matthew.

'What about intel? Do you know where he is, or where he's transmitting from? Damn it, we must be able to do something!' said the president, thumping the desk so hard that a picture frame fell over.

'We're tracking him. He's in Vancouver at the moment and the CIA are trying to get a fix. There's a shoot-to-kill order on him.'

'It's not good enough, Piers. I want him captured or killed. Make it a priority.'

'Mr President, he's in a foreign country. Even if we manage to assassinate him, it could be seen as an act of aggression against a foreign power. If any of their citizens were hurt in the process it would have serious international ramifications,' said Mr Andwell.

'To hell with Canada. If you get a chance to hit him then do it. Any harm to others will teach them not to interfere in America's affairs. I am not going to criticise you if there is collateral damage. Canada knows exactly what Stone is doing! We can't even stop our own media talking about this green make-up business and people are laughing about what they already call Baltimore Dyegate.'

The president stood, causing all of the visitors to jump to their feet.

'I am disappointed in all of you. Get out of my office and find ways to get Stone, Beech and Mayne out of my hair… and quickly! Now go, get out!' the president shouted as he turned towards the window and stared into the distance.

«««O»»»

[Taken from Paula Wilson and Harcon Trestogeen's files. RBB]

A familiar muffled pop announced that the ambassador had materialised in Lara Horvat's office in the British Ministry of Defence. With him was Yol Terend Stograther, an olive-green humanoid figure with short legs and four arms. He was dressed in violet trousers and a lavender jacket, with a white shirt which had wings wrapping his long neck and trailing over his back. He stood just short of average human height, maybe five foot four.

'Yol Ambassador, a pleasant surprise,' Lara said.

'This is my deputy,' said the ambassador.

The ambassador handed over a small device to the secretary general. 'This is a communication device. You press it once to communicate with me. I have been given permission to become further involved in bringing the Federation and Earth closer together.'

'That is good news,' said Lara.

'I would like to meet with the Security Council on board my ship. Could you please advise them that they will be collected at midday British time tomorrow?'

'Certainly. I'd like my assistant there as she also keeps official minutes,' said Lara.

'Yes. No problem. The Federation president spoke fondly of you, Ms Wilson,' the ambassador said.

'Really? I was only with him a minute,' said Paula.

'He prides himself in remembering everything, but I suspect his Clueb might have a hand in that. There is something else. I will be handing over my ambassadorial duties to Yol Terend in the near future. He feels about Earth the same way I do, so will always deal with you sympathetically'

'You've been reprimanded for breaking the prohibition?' asked Lara.

'No. My life is coming to an end.'

The two women were shocked at this sudden announcement.

'Oh. I'm sad to hear that. Can nothing be done?' asked Lara.

'Don't be too sad for me, Lara. The last act of the male of my species is to spawn. We get around the problem of death by being protected from the females during the process and then we are regenerated medically. The process can only be used four or five times, though, and I have already used it on five occasions. This time I shall die.'

'That's dreadful,' said Paula.

'Well, yes and no. It is also the most rapturous event. The spawning is the most important factor in our lives. My sixth will doubtless be the finest, with nothing to protect me, and the only regret I have is not being able to discover what will happen to your lovely planet.'

'It is, nevertheless, tragic,' said Lara.

'Try not to see it like that, Lara, it is my crowning achievement. I'll see you tomorrow,' the ambassador said, and the two of them promptly vanished.

«««o»»»

One at a time, Presidents Yang, Olov, and Ramseur, Prime Minister Church, the secretary general, and Paula Wilson materialised in a large conference room on the Eskorav. Immediately overcome by the view of Earth from orbit, each of them walked to the long glass wall and stared in wonder at their first view of their home planet from space. All but Paula, of course, because she had seen many planets during her time with Secretary General Okafor.

The door opened and in walked the ambassador and his deputy.

'Welcome all,' said the ambassador. 'This is my deputy, Yol Terend Stograther from Dihethror. We're both so pleased we have been allowed to help Earth make some progress.'

Each of the leaders introduced themselves to Yol Terend who acknowledged them in a rather tinny voice, as if it was electronically produced.

'I should explain,' said the ambassador, 'that Dihethrors don't normally produce sound to communicate, so they wear electronic implants if they are off world or meeting other species.

'Please sit,' the ambassador said, while settling himself into his specially adapted chaise longue. 'I'm glad you could all attend.'

He waited until everyone was seated, then continued, 'I have a very, very serious question for you first. It is crucial to how we will proceed.'

'Ask away,' said President Marat Olov.

'Two days ago, I attended a full cabinet meeting of the Federation which included President Dimorathron. What I am about to explain to you is absolutely unique in terms of the Federation. Never before has part of a planet been treated as if it is an actual planet of its own. The permission was granted, but there are sceptics in the cabinet who have not objected, because it has piqued their curiosity. It is unique. If I, or you, make a mess of this opportunity, I'm sure it will never be attempted again.

'This is my crucial question,' said the ambassador taking a drink of water from a large urn on the table. 'If we are going to contemplate allowing one nation on Earth to remain independent of the Federation, how sure are you that the rest of your world will join?'

The leaders looked at each other and Lara answered, 'Since our last meeting, we have considered this, Yol Ambassador. We think that all nations with the exception of North Korea and Israel will want to join.'

'We cannot have more than one nation opting out. How will you go about convincing those two countries, because you *must* do so? What can we do to help? Are there any compromises they could live with?' asked the ambassador.

'Israel's concern is primarily about its borders and having control over who can live within it. It is considered to be the promised land, promised by God to them as a race,' said Lara.

'They are a democracy, yes?'

'That's right.'

'Okay, if we took a hundred pro-Federation Israelis and a hundred anti-Federation Israelis and showed them half a dozen of our worlds, would their government allow them to promote their views freely to the rest of the population? If so, would they allow a free vote and honour it?'

'I really don't know,' said Lara, shrugging and looking to the others.

'I would think it was a possibility, Yol Ambassador. We could ask and see what they say,' said Prime Minister Maureen Church.

'Hmm,' said the ambassador. 'What about the North Koreans?'

'More tricky,' said President Che Yang. 'They are a totalitarian regime, something, in the past, both China and Russia accused of, but in their case, rule is from top and no one dare speak out against leadership.'

'Well, frankly I need you to visit both countries and persuade both of them to accept the Federation. We cannot mess around with a hotchpotch of small independent countries. That would never work,' said the ambassador.

'That offer of taking the Israelis to visit other worlds, would that still be available?' asked the secretary general.

'Yes. And we'd offer to do the same with the North Koreans, but it sounds as if it wouldn't work with them. Maybe I should speak to their leaders. What do you think?'

'You could certainly try, Yol Ambassador,' said President Yang.

'What would ze plan be zen, if zey both agree?' asked President Ramseur.

'I will arrange a large fleet of passenger liners and we will take all the leaders, their deputies, senior government advisors and officials to visit a few worlds. Not all at the same time, obviously, but spread over a couple of weeks,' said the ambassador.

'You're talking about thousands of people,' said President Olov.

'Yes, that is not a problem. I think even those of you here have not quite realised the scale of the Federation. Some of the larger passenger liners carry thousands, although we'll probably use ships which take three to eight hundred. More manageable. During their trips they will all be esponged with Galactic Standard and, once the trips are finished, I would expect you to hold a General Assembly to pass or reject membership for the entire world except the USA.

'In fact, I have trouble understanding Yol Ramseur and, occasionally, Yol Yang, so, when we finish this meeting, Yol Terend will arrange for you to be esponged with Galactic Standard.'

'If passed by the UN, the next stage will be to set up hard borders between the US, Canada and Mexico. I will then offer the USA independence from the Federation if they give up their island protectorates. I'd like them to relinquish Alaska too, but would be prepared to compromise as it has just the one border with Canada.'

'How borders will work, Yol Ambassador?' asked President Yang.

'The Federation border will allow free flow inwards. The USA would control anyone wishing to enter, either to move to the USA or visit for tourism. Initially the afed would match the dollar and we'd let the market find a true exchange rate.'

'Zat would cause 'uge volatility!' said President Ramseur.

'True,' said the ambassador, 'but it would not affect the Federation and it would be up to the USA to do whatever is necessary to control their currency. I would imagine the dollar will weaken quite rapidly over a short period, but we might artificially inflate it. The cost is negligible on a Federation-wide scale.'

'So, they could buy from the Federation using afeds they collect from tourists and any products they sell. What would they sell, I wonder?' asked Prime Minister Church.

'There are sure to be many products in great demand,' said Yol Terend. 'Alcoholic drinks, speciality foods and so on. There'll be no market for their agricultural equipment or other vehicles, nor bulk foodstuffs like grain, vegetables and meat except, again, speciality items and processed products. One of my projects will be to analyse which products the rest of the world would like from the USA.'

'What about them importing?' asked President Olov.

'That is more problematical,' said the ambassador. 'I don't think we'll want them buying our technology, robots or autonomous vehicles. How about tourism? What will USA citizens have to pay to visit places of interest in the rest of your world? Probably we'll subsidise tourism to encourage them to see how the rest of the world is doing under the Federation economic system.'

'Excusez moi, but 'ow will you get zem to agree to zis?'

'Now that you have agreed that Secretary General Horvat can represent you all, she will join me in meeting them to discuss the details. Logically, we think they will agree.'

'Would not be too confident over that,' said President Yang. 'You know there uprising underway. At least half Americans disagree with Slimbridge. Might be disappointed with decision allow independence. Certain you need speak both sides.'

'You think so?' asked the ambassador.

The leaders looked at each other. There were various nods. 'We seem to be agreeing that President Yang is correct,' said Lara. 'Can you arrange to meet both sides? Might be best to see the Free America group first.'

'Free America?'

'The name the uprising is using.'

'Why them first?' the ambassador asked.

'Because if you do a deal with Slimbridge, Free America might not recognise it and the uprising will continue,' said Prime Minister Church. 'Peter Stone is coordinating the media in the USA and he says that Free America is not intending to kill or maim, but it is in the early stages.'

'I see,' said the ambassador. 'I'll take your advice.'

'So, where do we go from here?' asked President Olov.

'You get North Korea and Israel to accept the position. I, with Lara's help, will visit both sides involved in the standoff in the USA. When you need us to take people to other worlds, Lara has a communication device.'

President Yang stood and walked to the window on the world. 'Excuse me,' he said. 'If this meeting about to end, I want enjoy looking at world from space for while. Maybe see China.'

'Oui, me too,' said President Ramseur.

They all stood and went to take in the view.

'Amazing,' said Prime Minister Church.

'Truly,' said President Olov.

'If we can make this work,' said the ambassador. 'Our worlds are your worlds. I came across a strange saying in an Earth book. I can expand upon it. The universe is your oyster! What it has to do with shellfish defeats me, despite my origins.'

Paula Wilson, Lara Horvat and Maureen Church laughed then began explaining to the others.

'Yol Terend,' said the ambassador, 'ensure they get home safely when they are finally sated by the panorama and esponged with Galactic Standard.' He made a strange giggling sound and left the conference room with five mesmerised humans watching Africa passing by beneath.

19 Free America HQ

[From Brad Gregg's, Jim Collins', and Hareen Trestogeen's files. RBB]

Jim Collins walked into the kitchen, where Dick Beech, Bob Nixon and some of the others were enjoying a cooked breakfast. 'I've just had a rather odd call from my wife on one of our burner phones,' he said.

The general was instantly alert. Anything "odd" could be dangerous. 'Why odd?' he asked.

'Whoever it was, provided her with a number and asked me to get either Charles or you to call it on a matter of some urgency,' said Jim.

'How long were you on the call?' asked the general.

'Twenty seconds, max.'

'Too short for a trace,' said Charles.

'Bring me a fresh burner, Eric,' said the general, and a soldier disappeared into the adjacent room, returning shortly afterwards with a new cell phone.

The general dialled the number.

'To whom am I speaking?' asked a very slightly foreign voice on the other end of the line.

'Beech,' the general said, curtly.

'Lara Horvat here. The Federation ambassador wishes to meet you.'

'When? Where? Be quick or I'll terminate this call.'

'Ambassador Trestogeen will contact you using their methods.'

'Okay. Goodbye,' said the general and cut the connection. 'Eric, take the SIM card and battery from this phone and drive into Jacksonville. Dispose of the phone and card a mile or two apart. Smash the phone and break the card. Keep the battery with the others.'

'Yes, sir,' said the soldier and left with the phone.

The general told the others what the secretary general had said.

'What are their methods, I wonder?' said Charles.

'What do you think they want?' asked Brad. 'Heard nothing about them since the nuke.'

'Lara is trustworthy,' said Jim. 'Charles and I had a meeting in Washington with her. She was on her way to try to reason with Slimbridge.'

'What happened?' asked the general.

'Brick wall, I think,' said Jim. 'She was strip-searched when she arrived in Washington.'

'What? No respect! Let's be prepared for a call when it comes,' said the general.

A matter of minutes later, there was the muffled sound of air being disturbed and a voice said, 'I am the deputy ambassador, Yol Terend Stograther. You are General Beech, yes?'

Dick Beech turned so suddenly that he almost fell off his barstool. Most of the others jumped and two grabbed their weapons.

'You have nothing to fear from me,' said Yol Terend and those in the kitchen visibly relaxed, although they stared at the strange looking four-armed, olive green figure.

'Welcome, Yol Terend. I'm Charles Mayne.'

The alien materialised his secradarve and studied it as it floated before his face. 'Yes, I recognise you, the general, Jim Collins, Brad Gregg and Bob Nixon from this device. The ambassador wishes me to take you to a meeting.'

'Travelling can be dangerous for us,' said the general.

'Not with me. You will be safe in my company,' said the alien.

'With respect, if we are even seen travelling, it could cause us to be betrayed.'

'You will not be seen, General. Rest assured, no one outside this room will know you have travelled to meet with the ambassador.'

'Okay,' said Charles. 'When do we leave.'

'Now,' said Yol Terend, and the six men were no longer in the kitchen in Florida, but suddenly in the conference room aboard the Eskorav.

The view impacted all of them, as it had with the members of the Security Council. Even Bob Nixon, who had been aboard Federation ships before, had his breath taken away by the amazing view of Earth below.

'Hello, Charles, Jim,' said Lara who was already on board. 'This is Yol Ambassador Hareen Trestogeen. Also my assistant, Paula Wilson.'

The general, Brad and Bob introduced themselves and shook the ambassador's fin.

'This is some meeting room you have here, Ambassador,' said Charles, admiring the view as India and the islands of the Far East passed beneath them. 'Stunning.'

'Welcome aboard the Federation rapid-reaction ship Eskorav,' said the ambassador.

'We are so sorry about the diplomatic team you lost in New York,' said the general.

'Most regrettable,' said the ambassador. 'When you have finished taking in the view, please take a seat. No hurry though.'

Shortly, the entire party was seated around the oval table, with the exception of the ambassador who lounged in his chaise longue.

Lara Horvat opened the meeting and explained the plan for the USA remaining independent of the Federation.

'I don't like it,' said Charles. 'If you assisted us to overthrow Slimbridge, we'd almost certainly want to join, or at least investigate the possibility in greater detail.'

The general jumped in, 'Can you not "beam him up" as you have with us, then we'd know exactly how to deal with him.'

'Sorry, General,' said Yol Terend, 'that is not the sort of intervention we are allowed to make.'

'The plan,' said Lara, 'is that the isolation of the country will soon cause the people to realise that they are far worse off than they would have been as members. They will then willingly join. But, it is a Federation rule that they will not interfere militarily.'

'Ambassador,' said the general, 'we've spent time and money, and risked our lives to build a Free America organisation which will, eventually, overthrow Slimbridge. Are you asking us to stand down and telling us that we've wasted our time?'

'No, General. Once the rest of the world has joined, we can give you far more logistical support than we can while you are seen as a rebellious organisation,' said the ambassador.

'*Uprising!*' said the general loudly. 'A rebellion is against a legitimate government! We are rising up against a usurper and unelected government! There is *nothing whatsoever* legitimate about Slimbridge!'

'I hadn't appreciated the distinction. Even so, we cannot assist in the manner you wish,' said the ambassador. 'We are not asking you to stop your campaign, but we do want you to understand why the rest of the world will be joining us, with the USA as the exception.'

Charles said, 'This policy of yours leaves most of America in the grip of an evil, murderous regime. We'd be better without your assistance.'

'I agree with Congressman Mayne,' said the general. 'Either you help us or you don't, but if you are not going to help, then we'd like to be returned home to continue our campaign.'

'Ambassador,' said Bob Nixon, 'I worked for President Spence. He was a practical man. He knew that membership of the Federation would leave him out of office and much poorer, yet he had come to believe it was best for the ordinary citizens of the United States and was prepared to make that sacrifice... as was I. He would be horrified that you are actually propping up Slimbridge, his murderer, in the office he loved.'

'We are, most certainly, *not* supporting him or "propping him up" as you call it,' said Yol Terend, 'but we cannot intervene by overthrowing him or assisting you to do so.'

'Then what is the point of inviting us here?' asked Charles.

'Please. One moment,' said the secretary general. 'The main purpose for us being here was to keep you informed. The ambassador and I will be visiting Slimbridge and feeling him out on the independence option.'

'But you'll be negotiating with a mass murderer,' said the general. 'There must be repercussions for what he did... surely?'

'He has, of course, broken Federation laws,' said the ambassador. 'Once the agreement is in place, I will apply to have him arrested, but until an agreement is settled, this is a sovereign world and we can do nothing about him.'

The general stood up and, as always, he commanded everyone's attention. 'Consider this – if this were the leader of a rogue country who murdered our president and a United Nations diplomatic team, we would most certainly declare war and invade. Why can't you do that? Surely the Federation has had to fight for its principles in the past.'

The secretary general said, 'This was discussed with other nations, General, and war was considered not to be an option because Slimbridge was threatening a full nuclear retaliatory strike.'

'But that does not apply to the Federation!' said the general forcefully. 'From what we've heard, you could wipe him out without anyone firing a shot and you could negate his bombs!'

'That is true, but it is not an available option for us for the reasons I've just given,' said the ambassador.

'Then, Mr Ambassador,' said Charles, 'you leave us no option other than to escalate our actions and, if necessary, use violence to achieve our objectives. So far, we have tried not to hurt individuals. Yes, there have been some casualties, but they have been minimised. We can promise that no longer!'

'Can you not just *accidentally* beam Slimbridge into our headquarters?' asked the general. 'We'll look after him from there. It would create the minimum disruption to the country... and to the world... and, for that matter, to the Federation.'

'Allowing an independent nation within a Federation world cannot be something simple to organise,' said Bob.

'Okay. An end to this meeting!' said the ambassador, now realising that it was not going to be as simple as he'd imagined. 'We have notified you of the plan for an independent USA. We have told you that we believe that will lead to the USA wishing to join the rest of the world in the Federation. If your venture can shorten that timescale, that is fine, but we cannot help you.'

'Yol Ambassador, the information trips,' said the secretary general.

'Oh, yes. Nevertheless, if you would like us to take some of your people on Federation visits to other worlds, contact Secretary Horvat and she'll let us know and we'll make arrangements. They could be anyone within or outside your organisation. We will not have a problem with numbers.'

'I'd certainly want one of those,' said the general, 'but I cannot leave yet.'

'Me and Jim too,' said the congressman.

'Let Secretary Horvat know when you are ready and we'll arrange it,' said the ambassador. 'Yol Stograther, please return everyone except Lara and Paula to their point of origin.'

Everyone stood. The uprising leaders' faces bore grim expressions. In an instant they were gone.

'That didn't go down very well,' said the ambassador.

'No,' said the secretary general. 'Where do we go from here?'

«««0»»»

[Taken from Ambassador Trestogeen's office files and notes. RBB]
The Eskorav continued its graceful two-hourly orbits of Earth. Ambassador Trestogeen and Secretary General Horvat, together with Paula Wilson and Yol Terend Stograther made their way through its corridors to a room near the rear of the ship.

A windowless steel cell containing a long copper-topped table greeted them. At the far end there was a single seat. By the room entrance, several more seats were available including a chaise longue which would suit the ambassador. Either side of the table was a soldier in full dress uniform. One a female Purrs and the other a tall Racutaan. Both carried weapons.

Sitting in one of the chairs at the entrance area of the room, was a Teratonian, the mind control species. He sat with his long fingers constantly interlacing and separating, almost in time with his phasing in and out of existence.

The party entered and the four sat with the Teratonian, Yol Trestogeen occupying the head of the table in his special seat. The other end of the room was empty.

'Are we all ready?' asked the ambassador and everyone agreed.

Suddenly the far end of the room was no longer empty. John Slimbridge materialised beside the far wall, leaning forward against it and trying to regain his balance as if he'd been plucked mid-stride from the White House. He quickly recognised that something untoward had taken place and that this was not the wall of the Oval Office. It was steel. He ran his hand over it then turned to see where he was. On seeing the others in the room, he was clearly shocked and backed into the wall.

'John Slimbridge,' said the ambassador. 'You are aboard the FEU rapid-reaction ship Eskorav. You are behind a force field to protect us. Please sit.'

'How dare you kidnap the president of the United States of America?' he said.

'Please sit,' the ambassador said again.

'I demand that you return me to my office.'

'Please sit.'

Slowly realising that his demands were being ignored, Slimbridge made his way to the chair at the far end of the copper table. 'What do you want?' he asked, looking daggers at the secretary general.

Lara Horvat answered, 'President Slimbridge, this meeting is to keep you advised of the rest of the world's actions regarding the Federation.'

'Ms Horvat. You do not speak for us!' said the president.

The ambassador said, 'It would be better if you listened and thought before answering.'

'Don't you tell me what to do, *fish*!' he said venomously.

The ambassador signalled the secretary general to wait. No one spoke for nearly three minutes, which is a much longer time than it seems when waiting for something to start or continue.

Eventually, impatiently, John Slimbridge said, 'Well, what do you want? Say what you will, then return me to Washington.'

'Then I suggest you listen, Mr Slimbridge,' said the ambassador.

Secretary Horvat continued, 'Arrangements are being made for the rest of the world to join the Federation, leaving the USA as an independent, isolated nation. However, it requires your cooperation.'

'What cooperation? Don't expect any cooperation from me!'

'If you agree to what we are suggesting, you will be left, unmolested, by the Federation. There will be borders with Canada and Mexico where you can trade with the Federation. You can give permission, if you wish, for tourists to enter the USA and to import certain Federation goods and services, although they will be restricted. You may export anything to the rest of the world except for products on this list.' The secretary general passed the list through the forcefield. The president studied it – it was extensive and included drugs, guns, oil, gas, explosives and other items which would never be wanted or allowed in the Federation.

Secretary Horvat continued, 'US citizens wishing to visit Federation territories on Earth or worlds in the rest of the Federation will be permitted to do so. An exchange rate between the afed and the dollar will be established. You can allow anyone to immigrate to the USA if you wish. That is up to you.'

'Ha, we'll be flooded with escapees from your regime!' said the president loudly.

'You have the final say on immigration. There will be conditions, though.'

'What conditions?'

Lara continued, 'You will give up all of your island protectorates and Hawaii, as their borders would be too difficult to manage.'

'And?'

The ambassador spoke, 'There is no "and". That would be the end of the matter, but one word of caution…'

'What?'

'Any aggression towards any part of the Federation would be considered an act of war. That includes any aggression against visiting Federation citizens entering your country for tourism or meetings. That includes both humans and aliens. You do not want to contemplate starting a war with the Federation.'

'You can't threaten me or my country!'

'It was a word of caution,' said the ambassador, 'not a threat.'

'When is this happening,' barked the president.

'The secretary general will advise you. It will take some time,' said the ambassador. 'Do you have any questions?'

'Hundreds, but I'd need time to consider them.'

'We can arrange another meeting when you are ready. Just contact the secretary general,' said the ambassador. 'Do you have any further questions at this time?'

'No.'

'I'll send you details of the plan as it develops,' said Lara.

No one spoke.

'Goodbye, Mr President,' said the ambassador and John Slimbridge vanished from his cell.

'Horrible man,' said the secretary general. 'He should be locked up for life.'

'If Free America succeed, I am sure he will be,' said the ambassador. 'We can never allow him freedom in the Federation, so if America ever joins, it is inevitable that he will be punished for his crimes.'

'It can't come a moment too soon,' said Lara.

'Let me know when you've drawn up the document for the segregation and we'll meet again to ensure everything has been taken into account,' said the ambassador.

'Thank you,' said Lara and both she and Paula disappeared back to their room in the Ministry of Defence in London.

20 White House

[From White House tapes. RBB]

The president was so furious, one could actually imagine the smoke rising from his ears, nose and mouth.

'Damn it all! Can you not get rid of that stain?' asked the president.

'No, sir. It's the type of indelible dye used in bank vaults and security systems. It should fade in about a week,' said General Alexander.

'I tried covering mine with make-up yesterday, but it was still visible,' said Matthew Brown.

'Is it true that people are deliberately marking themselves with this green stuff to show support of the insurgency?'

'Yes, Mr President,' said Admiral Mann.

'I want them punished. How can we do that?'

'Sir, there are too many to punish and the numbers are growing,' said the admiral.

'Matthew, what do you recommend?'

'Mr President, I still think you should hold a referendum. At the moment, I think we could win an anti-Fed vote, but if we leave this insurgency unchecked, it will become harder and harder to make our case. I can write some incredible speeches against the Federation right now, while news of the rest of the world capitulating to them continues.'

'What if we lost?'

'Do it now and it won't happen.'

'How can you be sure?'

'Generals, Admiral, can you leave us for a moment?' said Matthew.

The two generals and the admiral looked at the president. He nodded and they left, exiting through the secretary's door and giving each other puzzled glances.

'Well?' asked the president as the door closed. 'What can you not say in front of my most trusted military advisors?'

'I can explain, Mr President,' said Mr Brown. 'Firstly, we'll organise the debates and I will choose who speaks for each side. I'll select someone who can put on a good show for the Federation, while failing to win arguments on many of the issues,' said Matthew.

'So, not Mayne then?'

'Not a chance! We'll not let any *real* Federation supporters near the debate. We will control every facet of the event. Secondly, we'll have the vote quickly, so as to not give Mayne and his crew time to react.'

'But what if we lost?'

'If we lose, I will ensure we win.'

'Eh? How?'

'Mr President, you don't want to know. Trust me.'

'Are you sure? Fail me on this and… well, if you fail me you can imagine the consequences.'

'Sir, I will not fail. You can trust me. I'll deliver.'

'Deirdre!' shouted the president and her door opened. 'Show the joint chiefs back in.'

«««O»»»

[From Brad Gregg's and Jim Collins' notes and recordings. RBB]

'Damn it all,' said Charles Mayne, thumping the table. 'They have the ability to remove Slimbridge and his collaborators from office and allow a new election to take place, and what do they do? Nothing!'

'If they're giving Slimbridge the same information, what will he do, do you think?' asked Bob Nixon.

General Beech cleared his throat and it stopped Jim Collins from starting his reply.

'We need to get our White House and media sources to keep us informed. Brad, get on to Winston and tell him to listen for whispers,' said the general.

'There's a presidential address tomorrow evening. That might give us a clue,' said Brad.

'Hmm,' said the general, 'if I were him, in his position, I'd be trying to make the country think that there is an almost forcible takeover going on in the rest of the world'

'No, Dick,' said Charles. 'You see, he and I are politicians. From the political standpoint he is the leader of the free world and has terrorists fighting against him. While he has majority support, I'd call for a vote.'

'Presidential election?' asked Jim.

'No. A vote on supporting the United States either remaining free or being taken over by the aliens!' said Charles. 'With the right approach, if done immediately, he could win. I think he'll call a referendum.'

'Not if we get the chance to put our side of the argument,' said Bob.

'And how will you do that?' said Charles. 'You think he's going to allow a fair fight?'

'Charles is right,' said the general. 'He's going to call a referendum and, win or lose, he'll win and there will be nothing we can do about it. I'd wager that is what the broadcast will announce.'

'Clever bastard,' said Bob.

'As long as he remains predictable, we will always have a chance,' said Charles.

'We can't spray him green on live television, can we?' asked Jim.

'Don't think we can organise anything that sophisticated so quickly, but I'll get one of our tech guys to look into it,' said General Beech. 'Where will the broadcast come from, Brad?'

'Almost certainly the Oval Office.'

'In that case we can't do anything in the timescale. Sorry,' said the general.

«««O»»»

[Broadcast video recording. RBB]

The sun had set, and the White House was bathed in twilight's last gleaming.

President Slimbridge sat behind the famous Resolute desk in the Oval Office, smiling into the camera. He was into the last part of his presidential address, specially written by Matthew Brown. He considered that, so far, it was going down well with the nationwide audience, guaranteed by the government's recent imposition of control over what was transmitted as news or documentaries.

'In common with the rest of the world, we wish to ensure that you have the right to choose whether to remain independent or be absorbed and become part of the enormous Federation. As an independent nation, even if the whole of the rest of the world joined up, we would be able to carry on living the American way. Jobs will not be affected, and neither will our way of life. We will even be able to trade with the Federation so those of you in export industries will hardly notice a difference.

'But I am not an expert on the Federation nor in presenting the differences between the two systems. For that reason, there will be two information broadcasts on the next two evenings. The first will be by the pro-Federation expert and supporter, David MacNamara and the second will be by the White House economist, Matthew Brown, who believes the Federation will bring nothing but harm to the nation and its people. I would encourage everyone to watch both of these broadcasts to get a balanced and unbiased view of the reason for the referendum.'

The president smiled confidently into the camera, laid a sheaf of papers on his desk, loosely clasped his hands, and finished, 'The United States of America is a bastion of truth and freedom. Make your decision wisely. God bless you all, and God bless America!'

Superimposed flags were suddenly blowing in a gentle breeze behind the president and the rousing tones of the national anthem began to play. Gradually, the interior of the Oval Office and the president himself faded from view, leaving only the vista of the stars and stripes.

«««0»»»

[From Brad Gregg's and Jim Collins' notes and recordings. RBB]

Brad turned off the television as President Slimbridge faded into the American flag and the *Star Spangled Banner* played the presidential address off screen.

'Winston had it right then,' said the general.

'Who, exactly, is Winston?' asked Jim.

'General Winston Delve. He replaced General Braun, he's one of us.'

'Wow! I didn't realise it was someone so close to the president,' said Jim.

'Who is this "MacNamara" that Slimbridge mentioned?' asked Charles.

'Winston says he's just some anonymous stooge,' said the general.

'So, they're going to distort the Federation message and only promote independence?' asked Jim.

'Sounds like it,' said Charles. 'Just as he said about wanting to be independent or be swallowed by the Federation. The message will be totally distorted in favour of independence.'

'So, he could win the vote,' said Jim.

'Don't be naïve, Jim! *Of course* they will win the referendum, even if they have fewer votes!' said General Beech.

'Can't we do something?' asked Bob.

'What, exactly?' said Beech. 'I think we just carry on with our own plan. There's a big dinner in Washington on Friday. We'll be making a splash there and it'll be green!'

«««O»»»

[Broadcast video recording. RBB]

David MacNamara, in casual, tan coloured chinos and open-neck, marmalade-check shirt, sat in one easy chair in the studio and the well-known political journalist, Tanya Shay was in the other, tablet in hand, as the programme began. The camera closed in on her. She looked immaculate and exceedingly professional in a smart, indigo pinstripe, business skirt-suit, legs crossed and wearing matching high heels. Her beautifully styled bronze coloured hair cascaded over her shoulders. She made MacNamara seem almost grubby.

She looked to the camera, 'Good evening. It has been agreed that David MacNamara, a long-time supporter of the Federation, will represent the alien Federation point of view tonight, and Matthew Brown, the White House economist, will talk for the Independence movement tomorrow. Each will have a minute to give the bones of their cases and then they'll be questioned by me.

'So, David, why don't you get the ball rolling…'

The camera closed in on Mr MacNamara, revealing a recent shaving wound in a clump of stubble. As he spoke, his yellowish, uneven teeth made the first impression.

'Good evening, everybody.

'The Federation is an empire of a quarter of a million worlds. All follow the same tight regime of rules and trading agreements. All businesses are run by the government so there is no competition between them. Also, they are all staffed and managed by robots. There is no place for human managers or workers. People live in apartments and homes in residential areas of the cities, with virtually nothing to do except relaxing or joining clubs and associations. So, a life of luxury for those who prefer not to have to work and live off the state. Mind you, there are plenty of handouts. The Federation is not miserly in its provision of money which people can spend however they wish – dining out, attending sports events and even for interstellar travel.

'Strict gun laws prevent anyone owning or using a firearm and this does mean that Federation cities are very peaceful. Squads of robots, ranging in size from smaller than a fly to larger than people, keep the peace and anything deemed illegal by the Federation is easily policed. Anyone guilty of any crime then suffers the torture of being held in a vice-like stasis where they are forced to do something which they would otherwise find unpleasant. It does seem to work, as crime is almost non-existent.

'So, if you like to have plenty of spare time, are not too ambitious financially, and are happy to be watched over by the police squads, the Federation is ideal. It has been described as being communism wrapped in velvet gloves, but if you don't mind the regimentation, it is almost idyllic.'

'And, thank you, David,' said Tanya, looking at her watch and smiling. 'Almost exactly a minute. Now, let me ask a few questions – firstly, you say that all businesses are run by the government – what would happen to someone on Earth who, say, has a successful plumbing business or farm, garage or craft shop?'

'Well, Tanya, the Federation would allow them to continue to trade while automatons, robots, learned how to do their jobs. At that point the business owner would be retired.'

'That seems most unfair to someone who has spent years building up their business.'

'Well, not really, because the owner would receive their full earnings the next year and it is only after that they would find their income reducing to the same as everyone else. It could take five years.'

'And their employees?'

'It would be great for them. They would continue to get the same or better pay and would never have to work again. A retirement which lasts a lifetime.'

'Yes, I suppose so, if you have no ambition. What about if you are an inventor and want to make money from your inventions or products?'

'Well, again, the Federation helps by producing your invention or product for you and then selling it throughout the empire.'

'So, you still become wealthy.'

'Well, everyone earns the same, so everyone has enough to live. You don't get anything special for your new idea or invention, but there is the satisfaction of knowing you have produced something which has improved the lives of everyone else.'

'Doesn't seem too good to me, David. You're saying that Brian Goodge who made that incredible vegetable cleaner we all use, would no longer be a billionaire, but would be as broke as everyone else.'

'The Federation does give bonuses for great inventions, but, Tanya, you are looking at it from the wrong perspective. The inventor becomes a celebrity for his or her good works. They don't become rich, but they make the whole Federation a little richer for everyone.'

'I understand what you're saying, David, but it doesn't seem very American. What else will the Federation do for us?'

'War would end, starvation would end, disease would be reduced, intolerance would be stopped because discrimination is one of the crimes which would be punished by stasis. Tanya, imagine a world without war, without starving babies in Africa, and with most diseases wiped out.'

'That does sound wonderful, David, but would we not all be paying the price of stagnation, unable to advance ourselves or become wealthy by using our ingenuity? What would happen to ambition?'

'It is all rewarded by leisure time and the knowledge of everyone benefitting.'

'But why would I bother inventing a new way to treat cancer or a new gadget to make life better, if I knew there was no reward for me personally at the end of it, David?'

'You'd have the satisfaction of knowing it was for everyone.'

'Sorry, David, but that doesn't sound like much incentive for innovation. Surely the most inventive people should be paid more?'

'But that is what, in the world today, causes the less able, or the underprivileged, or the less well educated to be stricken by poverty and to live in ghettoes or slums. The Federation is a world of sharing and giving and equality. The richer people, in intelligence, ability and skill should work not just for themselves but for all, Tanya.'

'The rest of us are being selfish or greedy or uncaring, then?'

'Yes.'

'And you want to reduce everyone to the same level?'

'No, not at all. The Federation wants to lift everyone up to the same level, by evening out the world's wealth.'

'Time is up, David. You've not convinced me. I've spent ten years working my way to the top of my profession. I am one of the highest paid journalists at DRC. I am not going to give all that away. I think I'll trust the US government to be peacemaker and provider for the poor. It is not a duty I wish to bear. Now, you are allowed one or two sentences to sum up why the free people of the United States of America would wish to give away their wealth, freedom and happiness, to help those from God knows where, to never have to work for a living.'

'Tanya, what you say is most unfair, but I would say to the people of America that the Federation offers an opportunity to see an end to war, famine, poverty, inequality and disease and that is why they should vote in favour of joining.'

'Thank you, David MacNamara.'

«««O»»»

[From Paula Wilson's files. RBB]

'That was so, so biased,' said Paula as the closing credits appeared after the first of the two presentations to the American people.

The video had arrived from Peter Stone who circulated it from Canada. It had only been broadcast in the USA and Peter had distributed copies he'd obtained via the black web.

'It appeared so one-sided,' said Lara. 'Do you think the people will believe that was a genuine pro-Federation broadcast?'

'I think they might, ma'am, people are so gullible these days. If the media tell them it is so, they'll believe it. I guarantee the anti-Federation presentation will be far more effective. And did you look at the man. He looked scruffy, hadn't properly shaved, there were long hairs sticking out of his right nostril and his teeth looked as if they hadn't been cleaned for a month. Even his shirt collar was frayed.'

'Yes, I noticed the collar and his teeth. Looks as if he was selected by Slimbridge.'

'Didn't take Slimbridge long to organise the referendum, did it, ma'am?'

'No. I think he is aware he needs to move quickly before Free America can spring into action.'

'Ha. Did you see the business about that Washington dinner?'

'Yes, Paula. Plenty of green faces! Free America used the fire sprinkler system that time. Ingenious.'

'Yes, brilliant, ma'am. They are so innovative. I liked that General Beech.'

'Me too. It is such a shame the Federation can't help them more. They must feel as if they're fighting with one arm tied behind their backs.'

«««O»»»

[Broadcast video recording. RBB]

Matthew Brown looked incredibly smart in his charcoal grey suit with crisp creases and brogues in which you could probably see your face. His white shirt with slate stripes was complemented by an azure tie with small white motifs. The Windsor knot was flawless and the collar irreproachable. The only strange feature of his appearance was the fading green complexion.

Tanya Shay was once again immaculate, but this time in a garnet red suit and shoes, revealing even more of her legs than she had on the previous evening. The whole interview looked as if it was going to be a far more professional show than the previous night and that, of course, had been Matthew Brown's intention.

'Good evening, Matthew. I guess I need to ask why your face looks as if you've eaten some bad shellfish?'

'Ha ha, yes. I was caught up in one of the terrorist events organised by the pro-Federation movement and it stained my face. Many came off worse than me.' His face and voice showed pain. 'Some were killed or wounded. The terrorists were trying to assassinate our president and only the swift action of the FBI saved him from injury. These alien-loving fanatics claim they want a free America, when in fact they are working for the exact opposite – they want us to be ruled and perhaps enslaved by the aliens. Madness!'

'Yes. Maybe we could come back to that. For now, you have a minute to explain why you want the United States of America to reject rule by the Federation.'

The camera closed in on Matthew Brown with his close-shaven skin, even, pearl white teeth and charming, natural smile. The greenness didn't detract, it just added to the fact he was a patriot.

In a soft, friendly voice he said, 'Fellow Americans, you are about to be asked to make the biggest decision you will ever make in your lives. Either you will support the America you love, remaining free and independent of foreign and alien interference, or you will vote to invite a communist regime to come in and take over our country.

'It has often been said that communists will take over America without even having to fire a single shot. If you vote to support the aliens, you will be the method by which they achieve that objective!

'The Federation wants to remove your right to continue to work for a living, to be promoted and to gain the rewards you deserve from your hard work and diligence. The Federation wants the lazy, good-for-nothing people who have never done a hard day's work in their lives, to receive the same income as you! Why should they? Choose wisely or regret it forever.'

'And, thank you, Matthew for that excellent introduction to your case for independence,' said Tanya. 'Now, let me ask a few questions – firstly, you say that everyone will earn the same, but isn't this a good thing. Those less able or disadvantaged deserve the same rewards in life, surely?'

'Yes, Tanya, and our country works towards that, ensuring there is always a fallback position for the disabled, the sick, the people who are intellectually challenged. But the way to do it is to create a wealthy country which is able to provide the resources for such welfare. If we shut off the way for people to make money, then we are also shutting off the source of the wealth to pay for Medicare and social welfare.'

'I see your point, Matthew, but doesn't the Federation offer the end to war, famine and poverty?'

'Yes, it does, but the USA has been the largest influence for a peaceful world for over seventy years. We have always fought for the oppressed and sought to rid the world of tyrannical leaders like Hitler and Saddam Hussein. We did not do that only to replace them with a multi-tentacled, technicolour alien with delusions of grandeur! The United States is a wealthy country with incredible resources. We are well able to look after ourselves, feeding ourselves, caring for each other and, through the ingenuity which comes from being free and offering proper rewards for invention, we will continue to improve everything about America.'

'The Federation is offering people the ability to travel to other worlds. That sounds very exciting,' said Tanya.

'Yes. It will be, but we will not be stopping that. We will actively encourage it. We do not need to join the Federation in order to take advantage of what it could offer us. The difference is that, if you vote for independence, we will still be able to trade with the Federation and there is still every opportunity for citizens to visit any of the Federation worlds.

'I would also like to point out that they have designs on some of the rights within our constitution. Guns – I know it is always a contentious issue, but the Federation will take your guns away from you – everyone – they'll remove our way to fight back when we realise we've made a dreadful mistake. An American way of life, the right to hunt for game, destroy pests and protect ourselves and our families will be gone. How many more rights will they take from us?'

'You've sold it to me, Matthew, and we are now close to the end of the programme. Perhaps you'd like to give us a couple of words to sum up.'

'Yes, Tanya. It is easy really. Americans love their country. It is not just the land, but the way of life. Rewards for the innovative and hard-working, yet a safety net for the unfortunate and disadvantaged. The United States has a tradition of being the land of the free. For goodness sake, that freedom is under attack! Don't allow alien forces to take over our freedom. It is like a bad science fiction film. We really must stop it! Vote for independence tomorrow!'

'Thank you, Malcolm,' said Tanya and the audience, strangely absent the previous night, burst into applause and chants of USA, USA!

Tanya had to wait nearly three minutes for the chanting to die down, then she said, 'As Malcolm said, voting takes place tomorrow, so be sure to get out of your home and vote. This is your opportunity to secure the country's future. Don't miss it. Polling stations will open at seven am local time.'

The screen faded and the credits rolled upwards.

21 Voting

[Broadcast media recordings. RBB]

Voting began energetically with long lines developing at some urban stations. People seemed to have taken on board the message and wanted to record their opinions early. Almost the entire country seemed to be enjoying fair weather which would encourage a high turnout.

Of course, there were pollsters outside a large number of the polling stations. Many were the media, but the bulk were government organised. President Slimbridge and Matthew Brown wanted an early indication on how the vote was going. For Matthew Brown, it was even more important as, if the vote were mainly for the Federation then it would be necessary for him to put "contingencies" into place – contingencies which would guarantee a win.

There were other pollsters too. Free America volunteers waited to speak to people as they headed home or to work from the polls. They had just two questions to ask.

'Excuse me,' one said to a couple leaving one of the polling stations in Jacksonville. 'Can I ask you a couple of short questions?'

'Sure thing,' said the man.

'How did you vote?'

'Independent.'

'I did too,' said the woman.

'Thank you. Can I ask what swayed you?' asked the person with the clipboard.

'No contest,' said the man. 'Who the hell would want to be ordered around by alien creatures?'

'Yes,' the woman said. 'No-brainer, really.'

The volunteer moved on to the next person. The response was often very similar. Those who voted for the Federation were in the minority, but those who did expressed the opinion that the presentations had been biased.

«««0»»»

[Independence HQ's files. RBB]

One of a couple of dozen assistants brought papers to Matthew Brown. He nodded at each, sometimes made a note on his tablet, and sent the assistants to the master information board.

It was good. It was fucking good. It couldn't have been better. He walked over to the whiteboard which showed a growing percentage of votes for independence.

Why had he worried? The case had been put so well by him and the defence promoted so ineptly, that the result was going to be a landslide.

The phone rang.

'It's the president, sir,' said a young woman, passing the handset to him.

'Is it as good as the media are saying, Matthew?'

'It sure is, Mr President. It's getting up to sixty per cent for independence.'

'Why's it so high?'

'I think we did a better job than we needed on both sides. You need to give MacNamara a bonus, sir. He was amazing. Made it sound real, but presented it so poorly that he helped our case no end.'

'But that still doesn't explain where the Federation supporters have gone.'

'My original estimates were thirty per cent for independence; thirty against and thirty don't knows. Seems the don't knows have bought our presentation better than I expected. Might change later. I'll keep a close eye on it, but we could be home and dry by mid-afternoon, sir.'

'Well done, Matthew. Well done.'

'Thank you, sir. My pleasure.'

«««0»»»

[From Brad Gregg's and Jim Collins' notes and recordings. RBB]
'The polls have closed in the east,' said Brad.

'Still as bad?' asked Charles.

'Worse. Our local pollsters are reporting between sixty-two and sixty-seven per cent against the Federation. In some areas it has been as high as eighty,' said Brad.

'California is better,' said Jim. 'Some stations are only showing fifty per cent although most are closer to fifty-five. I think the Federation has lost this one.'

'Do you think the statistics are real or distorted?' asked Charles.

'I regret to say that they appear to be real,' said Brad. 'Our own volunteers are getting the same result as the media pollsters.'

'With the sort of biased presentations we saw, it's no surprise,' said the general. 'I think we'll carry on doing our own thing.'

'Trouble is, we're losing some of our legitimacy because of this landslide,' said Charles.

'Nonsense!' said Dick Beech. 'You're forgetting that we are standing against a murderous illegitimate regime. Slimbridge killed our president and murdered around eight million New Yorkers, as well as most of the world's heads of state. The uprising is not about whether or not we join the Federation, it is about whether we're prepared to let a tyrant take over our country.'

'Yes, you're right, Dick. Thanks for the timely reminder. I think I lost focus over this referendum,' said Charles in a rather subdued manner.

'Not at all, Charles. This referendum was sent to try us. We are battling through it. The parade in Memphis will make you feel much better,' said the general, and laughed.

22 North Korea

[From Paula Wilson's tapes, notes and biographies. RBB]

'The whole thing is going pear-shaped,' said the secretary general, holding her head in her hands.

A blond giant, Lara's deputy, Lars Eriksen, finished reading the dossier on North Korea. 'I cannot believe Kim Lung-min turned the offer down. He'd have been able to live in luxury for five years instead of the usual three.'

'He must know that he can't hold out. President Yang was furious,' said Lara.

'So, what's next?' asked Lars.

'The ambassador was quite clear. It is up to us to solve the North Korean and Israeli problems ourselves.'

'How is Israel coming along, ma'am?'

'Quite well, actually, Lars. President Ramseur has visited them twice. He's rather stretched the parameters of the offers we're allowed to make, but I think the ambassador might accept them.'

'What's he done?'

'He has agreed that Israel's borders can be controlled by them.'

'But that's way beyond what's permitted.'

'That might be the case, but the way President Ramseur put it to me, once we're all in the Federation, the borders will naturally become more relaxed. He thinks that President Avraham will soon leave office after integration and the new administration will want to remove the controls because they will not be necessary. Also, President Ramseur has suggested that the ambassador will put similar restrictions on Israelis wanting to leave Israel.'

'How does that help?'

'Obvious, really, Lars. If you are an Israeli and want to live somewhere else and your government is stopping you doing that because of their own rules on immigration, you'll soon become very dissatisfied and the government will change their rules.'

'Sorry, ma'am. If they do that, will they not be flooded by millions of Palestinians wanting to return to their native lands?'

'Not necessarily, but, you're right, it is an issue. We both think that President Avraham will not have thought through the repercussions of restricting his own people.'

'When is your next meeting with the ambassador, ma'am?'

'Probably next week. The Security Council meets in two days and we'll look at all of our options then. Disappointing result in the States.'

'Yes. Do you think the results were genuine, ma'am?'

'Surprisingly, there is no reason to disbelieve them and the Free America pollsters on the day showed very similar feedback to the actual result, if Brad Gregg is to be believed.'

'You don't think that could become contagious?' asked Lars

'What? That other countries will get cold feet, too? Not from reports coming back from the off-world visits. How did your group do?'

'Absolutely fantastic, ma'am. The first world we visited was entirely put down to food production. It had never had any intelligent indigenous people. They lived on a nearby world. There were three Earth-type planets in the system.'

'Three?'

'Yes. We held in orbit over the food planet and it gave us all a chance to see that the entire world, with the exception of mountainous areas and rainforest, had been cultivated. We dropped out of orbit and settled close to the most enormous warehouses.'

'How many of you in the group?'

'One hundred and sixty. Gradually we all disembarked onto an enormous floating platform which then set off across the countryside. Some fields were more than fifty miles across. Giant cultivators could be seen in some areas, or watering machines, pickers, weeders, transporters. In another field there was ploughing and seeding underway. All automated. Not a person in sight.'

'Did you see inside the warehouses?'

'Oh, yes. Amazing. Some buildings were for sorting and packing. Others were separating off seeds for storage and the food was being conveyed into ships, ten times the size of our liner. We didn't actually see one leave, but there were several being filled at just one warehousing terminal of which, we were told, there were over a thousand.'

'Incredible.'

'Interestingly, given our own problem with plastics, all produce was shipped in cardboard cartons and trays with a transparent vegetable protein sheath. A special gas preserved the contents. No single-use plastic at all,' said Lars. 'And the next world was amazing, but in a different way. It was an actual holiday world.'

'What no indigenous people again?'

'Oh, no, there was a population, but much of the surface had been put down to amusement parks. Ships were coming and going all the time we were there.'

'What sort of entertainment?'

'Anything and everything. Treetop walks, helter-skelters, all the fairground rides you could ever imagine plus motor racing, automaton riding…'

'What's that?'

'Robots like horses, lions, elephants and even sauropods which you could ride on or race. We all had a go on something. I particularly liked climbing sheer cliffs.'

'Safely, I hope?'

'Oh, yes. Force fields stopped you falling. Not instantly though. You had the sensation and thoughts about having failed, but you could get back on and try again. I'll have to go back sometime as there was an overhang, just like the Preikestolen at Lysefjord.'

'The what?'

'The Preikestolen or Pulpit Rock. A famous Norwegian landmark, over five hundred metres above the beautiful Lysefjord. Very scary, but this one was there to climb.'

'Wouldn't fancy that, Lars. Vertigo would get me.'

'I suppose everyone likes something different and Fotpiz, I think the planet was called, has everything you could ever dream of. The upshot was that everyone on board loved it.'

'How did it come about?'

'What? It becoming a holiday world?'

'Yes.'

'Well, I don't know the history, but I got the impression it has concentrated on providing fun for a long time. Fotpiz has been in the Federation for thousands of years. It is amazing how old the Federation is. Earth really is a baby by comparison.'

'Yes, with all our primitive attitudes, hatreds and conflicts.'

'The next world was in transition; they'd only been in the Federation for eighteen years. People were still doing a small amount of physical work, but they told us that there was an increasing population of robots who now did all the messy or difficult jobs, leaving them to just pick up some of the more pleasant, interesting or challenging tasks. They were gushing with the difference it had made to their lives since they'd signed up.'

'That will work in our favour.'

'One world you really must visit sometime is Kasettod. We split into small groups on arrival and travelled in secure pods to protect us from the animals and environment. It was a prehistoric world. Giant dinosaurs roamed the land. It was fascinating to watch Lost World events playing out before our very eyes. The guide was telling us that Kasettod is only one of more than a hundred worlds which are now specially protected, and visitors are no longer allowed to interact with the native creatures.'

'Does no one live on these worlds?'

'Some, ma'am. There were some domed towns in the forests, and these were mainly home to university students and lecturers from throughout the galaxy and, guess what, we were told that more than thirty per cent of the students are mature. Older people using their free time to learn more about natural history and prehistoric environments. I don't mean just pensioners. By mature I meant thirties upwards and they were loving it. Such a boon which would be unavailable to people on the current Earth where mundane work occupies the bulk of our lives until old age.'

'Gosh, yes, Lars. Imagine what we could all do if we were not imprisoned in our places of work until retirement. A great benefit to being in the Federation. We must make mention of that in presentations.'

<<<O>>>

[Taken from Paula Wilson's minutes. RBB]

The Security Council meeting once again took place in one of the cabinet briefing rooms in Downing Street. Within a couple of minutes, all of the delegates had switched to Galactic Standard.

Lara said, 'President Avraham has declined an invitation, but did send a communication that he had agreed the deal organised by President Ramseur if the UN were prepared to officially endorse it. Lu Cheng is standing in for President Yang. Can you understand us, okay?'

'Yes, I have also learned Galactic Standard. President Yang organised it for all top government officials.'

'Hmm. Good idea,' said Prime Minister Church. 'We must look into doing the same.'

Others present were the secretary general's deputy, Lars Eriksen, Malcolm Gorman, President Ramseur, President Olov and Paula Wilson.

Lara called the meeting to order.

Lu Cheng said, 'President Yang apologises for his absence, but he has been unavoidably detained. He has told me that he will provide some interesting information for you soon regarding an event taking place in China today.'

'Ha,' said President Olov, 'you mean the invasion of North Korea. We've been following the action during the night.'

'Malcolm, what is this?' asked Prime Minister Church.

'We've been monitoring a lot of fighter activity over the Yellow Sea,' Malcolm said. 'It started very early in the morning local time and has been almost continuous – Chinese planes flying to and from North Korea. There was also a considerable explosion in the northern mountains and we're assuming a nuclear accident or a nuclear facility being destroyed. That's all we know so far.'

'There'll be more information shortly,' said Lu Cheng.

'What's happening, Lu? You must know,' said Maureen Church.

'I'll tell you as soon as I'm able.'

'Okay,' said Lara. 'Over to President Ramseur to give us some good news from Israel.'

'Yes, I was hoping Daniel Avraham would be here to ratify what we'd agreed, but he is happy for us to confirm by written communique.'

'What, exactly?' asked President Olov.

'They requested that they control their own borders. I have just had a reply from a communication to Ambassador Trestogeen that he is comfortable with what I've arranged. We need to keep it secret from the full General Assembly until the vote has been passed to join the Federation.'

'Those of us here need to know,' said President Olov.

'Sorry, Marat,' said Lara. 'The arrangements are rather unique and delicate so we would rather not share the information at this time. It is very temporary and could only complicate arrangements in other countries if they were aware of the details. They will be released after the vote.'

'Let me register a protest about this then, Lara,' said Marat Olov.

'So noted.'

Lu Cheng's telephone rang.

A conversation then continued for several minutes in Chinese. Although Lara had some knowledge of Mandarin and Cantonese, the dialogue was at such a speed as to render any content meaningless to her.

'That was President Yang,' said Lu Cheng.

'And…?' asked the secretary general.

'North Korea is now an annexed addition to China. Kim Lung-min has been captured and will be handed over to the International Court of Justice in the Hague.'

'Guessed as much,' said Malcolm.

'Yes, we'd had some intel to that effect,' said President Olov.

'That answers the two challenges we were handed by the ambassador. Lars tells me all countries have reported that they are ready for a General Assembly vote. Shall I call the ambassador?'

There was general agreement.

«««O»»»

[There are no records of the details of this event, so I have had to work from hearsay and news bulletins which may or may not be accurate. RBB]

No one knows exactly how the invasion began, but it is assumed that an enormous build-up of troops and weaponry on the north-western border was where the advance entered North Korea. That no one was aware of the massing of troops is extraordinary.

Conventional missiles were over the border and striking their targets before anyone in Pyongyang had awoken to what was happening.

The strikes took place from four in the morning, destroying North Korea's weapons plants and stocks of nuclear warheads. This included a small nuclear explosion in the central northern mountains near Pukchin. The bulk of the action was with conventional armaments, then a four hundred thousand strong Chinese army was over the Yalu River either side of Dandong. Dozens of floating bridges were installed and being used in less than an hour, carrying tanks and armoured vehicles. It was, perhaps, the largest army ever to take part in an invasion of a foreign country.

The ground troops made rapid progress towards Pyongyang. The support was by hundreds of gunship helicopters and fighter jets whose task it was to destroy any military bases and weapons stores which were likely to hinder their attack. The gunships also dealt with the North Korean military as it started to react to the invasion. They didn't really have a chance.

The bulk of North Korea's forces, located in the south of the country for the always anticipated advance of western armies over the South Korean border, were caught by surprise as the aerial attacks from bases across the Yellow Sea destroyed parked vehicles, helicopters, and planes on the runways. Hundreds of missile launchers, also caught unawares, were knocked out by air strikes.

What little resistance there was, was quickly overcome and it soon became clear that the Chinese army was under strict instructions to avoid casualties, civilian or military as far as that was possible in such an offensive.

In an hour, the Chinese were in Pyongyang. Kim Lung-min had evaded the incoming forces and there was an instant hue and cry which resulted in his capture by early evening.

Within fourteen hours, by six o'clock, the war was over. China had annexed North Korea.

«««0»»»

[From media recordings. RBB]

Matthew Brown's skin had almost returned to its normal colour, but there was still the ghost of a green pallor remaining.

'You did well, Matthew. Sixty-seven point five per cent for independence was a tremendous result,' said the president.

'I only wish we'd given someone like Charles Mayne the chance to speak for the Federation, sir. We'd still have won, but would not now be criticised for a biased election.'

'I don't care about that, Matthew. There is a certain irony at pro-Feds accusing us of bias when the majority was so enormous. If you remove the "don't knows", fewer than twenty-five per cent were pro-Federation. Their complaints against such a landslide are rather foolish.'

'Yes, sir. Huge win!'

'Now. How are we going to deal with Beech and Mayne? If we could get them out of our hair, I'd feel a lot more comfortable.'

The intercom buzzed. The president picked up the handset, listened for a second and put it back onto its cradle. 'The joint chiefs have arrived plus the FBI director. Now we'll see what they've come up with.'

A few seconds later, the door opened and the four men walked into the Oval Office. They all said good morning and took their seats in the lounge area around the coffee table. Deirdre brought in coffee shortly afterwards.

'So, how do we get Mayne and Beech?' the president asked.

'We are fairly sure they are operating from a base south of Jacksonville, Mr President. It is just a matter of time before we find them,' said David Mendoza, the FBI director.

'And what about Walter Braun and Buck Burko? What progress there?'

'None yet, Mr President, not a whisper about either of them. They might be dead, sir.'

'I don't believe they're dead,' said Admiral Mann. 'The kidnaps were so well organised. If they'd wanted them dead, a bullet would have accomplished that. They are being held somewhere, Mr Mendoza.'

'What's the plan when you locate Beech and Mayne?' asked the president.

'That's down to us, sir,' said General Delve. 'We have a considerable force ready to move, and General Alexander has helicopters ready to react if they attempt to escape by air. It really is just a matter of pinning down their location.'

'Won't be long, General,' said the FBI director. 'We're sure they are somewhere southeast of Jacksonville and we're working through the area one property at a time.'

'Well, the sooner the better,' said the president.

An alarm sounded.

Outside, armed forces were strategically placed around the grounds of the White House and were keeping their eyes peeled for anything untoward, but although they were alerted to the jet powered drone soon enough, it was travelling too low and too fast for anyone to take it out. Somehow it had broken through the electronic no-fly zone which was designed to prevent ordinary drones entering White House airspace.

Sirens went off in the building and the president and others in the Oval Office ran into the chief of staff's office which had armoured walls for extra protection. The initial alarm had told them there was no time to head to the basement.

As the drone crossed into White House property, it began a vertical climb to about two hundred feet and exploded. Twenty gallons of green dye was atomised and fell like drizzle on the target beneath.

After a delay for security protocols, Secret Service officers arrived at the protected office and told the president's party that the coast was clear.

Outside, spectators on Pennsylvania Avenue were recording the scene and the images went viral. The White House was white no longer.

«‹‹0››»

[From Brad Gregg's and Jim Collins' notes and recordings. RBB]

'Burner call for you, General,' said a soldier as he rushed into the kitchen where General Beech, Charles Mayne, Jim and Brad were sitting at the breakfast bar.

'Beech,' the general said and listened intently for almost a minute. A long call indeed to receive on a burner phone. The general passed the handset to the soldier, 'Remove the battery and dispose, soldier.'

'Yes, sir,' the soldier said and left the kitchen.

'News?' asked Charles.

'Yes. They're on to us. That was Winston Delve,' said the general. 'We need to get out. *Captain!*' he roared the last word.

Captain Wooller rushed into the room, 'Sir!'

'Put in place evac one,' said Dick Beech.

'Yes, sir. When, sir?'

'Now, captain. Tell me when we're ready to go.'

'We have to go now?' asked Brad.

'Yes. We'd better all jump to it. One bag each. Don't leave any papers.'

They all hastily left the room.

23 Escape

[From Brad Gregg's and Jim Collins' notes and recordings. RBB]
'Ready to depart, sir,' said Captain Wooller.

'Thank you, soldier. We'll be out shortly,' said the general. 'Send Sergeant Potter in to me.'

The captain disappeared back through the house and a moment or two later the sergeant arrived.

'Linda, I've just used this phone to call the congressman's home and office. I want it left switched on. It has a new fully charged battery. I'd like you to take it and find a truck which is heading down the Keys. Try interstate rest areas. Tape the phone to it and wait to ensure it leaves southwards. Then head to rendezvous four. Understood?'

'Yes, sir,' the sergeant said, taking the phone.

'If you're pursued before you find a truck, do what you think best. Any truck is better than no truck.'

'I understand, sir.'

'Good luck. Go. Now!'

'Yes, sir,' she said and left the house at the double.

General Beech called up the stairs, 'We're leaving. Now! *Right now!*'

Charles, Jim, Brad and Bob made their way out to the Atlantic Jet Ski Adventures minivan. As soon as they were on board, it pulled out of the turning area and headed down the driveway. They turned right towards Jacksonville. Two miles later they passed a convoy of army vehicles travelling the opposite way. Their driver studiously obeyed all speed limits and road signs. Now was not the time to be pulled over by a traffic cop.

«««o»»»

[From White House tapes. RBB]
Squads of painters were all over the White House and its outbuildings, returning the property to its traditional colour. Now preposterously emerald-coloured, Eleanor Roosevelt's historic rose bushes were being pruned, or grubbed out of the flowerbeds. Many would have to be replaced. The soil was also turned over to hide the dye. Only the grass did not need attention. Jet washers, using abrasive liquids

were working hard to return paving slabs and concrete to their original greys, while gravel on other pathways was being scooped up by mini-excavators and replaced with pristine material arriving in a convoy of trucks.

President Slimbridge looked through the windows of the residence at the feverish activity. His junior assistant knocked on the door and entered, 'It's General Delve, sir.'

'Right,' he barked in reply.

'Good news, sir,' said the general as he entered.

'About time, Winston. What is it?'

'We're on to them. They're in a mansion on the Florida coast, just south of Jacksonville. I have a battalion heading their way right now and Marines leaving for a helicopter approach to coincide with our arrival.'

'You really think it is Beech?'

'Pretty certain, sir, and Mayne too.'

'Thank you, General. Keep me posted.'

The president turned back to the window as another trailer load of rose bushes in full flower passed across the scene. *How dare the terrorists do this to the White House?*

«««O»»»

[Taken from Paula Wilson's minutes. RBB]

The secretary general, Caroline Stoddart, the British UN representative, and Paula Wilson entered the hall and were astounded by its grandeur.

'I've never seen it empty,' said Caroline.

'Magnificent,' said Lara. 'I've seen television programmes of concerts held here, but never actually been inside.'

'It was Queen Victoria's statement of love for her late husband, Albert,' said Paula.

'And that was him in the monument we saw outside?'

'Yes, ma'am.'

'You're sure it is available on that list of dates, Caroline?' asked Lara.

'Yes, Madam Secretary. The General Assembly will be thrilled to have such a major event staged in the Royal Albert Hall. It is such a stunning venue. How have the familiarisation trips been going?'

'Paula's been monitoring them,' said Lara.

'So far, over half a million politicians, officials and ordinary citizens have taken trips to a couple of worlds, and twice that number still to go before the end of next week.'

'What reactions are you getting?' asked Caroline.

'Most people are staggered by the scale of what they are seeing,' said Paula. 'The enormity of the space liners, the diversity of the planets. The ambassador has ensured at least one administrative hub planet has been included, which means the variety of aliens encountered has been enormous. The reaction has been overwhelmingly positive.'

'Any adverse reactions at all?'

'Surprisingly, none. There has been some disbelief at the multifarious automatons. The ambassador built in time during the interval between visits to let people question the robots and ask about their functions, abilities and responsibilities. That went down very well with everyone,' said Paula.

'I think the Albert Hall is perfect, Caroline. Can you let me and Paula know the availability for the second half of next month in case we need to change dates?' said Lara.

'Certainly, Madam Secretary.'

«««O»»»

[From White House tapes. RBB]

'No one? None of them?' said the president, banging his fist down upon the old Resolute desk.

'No. There were signs it had been evacuated that very morning. We could only have missed them by a matter of half an hour,' said General Delve.

Deirdre knocked and opened the door, 'Mr Mendoza, sir.'

'Yes. Yes, show him in.'

David Mendoza hurried into the room. A small man, belying the power he wielded as director of the FBI. He walked around the desk and sat beside the general. 'We're tracking them. Someone left a burner phone switched on.'

'How'd you know its them?' asked the president.

'A call was made to Mayne's office in Pittsburgh and also to his home. As usual we then checked the number and discovered it was the same phone which made both calls. At the moment we're assuming it was used by Charles Mayne, probably to tell his wife and office that they were about to move, but he left it switched on.'

'Where is it?'

'Currently it is on ninety-five heading south. We have a car in pursuit, followed by some agents playing catch-up. Can't understand why they'd go south. Closes down options for them. It might turn out to be a decoy, of course.'

'Okay, but how did they know we were on to them?'

'Has to be a spy in the White House, sir,' said General Delve.

'Suppose so, but who? David, put a hundred agents onto it if you have to, but I want to know who leaked the plans.'

'Yes, sir.'

24 The Spawning

[From Paula Wilson's notes and recordings. RBB]

The Federation device let out a chime and vibrated.

'Yes. Lara Horvat here.'

'Secretary Horvat, this is Yol Terend,' said the familiar tinny voice. 'I have a personal message from Yol Hareen for you and Ms Wilson'

'Yes, one moment,' said Lara and pressed the intercom button. 'Can you come in, please, Paula.'

'Hello Ms Wilson,' said Yol Terend.

'Good morning, Yol Stograther,' she said as she entered the room, looking around the room for Yol Terend, and seeing Lara point at the communication device.

'Yol Hareen regrets that he will not be able to see you again and I am now the Federation ambassador. However, he did ask me to see if you would like to attend the spawning. When it is to be someone's last spawning, they often invite family and friends to attend. Yol Hareen must have been very fond of you both.'

'What is involved, Ambassador. I'm not sure that I would want to watch someone die,' said Lara.

'The event is held at a private sea pool which will be near Yol Hareen's home. It is a unique occasion. He will be laid to rest very simply at the end and people will disperse. There is nothing unpleasant to see.'

'I don't understand why he asked. It sounds like a family occasion,' said Lara.

'He respected you both. Nothing more nor less. Only people he liked will be present.'

Lara looked towards Paula and said, 'I'll go if you'll accompany me.'

Paula nodded.

'Tell him, thank you. What is necessary for us and what should we bring, how do we dress et cetera?' asked Lara.

'Dress smartly. There is nothing to bring.'

'No flowers or anything?' asked Paula.

'Nothing is normally taken. I'll collect you at six tomorrow morning.'

'We'll be ready,' said Lara.

««‹o›»»

[From White House tapes. RBB]

All signs of the squads of painters had vanished. The White House was, once again, white. President Slimbridge stood in the ivy-covered walkway outside the Oval Office, the rain cascading down and running off the variegated plant and falling through his field of vision in heavy droplets.

It was all going so badly. How had he got himself into such a mess? Two generals kidnapped, Free America seemingly hitting every parade, sports event and rally with their green paint, Mayne and Beech wanting him dead and a spy in his inner circle to boot.

'Mr President,' said Deirdre's voice from behind him.

'Yes. What is it?' he snapped.

'Mr Mendoza is here, sir.'

He turned and saw his flustered secretary standing in the doorway. He'd torn a strip off her earlier for telling him someone was waiting while the door was open, and the visitor could hear when he said he didn't want to see him. John Slimbridge, however, was not the quickest to offer an apology for his increasingly regular outbursts of bad temper. 'Show him in.'

She vanished from the doorway and he entered his office and sat behind the famous desk. David Mendoza entered, wished him a good afternoon and pointed at one of the visitors' chairs.

'Yes, sit,' said the president impatiently. 'I hope you've got some good news.'

'Well, sir, yes and no. The phone we were tracking en route for the Keys *was* a decoy, pushed under the tarpaulin of a truck.'

John Slimbridge raised his hands from the desk in despair and allowed them to fall again.

'We have no new intel on the movements of Mayne or Beech, but we are still looking into it. Give me time.'

'And the good news, man. What is it?'

'It depends how you look at it, Mr President. We've found the spy.'

The president sat bolt upright in his chair, then leaned forward, 'Who?'

'Delve.'

'Really? General Delve!?'

'Yes, sir. He's been feeding information to Beech for some time.'

'God damn him! Where is he now?'

'He's with one of his battalions looking for the insurgents. Somewhere north of Jacksonville. Our failure to pin them down could well be because he's been working against us.'

The president hit the red button on his intercom. 'Deirdre, get Mann, Alexander and Delve back here asap.'

'Yes, sir,' said the tinny voice from the intercom. 'Is there a particular reason?'

'Tell them Mr Mendoza has come up with something we need to discuss.'

'Yes, sir,' she said, and the intercom died.

'What's the plan, sir?' asked the head of the FBI.

'I'll get Deirdre to tell you when they'll all be here,' said the president, wringing his hands as he plotted. 'Have ten armed men ready to come in and arrest Delve on my signal.'

'Yes, sir. Is there anything else right now? If not, I'll get things organised.'

'No. That's it for now, but see if you can make some progress on Mayne and Beech.'

'Yes, sir. Without Delve's interference, we might be more successful.'

«««O»»»

[From Paula Wilson's notes. RBB]

Lara and I were transported directly to the bridge of the Eskorav where we were welcomed by both Ambassador Terend Stograther and Captain Ya Istil Sperafin. Terend looked his usual dapper self with everything complementing his olive-green skin. Istil was naked. Her somewhat disturbing sac-like body providing all the colour which could ever be required. I had chosen a short black cocktail dress and white cape, while the secretary general wore a dark hickory brown trouser suit.

I handed over a package to the ambassador. 'Ambassador Trestogeen told me he had an archive about Earth. This is my biography of Perfect Okafor. Could you ensure it is put with his files?'

'Certainly, Ms Wilson. I'll give it to a member of his family. They'll put it into his office where there will be a permanent record of his work over the years.'

'Thank you.'

'How long to Yol Hareen's home world? Pestoch, is it?' asked Lara.

'A few hours,' said Ya Istil. 'You three go and relax in the viewing lounge. I'll call you when we are approaching the star system.'

Spending some quality time with the ambassador provided many revelations about the thinking around an independent USA. Yol Terend was of the same mind as Yol Hareen and everything seemed to be on course for the rest of the world joining the Federation if the vote was positive. During the flight we worked through many of the border functions which would have to be set up to prevent technology leaking into America and to control currency transfers.

A light lunch was provided and a couple of hours later the captain called us back to the bridge. A beautiful world was hanging motionless before us, surrounded by glittering rings.

As we entered, I gasped at the magnificence of the scene, then said, 'I recognise that – it's Arlucian.'

'Correct. Arlucian is the third planet in this system and Pestoch is the fifth,' said Ya Istil.

'I recognised the rings.'

'Dazzling,' said Lara.

'You must visit the moon sometime, ma'am. It is absolutely gorgeous and some of the shrubs are astonishing. Remind me to show you some video on the journey back. I think I have it on my tablet,' I said.

'I will,' said the secretary general.

The view from the bridge suddenly changed as the Eskorav banked and swung to port, and then there was a brief slip into hyperspace, turning the cosmos emerald green with lemon flecks. It lasted barely four minutes before space returned to its natural black, only this time with a splendid, predominantly blue globe hanging centre stage.

We were both stunned into silence by the scene.

The right hemisphere of Pestoch exhibited the fairy-light effect of all civilised planets. Jewels of white, amber and yellow clumped together indicating coastal towns and cities, while the routes between them played like necklaces or chains of illuminated strands upon the black of the uninhabited continents at night.

The daylight side of the planet was ninety per cent water. White swirls and wisps of clouds set off the azure blue of the seas which was only broken by islands in various shades of green.

'Wow!' said Lara. 'Marvellous. How much of the world is water?'

'I'm not sure,' said Ya Istil, 'but I'd guess at more than eighty per cent overall. We're heading for that island which looks a little like a broken egg.'

The Eskorav slid down its invisible glidepath towards the island which began to show that it was larger than it looked from space. I estimated that it was the size of Ireland. The ship came to rest, hovering a metre above the ground.

'Air?' asked Lara.

'No problem,' said the ambassador. 'More oxygen than Earth so expect to feel a little lightheaded from time to time. Just stand still and take slow and shallow breaths if it affects you.'

The stairway awaited us, and the ambassador led us down to the ground where a Pestochian was awaiting our arrival. She was considerably larger than Yol Hareen but held out a fin in a friendly manner. We all shook it.

'I am Sloreen Trestogeen, one of Hareen's many sisters. Pleased to meet you. Follow me. The event will begin shortly,' she said.

'Will we understand what is happening?' I asked.

'I'll have one of my relatives, Ya Dolodreen, interpret for you,' Ya Sloreen said.

We left the landing area and walked about a hundred metres down to a harbour.

The land was covered in a short, spiny seaweed-green coloured grass. The harbour formed an almost closed letter C with the open side facing out into a turquoise sea. In the harbour, the water was very clear, but still had the shade of mint in colour. Dozens of large Pestochians were swimming in a coherent shoal, their iridescent scales sending sparkles of cobalt into the air and the spray which was being thrown up.

'Hi, I'm Ya Dolodreen,' said a much smaller Pestochian who joined us on the harbourside. 'I'll try to let you know what is happening.'

'Thank you,' said Lara, introducing herself and me.

'At the moment you are seeing a shoal of female Pestochians, none of whom will be related to Yol Hareen. Most are strangers, taking the opportunity to expand their gene pool, but there will also be good friends among them. They are building anticipation. The faster they swim and the more they interact, the more excited they become,' said Dolodreen.

'Have you taken part in one of these?' I asked.

'No,' she said and giggled, 'I'm far too young. But I will, one day,' Dolodreen seemed very excited but, I felt, somewhat embarrassed. I suppose, in a clumsy way, I had asked the Pestochian equivalent of a young virgin if she was about to take part in a breeding ceremony.

'Sorry,' I said. 'Didn't mean to intrude.'

'It is all right, Ya Paula, but it is supposed to be an ultimate experience, so, at my age, I can't wait.'

'Can I ask how old you are?'

'I'm seven.'

'How do your years compare with Earth's?'

'No, that is Galactic Standard years.'

'Ah,' I said, 'they are similar to ours. How old are the females who are taking part?'

'Anything from nine to thirty.'

'And what is your life expectancy?' I asked, determined to try to understand her coming of age.

'About thirty.'

Yol Terend said, 'Pestochians have very short lives compared to most species.'

That was so profound I fell into silence. Dolodreen was adolescent and Hareen had lived less time than I had myself. How tragic. An aspect to alien lives which had never crossed my mind.

'Where is Hareen right now?' asked Lara.

'He is preparing himself in the small building over there,' she said, pointing at a marbled structure on the side of the harbour.

The shoal swam faster, all breaking the surface twice during each harbour circuit and the now considerable crowd cheered at each sound as they hit the water after leaping clear of the surface. The silence of the crowd, the noise of the fish splashing at the surface, the leaping clear and the crashing back into the depths accompanied by everyone cheering was so exciting. Lara and I joined in as we heard Ya Dolodreen shout out her encouragement to the shoal.

All of a sudden, Hareen left the hut and stood on the harbour wall. The sight of him caused the shoal to break its circling and dash in his direction, each of the forty or fifty fish throwing themselves dolphin-like into the air before him. Once, twice, three times and again and again and again, they leapt five or six times their body lengths into the air, spraying him with the spume-laced water. The entire crowd was now screaming and chanting a strange song which was in their own language, not Galactic Standard. We didn't need to ask what the song meant. It was clear it was encouragement and each line ended with a deafening cheer and the shoal leaping into the air before Hareen.

In an instant the water was cloudy and the activity even more frantic.

'They're eggs being released,' said Dolodreen.

'Yes. Wow!' I acknowledged, staggered at being so privileged to be invited to watch this most intimate of events.

Hareen bent his body and launched himself into the seething mass of fish and eggs, regularly rising to the surface and screaming in ecstasy before being dragged down into the depths by the frenzied females who rubbed against him and pushed and pulled him around. The impacts and large number taking part looked as if it would kill him, yet time and again he broke the surface and gave a unique howl of obvious pleasure. I felt embarrassed. We were intruding here. This should be private. Should we even be watching?

It continued for fifteen or twenty minutes, with each breaking of the surface by Hareen gradually becoming weaker until he arose no longer and floated motionless at the surface, his sparkling scales morphing into a dull, lifeless grey as the shoal dragged him from the harbour further out to sea.

The spawning was over, the stilling water slowly clearing and the cloud of fertilised eggs drifting silently to the bottom. Huge gates closed across the harbour entrance and the crowd gradually dispersed.

I couldn't speak. I simply stood immobile, watching the sea, a little like the end of a regatta when the spectators began to amble back to their homes. Hareen was dead. We had watched a person die from an overpowering ecstasy. I really was intruding here. Dolodreen had gone too.

I turned to the ambassador and Lara somewhat traumatised. As Terend guided us back to the Eskorav, I choked up.

'So, that's it? Ambassador Trestogeen's dead?' asked Lara.

'Yes, he's gone. His family will go and find the body, cremate it and the ashes will be scattered in the family garden,' said Yol Terend.

'It seems such a waste,' I said.

'Not to him. He had to do it. An instinct,' said Yol Terend. 'In the harbour lie untold millions of eggs which will gradually hatch and swim out to sea. Pestochians' minds don't begin to develop until they are about a foot long. It is a dangerous time for them. The adults will then find the survivors and begin their schooling. Fewer than one per cent will reach adulthood.'

'What would have happened to Hareen on the five previous occasions?' I asked.

'He would have been rescued and spent a week in care, being regenerated.'

'Why not this time?' asked Lara.

'It has a debilitating effect and the body would not survive another encounter. He would have died in the next year or two anyway. Don't feel sad for him. He was looking forward to it and he died in absolute rapture – at least that is what he told me would happen. It is how Pestochians reproduce. Part of their way of life. In the past, before the regeneration process, males rarely lived beyond their first spawning. Often they were deliberately killed by the females.'

'Okay,' we both said, barely comprehending the enormity of Hareen's choice.

The return journey to Earth was a sober affair indeed.

25 The Monster's Beard

[From Brad Gregg's and Jim Collins' notes and recordings. RBB]
'Who gave us away, sir?' asked Captain Wooller.

'Don't know, Captain. Probably just good intel. It's not easy to hide even our small command team. People who live nearby hear things, start rumours and talk. It could've been as simple as someone on a yacht seeing a soldier in uniform on one of the balconies.'

'So, not a traitor,' said Mayne.

'No. Doubt that very much,' said Beech.

'I take it that convoy was heading to the mansion,' said Jim, looking out of the back window at the army vehicles heading the other way.

'Yes. Winston held back to give us time to depart,' said the general.

'Where are we heading now, Dick?' asked Brad.

'Washington.'

'Washington DC?' asked Charles Mayne in disbelief. 'Surely not.'

'Yes. We're going to hide ourselves in the monster's beard. It's the last place they'd look for us. And most of our orders are now issued via burners or the black web. We can keep ourselves hidden as long as nobody is stupid,' said the general.

The minivan proceeded northwards.

«««0»»»

[Taken from UN video and seminar notes. RBB]
The number of aliens and robots now working with the Earth governments grew rapidly as the date of the General Assembly vote approached.

It was only natural that there was anxiety among ordinary people and business owners. The latter knew that they would soon lose control, but the more responsible owners were keen to ensure as little disruption to supplies as possible.

'My business supplies bread and cakes throughout the region. How are you going to ensure continuity of the various components – flour, yeast, seeds, wrappers and so on?' asked one delegate at a Federation seminar.

An alien responded, 'We are relying on you and your staff to continue to place orders and ensure manufacture until robots can take over. What's your business called?'

'Niger Superloaf.'

A robot spoke into the alien's ear. He listened and then said, 'Ah, you are in list two for this region. There will be an administration robot with you tomorrow morning. A squad of baking and production line robots will be with you by the end of the week. At that time the admin robot will have taken over all supply and delivery organisation and the robots will replace your staff. If any wish to stay on in the bakery that is welcomed. They can leave when they are ready. There is no compulsion. You too can stay as long as you wish to oversee operations.'

'And if things go wrong?'

'I'm sure some will,' said the alien, 'and we hope you will offer a small amount of your time to help ease the transition.'

'There are over sixty businesses like mine in the city.'

The alien looked at his secradarve. 'Yes, I can see that. Within a few months they will all be amalgamated under one roof.'

'Does that mean you'll be scrapping most of the recipes for different breads? Parka loaf makes completely different loaves to us.'

'No recipes will be lost as long as there is demand. Because profitability is unimportant, the product selection can actually rise. Amalgamating factories, workshops and bakeries et cetera will not reduce the choice for the general public. You will be very welcome to stay on and ensure that the city's bread stays at the highest quality. Our systems will also mean that there will be no waste. By studying the supply chain and shoppers' needs, we will be producing almost exactly the correct amount of bread. No wastage, no putting up with the previous day's loaves. Freshness will be the watchword.'

The alien waved towards another person with her hand up.

'Social services. We provide services for disabled and elderly residents in the south of the city. Each person is visited between one and six times per day depending on their needs and disabilities. What will happen to us?'

'Again, we hope you will stay on to ensure that nothing slips through the net when our robots come onto the scene. Initially, our domestic and care robots will follow your schedules, but our factories are geared up to increase production rapidly. There will soon be a robot for every person. No visits. They'll be permanently available for individuals. Those with better mobility or who would like to remain independent for as long as possible will be able to ask the robot to stand down, at which point it will go to the recharging point and switch to standby. It will, however, be continually monitoring the individual for whom it is responsible and will immediately snap into action should there be a sudden need, like a fall, or some item the individual needs. Robots providing closer attention to more needy people will be continually on duty, charging when there is nothing to do. We would hope you will stay involved because we've sometimes found resistance when a robot takes on duties like washing or dressing the subject. You can help ease the transition by being present. Often it is shyness or embarrassment which is the problem. Having a human there initially will really help in those instances.'

'It seems too good to be true.'

'Yes, I suppose it does, but it will happen, and we'd be delighted for you to monitor its operation. If you think the robots are falling short on anything, you can talk to the senior admin robot and extra help will be put in place. It is also important to remember that robots do not experience emotions when criticised or corrected or chastised. They just learn and perform better in the future, passing on, if it is relevant, what they have learned to every robot with similar functions throughout the galaxy.'

Questions and answers continued into the early evening and such events were taking place several times each day in cities, towns and villages throughout the parts of the world who were joining the Federation.

«««O»»»

[From White House tapes. RBB]

David Mendoza, General Alexander and Admiral Mann sat in the lounge area of the Oval Office with the president. Mendoza had briefed the two military chiefs on the situation with General Winston Delve. Now they waited.

'Where is he?' snapped the president. He should have been here by now. 'Deirdre!' he shouted.

His secretary opened the door and looked into the office. 'Yes, Mr President.'

'Find out where General Delve has got to.'

'Yes, sir.'

They continued to discuss other matters, including the lack of progress on finding Charles Mayne and General Dick Beech. There was a knock on the door and Deirdre entered.

'Well?' the president asked.

'Apparently, sir, he stopped off to deposit his bag at the staff residence and vanished. Major Salford has been trying to find out where he is.'

'*Jesus Christ!*' shouted the president. '*Give me strength.* Mendoza go and find him and report back. It sounds as if he found out something was going on. Does that mean we have yet another spy in our midst? This is hopeless!'

«««0»»»

[From Brad Gregg's and Jim Collins' notes and recordings. RBB]

The doorbell rang at the large detached house in Wisconsin Avenue on the west side of Washington DC. Four soldiers in civvies jumped into action as Captain Wooller examined the CCTV.

He called through to the lounge, 'It's General Delve, sir.'

'Let him in quickly,' shouted General Beech who jumped up and was in the hallway almost before the captain had opened the door. 'Winston. You okay?'

'Sure am, but it was a close call. If I hadn't stopped off at the staff residence on the way to the White House, I'd have been caught. There was a message for me in my room. It simply said, "Run!" so here I am.'

'How'd they figure you were working with us?'

'Don't know, Dick. It has to have been Mendoza. He's got agents everywhere at the moment. Need to keep your heads down.'

'We will,' said General Beech. 'Come and meet the others.'

The two generals walked through to the lounge area where Dick Beech introduced Winston Delve to Charles Mayne, Jim, Brad and Bob Nixon.

'Winnie, lovely to see you again,' said Bob.

'You two know each other?' asked Charles.

'Yes, met several times at the White House when Jack was still president and grabbed a few drinks together when Winnie was out of uniform,' said Bob.

'Right. Better times. I see you're still making Slimbridge's life unpleasant, Dick. The Green House was classic.'

'Yes, we've over fifty cells now. The best one was the dinner party. The main course had been almost served and the sprinkler system poured out its green dye. Magnificent. Wish I could've seen it,' said Dick.

'Made him mad as hell,' said Winston. 'Okay, I'm stuck with you now. How can I help?'

«««0»»»

[Taken from UN video and minutes. RBB]

The Albert Hall was packed to the gunnels with representatives from every country and many more press and observers.

The secretary general called the assembly to order and said, 'It gives me the utmost pleasure to welcome you all to this first full General Assembly of the United Nations since the fateful day my predecessor opened her meeting in New York.

'Before we begin, could I ask everyone to hold a minute's silence in remembrance of those who died, which also includes the Federation diplomatic team and millions of innocent people in the city itself.'

A hush quickly fell over the crowd. Many prayed. Others just looked to the ground or the air while they remembered colleagues or opponents, friends and acquaintances who'd died in the nuclear explosion caused by people as yet unknown, although most were pretty sure who the culprit was.

'The Assembly is gathered today to debate Resolution four hundred and twenty-seven, that all countries of the world, with the exception of the United States of America, will join the Galactic Federation, whose capital is on the planet Arlucian. Ambassador Terend Stograther and his team are seated to my right and available to provide answers, as necessary, to any questions raised.

'Before beginning the debate, could you please press your red voting button if you still have issues to raise before you are ready to place your vote.'

Lara looked over her shoulder, where the bank of LEDs sat beside the name of each of the one hundred and ninety-three member countries. Only one was lit. South Korea.

'The Assembly recognises the representative of South Korea,' said Lara.

'We have an ongoing concern about China's annexation of the north of our country and would ask that it be given back to South Korea.'

'But Hwang Kang-woo, we have already discussed this matter at length,' said Lara.

'I want to hear what we agreed confirmed by you and minuted in the General Assembly,' said the South Korean president.

Lara covered the microphone and called Paula over. 'Do you have the agreement?'

Paula swiped across her tablet several times and passed it to the secretary general. 'Here it is, ma'am.'

'The document runs into many pages, but the agreed final line is this, "Once Federation membership is agreed, the country known as China will hand administrative control of the country known as North Korea to the country known as South Korea, so that they are in the same administrative area." That is now minuted. Is that to your satisfaction?'

'Yes, thank you, Madam Secretary,' said Hwang Kang-woo, removing his red light from the board of nations.

'Secondly,' the secretary general continued, 'we have representatives here from Palestine, Taiwan, the Cook Islands and Niue plus the Holy See. Can you raise your hands for us to show where you are seated?'

Hands rose into the air from the spectators' area.

'Can you please confirm that you are in agreement with the General Assembly should it vote to join the Federation?'

All of the hands were lifted again. Lara breathed a sigh of relief to see the Palestinian representative showing agreement, as the negotiations between them and Israel had been long and extremely fractious.

'Now the last point of order. It has been agreed with the United States of America that Hawaii, Alaska, Puerto Rico and all other US dependencies will join the Federation and become their own administration areas. Would the observers from those countries kindly raise your hands to show that this has all been agreed with you?' said Lara.

The relative hands were raised.

'Thank you. Does anyone else have questions or matters to raise before we carry out the vote?'

Lara looked around the room. 'The Assembly recognises Helena Martinez, president of Mexico.'

'We, and our friends north of the USA, Canada, still have concerns about maintaining the borders between our countries and the USA. We think this should be clarified for the benefit of the rest of the world.'

'Ambassador Stograther, would you like to answer this point,' said Lara, looking to the benches where the Federation diplomatic team were seated.

'Indeed,' said the ambassador, rising slowly to his feet and walking up to the lectern. A strange figure in this sea of humanity. His arm waved through the air and his secradarve materialised before him, seemingly balancing itself on one corner of the lectern. He swiped one of his hands across it.

'It is important to realise that there are not just two borders. Obviously, those with Canada and Mexico are easy to administer, but it must be remembered that both coasts of the US are also borders. The Federation is not concerned about people coming from the US into any other country. If they register wherever they arrive, they can become Federation citizens. If not, then they can visit Federation territories as tourists. Border scanners will record everyone moving into the US from Mexico or Canada. Any time spent outside of Federation territory will lose them all Federation income and benefits until they return.'

'That seems like a lot of red tape,' said the Canadian president.

'No, not at all,' said the ambassador. 'It is all done by robots and is instant. You walk across the line into the USA, your income stops, step back over and it starts again. Ten seconds or ten years. When things are recorded by automatons, nothing is too much trouble or too complex.'

'What about system failures?' asked Anna Tolberg, president of Sweden. 'We all know how unreliable computer systems can be.'

'I don't understand,' said the ambassador.

'Yol Ambassador,' said the secretary general, 'Computer systems can crash or be hacked or simply handle data in unexpected ways.'

'I see. Yes, this might be a problem you would have on your own world, but let me assure you, a few hundred thousand years of development has produced foolproof programs which are continually monitoring their own functions and reactions. When new systems are introduced, the automatons themselves find minor errors and correct them. Major errors do not exist. "Hacking" as you call it, if it did occur, would be recognised, tracked and traced. I cannot remember a single occasion where that has happened and you must understand that there is no hiding place. Punishment would be certain and, potentially, lengthy stasis would follow. Please, let us worry about that and I assure you I will lose no sleep over it.'

'But immigrants have to register if they are coming from the US?' asked the Mexican president.

'Yes.'

'What if they don't?' asked a delegate from Trinidad.

'They will be reminded by a borderbot. Once after an hour, then half hour, then ten minutes, then continually, like one of the annoying seatbelt alarms you have in your cars. It costs nothing to register and there will be no further intrusion. The Federation is not a police state, but having a single independent country on the planet is offering challenges even we have not previously encountered.'

'Excuse me,' said the president of Nigeria. 'If we are visiting America as tourists, where do we get our currency?'

'Again, this is new for us. We have told America that it is up to them to come up with an exchange rate and to set up bureaux de change at key points.'

'So, we don't get a say?' asked the prime minister of Australia.

'No, but you can barter. We think that if they lapse into the temptation to overvalue the dollar, they will eventually realise that the number of visitors will decline and that should cause the value to fall. As I say, it is experimental, but we have some economist robots who will monitor it,' said the ambassador. 'In fact, if anyone feels they are being cheated or exploited over the currency, see our borderbots. I'll arrange for them to be able to offer small grants if necessary.'

'Any other questions?' asked Lara, returning to stand beside the ambassador. She scoured the field of faces. The ambassador returned to his seat.

'In that case, I am calling a vote on Resolution four hundred and twenty-seven. Green for yes, red for no.'

The secretary general turned around and looked at the board of nations. A sea of green. One hundred and ninety-two green lights.

'Resolution passed!' she said and brought her gavel down upon the lectern. 'Federation administrators will now visit all countries and the transition will begin. The Earth is now about to enter a golden period in its history, and we have all voted ourselves into unemployment.'

There was laughter, applause and not a little cheering.

26 Federation Meeting

[Taken from Paula Wilson's records and Ambassador Stograther's files. RBB]

Yol Ambassador Stograther, Paula and Lara sat at an exceedingly large mahogany conference table in a Ministry of Defence meeting room. A Clueb sat on the back of the ambassador's chair. Yol Stograther's secradarve rotated leisurely in front of him, just above the highly polished wood. Another sat in front of Paula, motionless and colourless.

'I am really pleased you have both agreed to work as coordinators for us during the transition,' the ambassador said to Paula and Lara. 'This is my assistant, Ya Henedy Esrov. She's a Clueb and remembers everything… I hope, because I am sure I will lose track of events otherwise. This is an excellent place to work from.'

'Maureen was only too pleased to offer you the building as the Ministry of Defence is no longer required,' said Lara.

'Our pleasure, to help,' said Paula. 'We were both hoping to maintain an involvement during the period of change.'

'There will be a lot of useless professions which will have ceased. There will be more in the future. The department of sociobots is being set up on this floor and you must keep in contact with them at the first sign of depressive illnesses. There will be some. There will even be suicides. We are much better at spotting such people, but it varies by species. It is tragic that some individuals never get to appreciate the beauty of the new order. They miss the stress and antagonistic attitudes of colleagues they never really liked and had put up with for years. Defence departments are classic for creating that sort of misery when planets join the Federation. We will pump whatever resources are necessary into looking after the affected.'

'We'll ensure it is raised with each country we visit,' said Lara.

'My assistants will be joining us in a moment. I want you to know that you both have personal shuttles available to you. Twice a week we will all meet here, and you will head out around the world to discover anything which is not working properly and to report back. It is far better that this be handled by humans as there is sure to be some apprehension about the number of aliens and robots involved in transition. You have your robot assistants?'

'Yes.'

'Don't forget to give them access to your secradarves after each meeting so that they know what is happening. In fact, where is yours, Lara?'

'Whoops! Sorry,' she said as she waved her arm and the spinning globe materialised and hung in front of her, revolving slowly.

'You must use them, or your robots will soon become ineffective.'

'Yes. Just a matter of getting used to it,' said Lara.

'As far as anyone is now concerned, until administration elections take place, you, Lara, are effectively the leader of the Federation section of the Earth. Expect to be bombarded with questions. Your secradarve and other robots will be available for you,' said the ambassador.

'My sister would be happy to be your assistant, if it would help,' said the Clueb.

'Thank you, Ya Henedy. Please put her in touch,' said Lara.

'Okay. Henedy, can you call the others in,' said the ambassador. 'I should add that all of the roles of those now entering our meeting will eventually be handed over to volunteer humans, like yourselves, as soon as everything is running smoothly.'

An assortment of some twenty aliens, accompanied by their assistant automatons, entered the room and seated themselves around the table, except for one who travelled in a device similar to an open-topped Dalek.

'Welcome, everyone,' said the ambassador. 'Today we begin to turn Earth into paradise. Yol Prestegon, finances?'

Yol Prestegon Gerandor was a brown, hairy mammal-like creature with large bat-like ears and a pointed nose. Although he walked on all fours, he sat upright at the table and his hands were very similar to a human's apart from the hair and two opposable thumbs. His secradarve materialised before him and he studied the text. 'Africa, Middle East, Pakistan and India should be complete by this evening. Every person should be in possession of a month's supply of afeds. We should have Australasia, Far East, Japan, China and their neighbours supplied by tomorrow and Russia through to Great Britain by Thursday. That will leave Canada, Central America and South America plus a few islands by Friday night.'

'Excuse me,' interrupted Lara. 'Are you saying everyone in the world will be in possession of a month's supply of afeds in just four days?'

'Yes, Lara,' said Yol Prestegon. 'The delivery is a physical handover of printed cash. Over the following two weeks, as we install purchasing devices in shops, we will return to collect whatever afeds they have and convert them into electronic funds. That is when they have their financial chip inserted in the soft tissue between the thumb and first finger.'

'I'm amazed!' said Lara.

'Federation capabilities are always underestimated. Yol Prestegon has literally millions of robots working on Africa as we speak. They are simply handing over the money as they pass through the country. Detectors ensure no one is missed, and no one gets more than one supply. Remember, we have done this on thousands of worlds and transition robots are kept in storage to be used in such a manner when a new world joins. What seems incredible to you, is almost routine to us.'

'Simply amazing,' Paula said.

'Okay, let's move on. Ya Torendal Isfinmaredal, what is happening on health?'

And so, the afternoon progressed. The transition was staggeringly well organised. Within a week, all poverty had been erased, everyone was being treated for their medical problems, cars were given autonomous drivers until autonomous carbon-neutral cars could replace them, and polluting planes were dismantled for scrap as fleets of Federation shuttles arrived to replace them.

27 Presidential Rant

[Taken from White House tapes. RBB]

Matthew Brown listened to President Slimbridge as he ranted about what was going on in the United Nations. The media had pulled in the story from the Internet and had covered the unanimous vote to join the Federation.

'There is no need for concern, Mr President. The nation voted not to join. You have a mandate to remain independent and you shouldn't be bothered by them again. They did agree not to interfere as long as there was no conflict against other countries.'

'I don't like it, Matthew. We haven't been told what is going on. You'd have thought there'd have been a communique of some description.'

'I'm sure they will. Any sign of Mayne or Beech. I see they were at their annoying best at the Superbowl.'

'Not funny. How did they get access to the changing rooms, anyway?'

'Could have been any time in the previous six days. It was a fairly simple matter to connect the supply of dye to the sprinklers in each changing room.'

'We must find a way to stop them,' the president said and stood to look out onto the White House lawn.

'Mr Mendoza says they are beginning to understand the pattern and methods used in the attacks. They prevented one at a Californian event just yesterday,' said Matthew.

A muffled pop and increase in air pressure took place. Both men turned and stared at a delegation of four aliens and six robots standing against the far wall of the Oval Office.

'How dare you enter here unannounced?' roared the president.

'We are here to set up lines of communication for that very reason, Mr President,' said a short, cider-orange-skinned alien with tentacles.

'Okay, well on this occasion I'll forgive the intrusion,' said the president.

'This is a communication device which you can use to contact me,' said the alien, pressing a doughnut-shaped grey object into the president's hand. He snatched it away, avoiding any contact with the offering tentacle.

'My name is Yol Lorel Distern. I am from the planet Imhop and I have been appointed ambassador to the United States of America. It is the first time a Federation ambassador has been allocated to a single nation. I will provide as little or as much support as you wish, and I will mediate between you and the Federation which now begins at the Mexican and Canadian borders.'

'We don't need your interference,' said the president.

'That is up to you. We are in the process of acquiring an embassy in Washington and will be there to deal with any problems Federation citizens might experience in the United States. We assume that you will treat any Federation citizens, whether human or alien and any accompanying robots, with the same respect you would expect your own citizens to receive in the rest of the world.'

'Of course, as long as they don't commit any crimes. We're not at war with you,' said Matthew.

'Not yet!' said the president.

'This is Ya Iridold Vestormoron. She is the same species as your original ambassador, a Racutaan. She, and a number of assistants and robots, will assist you with your border security until your own people have everything in order. She is fully aware of every rule regarding visitors from your country wishing to cross the border and will help you set up whatever procedures you require on your side of the borders.'

'Okay. How will I contact you?' asked the president.

'I will provide additional communication details as soon as the embassy is established,' said Ya Iridold. 'That should be some time tomorrow or the day after. Until then, our border robots will not stop anyone crossing into the USA. They will be advised to wait until your own people grant permission to enter or not. Neither will our border robots stop anyone wishing to cross into the Federation.'

'How are you monitoring your borders now?' asked Yol Lorel.

'They are working as normal. What about ports and airports?'

'We will be asking you for terminals at ports and airports for people to take shuttles to anywhere else in the world. We will handle border security before they board the shuttles. That way we will not require border checks anywhere except in the USA.'

'What about flights out of the USA on our airlines?' asked Matthew.

'Your airplanes are too polluting to enter Federation airspace or be allowed over the oceans,' said Yol Lorel. 'Anyone travelling to the rest of the world will need to use shuttles.'

'That's outrageous!' shouted the president.

'You might feel that way, but we can compromise by making outward shuttle flights free of charge,' said Yol Lorel. 'That way there is no cost to you. Our robots will monitor border controls when passengers enter the boarding areas.'

'You are restricting citizens of the USA from using their own private jets or our airlines. That is not acceptable,' said the president.

'Mr President, you have chosen to isolate the USA. That means that everything more than fifty miles from your shorelines is Federation water and Federation airspace. We will not permit your aircraft to fly outside that area and your citizens are being given free travel on shuttles instead. Is that not reasonable?'

'Let me speak to the real ambassador – the fish creature,' said the president.

'Sir,' said Yol Lorel, 'I am your ambassador. Yol Hareen Trestogeen, to whom you refer, came to the end of his natural life. During transition, Yol Terend Stograther is the ambassador to Federation parts of Earth and I am the Federation ambassador to the USA.'

'What, I can't appeal to a higher authority?'

'No, Mr President,' said Yol Lorel. 'You can cut off diplomatic relations and we will leave. We will not set up an embassy and no USA citizens will be allowed across our borders. You can control your borders however you wish, but I would ask you to consider the fact that you would be cutting off all inward tourism! In addition, no planes or polluting cruise ships will be allowed outside your fifty mile coastal waters.'

'How dare you?' the president said, banging his fist on the desk and turning a rosy pink.

'It is your country who wishes to remain independent. The rest of the world has joined the Federation and nothing will be permitted which pollutes Earth's atmosphere or damages the ecology of the planet. Now, you need to make your choices! We are only too happy to provide all the assistance you could possibly need, free of any charge. What is your problem, sir?'

President Slimbridge was apoplectic with rage. 'I've had enough of this,' he shouted. 'Matthew, you deal with it,' and he left through his secretary's door, slamming it behind him so hard that a split appeared in the door jamb.

'Mr Brown?' said Yol Lorel.

'Give me a minute,' said Matthew. He left the room and two security men came and stood inside the Oval Office.

Five minutes later Matthew Brown returned. 'Okay,' he said, 'come this way.'

The aliens and robots left through the main door and walked through to a small meeting room.

'Can you use this location to come and go?' asked Matthew.

Ya Iridold materialised her secradarve and checked the coordinates. 'No problem,' she said.

'Okay,' said Matthew. 'I'll be your liaison. Give me some time to bring together a group of border security administrators and meet me back here at ten tomorrow morning. We'll then sort out the detail without having to bother the president. Does that sound acceptable? I need to be able to contact you.'

'Certainly, here is another communication device,' said Ambassador Lorel. 'Do you need anything else from us now?'

'No, not until tomorrow,' said Matthew.

'Thank you, Matthew,' said the ambassador and they all vanished, causing a plop sound as the air rushed in to fill the space they'd been occupying.

28 My Involvement

[This is where I enter the scene myself. RBB]

A friend on Arlucian contacted me at my university on Daragnen. I'd mentioned the enigma of the 'prohibited planet' Earth to him when we met at a conference on the capital world.

'You know that planet you were interested in, Rummy. Well I heard a rumour. It was Earth, wasn't it?' my friend said.

'Yes, that's it, Earth,' I said.

'Well, now don't mention my name about this, but I heard from a friend who works in the cabinet office that there is an odd experiment taking place there.'

'An experiment? What sort of experiment?'

'I don't know, but the whole cabinet were involved in the discussions.'

'Thanks. Think it's time for me to try to get there again,' I said.

It took me nearly a week to sort out my lessons and tutorials, handing over to a couple of robots to take responsibility during my absence. I spoke to the principal and he reluctantly let me leave.

That was the easy part. At the time, my children were still infants and my wife was not particularly amused at my intention to abandon her for what could be a lengthy research trip. She knew how important Earth was to me, though, and finally relented.

I managed to get a ship direct to Delarkon where I had to wait to find a freighter or something heading to Sol. If I could get to Mars, I'd be sure to find a way to Earth.

Everywhere I went I still drew an absolute blank on the mention of Earth although there was a rumour on Delarkon. I didn't know quite what to make of it.

[You need to bear in mind that, at this point, I knew virtually nothing about the relationship between the Federation and Earth after the time immediately before the New York atrocity. RBB.]

I entered a bar. My usual tactic was to become friendly with locals and then drop a mention of Earth into the conversation.

'Hey, wasn't that the place the Churmbin woman was blown up?' said one guy at the bar.

'Yeah, think it was. Nuclear bomb or something,' said his friend.

Now I had to be careful not to get too inquisitive and make them clam up.

'No one uses nuclear bombs,' I said matter of factly.

'Yes. It was a nuclear bomb. They never found her body. She was part of some diplomatic team trying to bring this Earth place into the Federation.'

'Oh, yes. I remember. Then the whole thing went belly-up and was eventually hushed up.'

'That's unusual,' I said. 'Why would anyone hush up a new member of the Federation?'

'Don't know, mate. I think they failed entry.'

'Yes,' the other person said, 'never heard any more about it.'

Each day, I headed to the spaceport and asked if anything was heading to Sol. Day after day the answer was negative, then, finally there was a crew member of a supply freighter standing in the ops room.

'Sol? Why'd you want to go there?' said a person wearing a junior officer's uniform.

'I'm trying to get to a place called Earth, but Mars would do. Where are you heading?'

'My ship is taking supplies on an aid mission to the planet Earth. Hush hush job,' said the crew member.

'Glad you don't talk about it, then,' said the person behind the counter who was delivering papers to the adminbot at the desk.

The crew member laughed and took me to one side.

'I can get you on board, but you'll have to stay concealed for a few hours. I think we'll be landing.'

'What? On planet Earth itself?'

'Yes, so I believe.'

'Fabulous. When do we leave?' I asked.

'Be here tomorrow at eight. One bag only.'

'Will do, thanks.'

«««o»»»

[Taken from Jim Collins' notes. RBB]

Brad was lucky, but Charles, Dick, Bob and me and half a dozen officers in the Free America organisation were not. When it happened, it took me back to a scene in the film, *Bonnie and Clyde*. I was sitting beside the front window and saw a couple of plain cars pull into the end of the driveway. Behind them a police squad car parked, and I could just make out a stationary black van beyond it.

We were rumbled. I ran through the house alerting everyone and looked out of the kitchen window. A SWAT team was making its way up the garden, using shrubs and apple trees as camouflage.

Now, in *Bonnie and Clyde*, they made a break for it, firing machine guns as they mowed down as many police as they could. Would we be so stupid?

'Okay,' said Dick, 'game's up. I've signalled Mike and destroyed the burner. We need not give them any opportunity to open fire. Bring me the bullhorn, Jim.'

Once he had the megaphone, Dick opened the front door and stood behind it. 'Let it be known that we can see your SWAT team at the rear and will surrender. We have all laid down our arms and will be in the dining room, the first door off the hallway to the left.'

The sound of the device had echoed around the house.

'Into the dining room, everyone. Captain, unlock the rear door and follow us quickly,' said General Beech.

Within thirty seconds we were all in the room. We spread ourselves around it and waited.

All of a sudden there were calls of 'Armed police, armed police!'

A SWAT officer looked into the room and saw all of us standing with our arms raised. He said, 'On the floor! Face down with your arms behind your backs. *Do it now!*'

We knelt, then lay down on the floor around the dining table and beside the fireplace.

'Don't move,' said the officer, then on his radio, 'I have ten of them in the dining room. No sign of resistance.'

Voices from elsewhere in the house shouted out 'Room clear!' then 'Upper floor clear!' and 'Second floor clear!' 'Kitchen clear!' 'Office Clear!' 'Lounge clear!' and so on until the final call of 'All clear!'

I could hear people in the dining room, moving around. My hands were roughly pulled and cuffed, and I assumed it was also happening to the others. I am sure all were as apprehensive as I… this was likely to end up in front of a firing squad, if we even got that far.

The leadership of Free America had been neutralised.

«««o»»»

[From my own notes, images and recordings. RBB]

It was really uncomfortable. I know he warned me that I'd have to remain concealed, but this was a tiny cupboard in the crew member's cabin. The freighter was not like the last rust bucket I'd travelled in a few months back on my first attempt to get to Earth. This was a modern ship, so there was no clue as to what was happening. No changes in gravity, or any movement felt through in-flight vector changes.

All of a sudden there was a change. The ship had been operating under Arlucian standard gravity and now we were a little lighter. It must mean we had landed on a different planet. Could it really be Earth?

'Rummy, you can get out now,' said the crew member.

I uncurled myself from the cupboard and stretched to ease my cramped muscles. 'What now?'

'Leave my cabin, run down the corridor to the left and take the door at the end. It will take you into one of the cargo bays. You're on your own from there.'

'Thanks. Much appreciated,' I said and made a dash along the corridor, hoping no one would leave their cabin.

In just two minutes I'd run four hundred metres and was now standing at the door. I cracked it open.

The hatch opened onto a gantry high above the storage containers. Dozens of robots below were sorting and loading transports which made their way out of the ship and onto some rough ground. This must be Earth. I'd made it.

There didn't seem to be any people about, just automatons, so I quickly descended from the gantry down an open, but shielded, vertical ladder. I began counting the rungs but gave up at fifty and, soon after, felt solid ground beneath me. Warily, I looked around the hive of activity in the cargo hold.

The robots were not interested in a person in their working space and just continued their frantic unpacking, loading and shipping of goods down the sloping platform to the ground below.

I could see pleasant sunshine. Being a Daragnen, the sort of temperature I was feeling was comfortable. It was humid so I removed a padded jacket I was wearing and stowed it in my bag. I slung it over my shoulders and marched down the slope into the sunshine.

There were dozens of medibots moving around a tented community.

I stopped one and asked, 'What is happening here? What is this place?'

'This is Mexico. Beyond that wall is the United States of America, which is independent, not part of the Federation.'

'But Mexico is? And why are they living in tents?'

'These are refugees from this central part of the Americas. Many in this camp are from Honduras. We have been assigned to bring them up to standard health and nutrition.'

'But why are they here?'

'They want to cross the border but the United States won't let them in.'

I was having trouble understanding. 'What did you mean by this United States of America being independent and here, Mexico, being part of the Federation?'

The medibot said, 'I don't know the full story, but this entire planet has joined the Federation except for the United States of America. They are not part of the Federation and so they control their own borders.'

Now I understood, but it seemed most bizarre. Is this what my friend on Arlucian had meant by Earth being an experiment? 'Where is their border control?' I asked.

'Do you see that queue over there? Those are people waiting to be seen by the border security people on the United States of America side of the wall.'

The line comprised about sixty or seventy humans; male, female and children. I made my way to the end of the line. The family standing there looked at me strangely and shuffled away from me. I supposed that aliens were not commonly seen here. We would be strange-looking people to them. Compared with a human, I am very short, standing about half their size. My skin is dark brown, a cross between these Mexicans and the few black people I see among them. I have the same number of legs and arms as they do, but my head is set very low on my torso with no appreciable neck although we can swivel it through more than two hundred and forty degrees. I was wearing the equivalent of a T-shirt and trousers which reached my ankles. My shoes were open, showing that I only had three toes on each foot. My hands, similarly, had two fingers and an opposable thumb.

'Why are you wanting to leave Mexico?' I asked the woman of the family, but she didn't speak English. I tried French but that didn't work either. 'What do you speak?' I asked, pointing at her and my lips.

'Ah, Español,' she said. It meant nothing to me. She walked forwards to a man four or five positions in front of her, tapped him on the shoulder and said a few words in Spanish. She waved me forward.

He turned around and was shocked at my presence. He looked me up and down, slowly. 'You alien?' he asked.

'Yes,' I said. 'I'm from Daragnen. I don't speak Español. I wondered why you are all leaving Mexico to go to the United States of America?'

'Ah. Si. We have relatives in El Paso,' he said a few words in Spanish to the woman. 'She too has relatives in the USA.'

'You are not leaving to get away from the Federation, then?' I asked.

'No. In fact, we in two minds. If you been here yesterday, this line would be a thousand people. Most have dropped out. We might. Now I have this,' and he pulled a wad of afeds out of his pocket.

It was rare to see actual cash in the Federation. 'How long have you been members?'

'Just yesterday. One day only,' he said.

'Is that only Mexico or the rest of the world?'

'Whole world.'

Amazing. I had arrived on the very day the Earth had joined, but with this strange situation of a single country remaining independent.

As the day progressed, the queue shuffled forward. Many dropped out and it was not long before I got to the border post. It comprised a building which had a walkway passing through it on the left and a glazed office section on the right. Inside, an obese, uniformed white woman sat looking down at me through the glazed panel. She shouted over her shoulder, 'Tell Jack I've got a weird one here!'

'What's your name, sonny,' she said.

I wondered what "sonny" meant and assumed it was a name you used if you didn't know someone's real name. 'My name is Yol Rummy Blin Breganin from the planet Daragnen, and I am a professor at Dinbelay University. I have an interest in other worlds and that is why I am here. I would like to visit the United States of America.'

She seemed to be taken aback by my fluent English and the fact that I was an adult. Maybe sonny meant child and she thought I was a child owing to my lack of stature.

'Okay, Mr Breggin. Wait a moment.'

'Breganin,' I said.

'Yes, Mr Breganin. Please wait a moment,' she said and turned to a human with an official-looking peaked cap. I couldn't hear what they were saying.

'Right, Mr Breganin. Do you have the entry fee of five hundred dollars?'

'I am sorry. I have no currency in cash. I have a microchip you can read to obtain that sum in afeds,' I said.

'Microchip?'

I raised my hands and pointed at the tiny bump between my thumb and first finger. 'This microchip can pay my entry fee.'

'One moment,' she said.

This time I could hear the conversation.

'He says he has a microchip in his hand to pay us, but no cash. What should I do?'

The man with the peaked cap replied, 'Aw, damn it! Just let him in. It was worth a try.'

The woman shrugged, filled out details on a card, checking the spelling of my full name and my planet. She handed me the card and I was permitted through the barrier into the United States of America, or USA as they all seemed to call it. I looked at the card and saw that it had a note on it – "to pay $500 on departure."

I saw a bus heading to the centre of El Paso, but they wouldn't let me on because I had no money to buy a ticket. I was going to have to get some cash from somewhere. I started walking along the dusty road. A sign said "16 miles". I wondered how long a mile was.

«««O»»»

[Taken from various sources. RBB]

On the seventh day of Earth's membership, some people were trying to leave the USA to enter the Federation. Many wanted to see what was happening, but some were already making a commitment.

The border was letting anyone through and categorised them as tourists or wanting residency. Currency was exchanged at a dollar for an afed at the border posts inside the Federation. In the other direction, exorbitant rates were being charged. It had become obvious that Mexicans had been given afeds in cash and, inside the USA border, they were being offered as little as twenty-five cents for an afed.

It would soon change, of course. Currently, it was easy-pickings for any unscrupulous person wanting to fleece the immigrants. Sooner or later the real exchange value would settle down, but for now it was "make hay while the sun shines". Of course, on the Federation side, there were now millions of nanobots keeping an eye on all transactions, preventing fraud and stopping people selling-on items they had received in aid. Short, sharp, shock punishments of an hour in stasis were stopping much of the crime and corruption, especially when it became known that repeat offenders were getting ten hours, then a hundred hours, then a month! Fewer and fewer individuals received ten hour punishments. They had enough afeds for their needs. Why bother trying to cheat the system? If you were spotted breaking the rules, which was becoming more and more certain, then you were punished.

Gradually, the nanobots could leave peaceful areas of the planet and they congregated at places where habitual corruption dominated life. Nigeria, Uganda, Zimbabwe, and Ghana were soon hotbeds of attention. At one point, over twelve per cent of people in central Africa were in stasis. It took time for them to learn but, within three months, most countries were gradually cleared of criminals and the system was working as it was intended. Everyone had enough to eat, and there was freedom of movement worldwide. African cities were soon developing, clearing slums and rehousing people, firstly in comfortable prefabricated buildings and later in individual cottages or apartments, depending upon the location in which people wanted to live. Corruption or exploitation using sex or intimidation was easy to detect and quickly stopped.

Similar corruption took place in the Middle East, eastern Europe, the Indian subcontinent and the Far East. There was less in Western Europe, but crimes there were of the more serious variety, again treated by stasis periods from an hour to a year. The odd murder meant a life sentence, with rape and grievous bodily harm attracting sentences of many years. The beauty of the legal system was that there were almost always nanobots as witnesses. They could not lie and could never reveal what they saw except in a court of law. Being virtually invisible, no one was ever aware they were living in their communities. Was the prevention of all crime worth the intrusion of these almost invisible automatons? Only time would tell, but it had certainly killed premeditated crime stone dead. Only spur of the moment or opportunistic crimes seemed to persist. After a few sessions of stasis, even those would be likely to diminish.

Civil rights groups objected to the intrusion of robots and nanobots but, over time, their activities faded into obscurity. Nanobots disappeared from conversations. When something does not intrude and never does anything but good, it is soon seen as inconsequential by any but the most pedantic of individuals. Yes, it would take years before they were completely forgotten, but it would happen eventually. Who would rather see a rape or violent attack take place when the presence of nanobots could ensure the arrival of policebots to stop the assault in minutes? The logic was undeniable.

29 Marine Barracks

[Taken from White House tapes, Jim Collins' notes and media recordings. Bear in mind that when I arrived on Earth, I did not have any of the information which appears in these header notes. RBB]

Marine One collected the president, Matthew Brown and some aides from the White House and delivered them to the nearby Marine barracks. The motorcade was never used now except in secret. The president dare not announce his itinerary for fear of Free America performing some relatively minor, but hugely embarrassing stunt.

The prisoners were kept in a single dormitory and saw Marine One settle onto the parade ground. The president and his party were hurried into an adjacent building and then the door to the dormitory opened to admit a squad of armed men, led by a major.

'On your feet!' he ordered.

In short measure, the prisoners were marched over to the building to meet the president.

He sat on one side of a large room, behind a desk with Matthew Brown beside him. The prisoners were lined up four metres away, guarded from the front and sides by the Marines.

'You are traitors to the United States of America,' said the president.

'You, sir, are a murderer!' shouted Dick Beech.

'Gag him,' said the major and a Marine tied a kerchief around his head. The general did not resist, he'd made his statement.

'We are showing leniency to all but five of you. Major, take the others away. We will deal with them separately. Leave Beech, Mayne, Gregg, Collins and Nixon here.'

The squad of Marines split in two and marched the others away from the leaders of Free America.

'You traitorous individuals will be shot, and I intend to make a spectacle of it on television. It might stop the stupidity of your rebellion,' said the president.

'*Uprising!*' shouted Brad. 'A rebellion implies you are a legitimate government, and nothing could be further from the truth!'

'Take them away. You'll finally be out of my hair.'

'The world knows what you did, Slimbridge. Your name will live in infamy forever!' said Bob Nixon.

'Ha. You and Spence were the greatest traitors of all. What are you waiting for, major? You have your orders.'

The major and remaining guards marched the prisoners out of the building and onto the parade ground. The president followed and stood nearby. In a minute they were all lined up in front of a red brick wall.

The order was given by the major. On 'Ready!' they began shouting various insults at the president. 'Mass murderer!' 'Murderer!' 'You're the traitor!'

'Aim!' ordered the major.

'Fire!'

The volley of shots rang out, hit a forcefield and fell to the ground. Ambassador Terend Stograther appeared in front of the five men and said, 'We cannot tolerate this action, President Slimbridge. These humans are now honorary Federation citizens and, as of now have the benefit of my protection!' As he finished speaking, all six vanished from the scene.

President Slimbridge was furious!

30 California Dreaming

[From my own notes, images and recordings. A serious dilemma was developing. RBB]

The USA was certainly a beautiful country.

Eventually, I found a bank which was prepared to spend some time getting me access to my bank account. They charged me a ridiculous rate for dollars, but at least I now had some money to spend on travel and accommodation. I made my way west from El Paso.

It seems I was a rare beast, an alien wandering the highways and byways of a country which had chosen not to join the Federation. I met no other aliens in my travels. When I arrived in the state of California, there was not a little unrest about the government.

The Free America movement faded from the news but, in California, the population was beginning to learn more about the potential benefits of Federation membership. Tourists were entering the state and speaking of their new lives, of not having to work, free health care, fantastic education, and opportunities to visit other worlds. It was far too soon for much of this "information" to be the actual experiences of the tourists. More likely it was the rumour mill. It meant that I was forever being quizzed about life in the Federation. Some hung on every word, but others were deeply suspicious of everything I said.

I needed to get out of the USA to see how the rest of the planet was coping with membership transition. The early period of transition would be a vital part of my study. As far as I was aware, papers on transitioning had always been produced by government officials. What about the effects upon and actions of ordinary citizens? It needed documenting. I needed to leave now.

I soon learned that there is nothing like Californians for becoming jealous of someone having a better lifestyle. I'd discovered that California had been one of, if not *the* most desirable location to live for over half a century. All of a sudden, everywhere else in the world was competing for quality of life in the imagination of Californians, if not yet in reality.

Governor Arnold Pattison was outspoken towards the federal government about missed opportunities but President Slimbridge was soon on his case and there was news that the dozens of military bases in the state had received orders to prepare for action. The president was not going to tolerate insurrection on a state-wide basis.

In my hotel room I watched the tension build as the rhetoric between Pattison and Slimbridge became increasingly bitter.

Then a huge surprise – on the 20th June, the morning I was planning to head for Los Angeles airport, Governor Pattison made a Unilateral Declaration of Independence and gave notice that California was breaking away from the United States of America and was planning to join the Federation.

With the work I'd already done researching Earth from my base at Dinbelay University, together with what I'd learned during my brief time in the USA, I saw a fascinating opportunity to now study insurrection on a massive scale, but if I did so, I'd miss the opportunity to study transition in the rest of the world.

I wished I knew more about the interstate structure. Would other states assist California? Would Slimbridge's forces just crush the rebellion? Many Americans owned weapons – some of them military grade. Would they spring to the defence of UDI? Would those from neighbouring states enter an armed revolt on one side or the other?

As far as I was aware, nothing like this had ever occurred in the Federation's history. My need to visit other areas of the world for comparison grew in importance. If I delayed in order to follow events in California, I would miss recording the everyday changes in the lives of people in the rest of the world. Which was most important? Should I stay or leave?

With tanks approaching the eastern borders of the state, I would have to make sure that I didn't become a victim of Pattison's declaration. Many called him crazy. Was there even a majority in favour of UDI? Increasingly, a violent conclusion was becoming most likely. Violence challenged all of my personal principles, but I'd become as much a pawn in events as the ordinary Californians.

Pattison was betting that the Federation would support his UDI initiative and the Californian military bases would swing in behind him.

Slimbridge was banking on the Federation doing nothing because they'd agreed to leave the USA alone.

Something would have to give! I needed to get out. I packed my bag and headed for Los Angeles airport.

----««oOo»»----

Released June 30th 2020:

HIDDEN FEDERATION

A Word from Tony

Thank you for reading *FEDERATION AND EARTH*. Reviews are very important for authors and I wonder if I could ask you to say a few words on the Amazon Review Page. Every review, even if it is only a few words with a star rating, helps the book move up the Amazon rankings.

Tony's Books

Currently, I have written six science fiction stories. ***Federation*** and ***Federation and Earth*** are the first two books in my ***Federation Trilogy***. ***Moonscape*** is the first in a series about astronaut, Mark Noble. The second book, ***Moonstruck***, is due for release around the end of 2019. My other books are all stand-alone novels.

More detail about each of the books can be found on Harmsworth.net.

THE DOOR: Henry Mackay and his dog regularly walk alongside an ancient convent wall. Today, as he passes the door, he glances at its peeling paint. Moments later he stops dead in his tracks. He returns to the spot, and all he sees is an ivy-covered wall. The door has vanished!

He unwittingly embarks on an exciting trail of events with twists, turns, quantum entanglement and temporal anomalies. It becomes an unbelievable adventure to save humanity which you'll be unable to put down.

The Door is an intriguing and unique science fiction mystery. It is endearingly British and covers the problems we face with the environment and the Earth's dwindling resources.

Discover the astonishing secrets being concealed by ***THE DOOR*** today!

FEDERATION takes close encounters to a whole new level. A galactic empire of a quarter of a million worlds stumbles across the Earth. With elements of a political thriller, there is an intriguing storyline which addresses the environmental and social problems faced by the world today.

The aliens' philosophy on life is totally unexpected. With the help of intelligent automatons, they've turned what many on Earth felt was a reviled political system into a utopia for the masses, but are they a force for good or evil, and will the wealthy make the compromises needed for a successful outcome?

A Daragnen university graduate, Yol Rummy Blin Breganin, discovers that Earth failed in its attempt to join the Federation, and, for some unknown reason, members are forever banned from visiting or contacting the planet. Rummy had never heard of a whole world being outlawed. Perhaps it would be sensible to leave well enough alone but no, he decides to investigate…

FEDERATION is the first in a trilogy of near-future, hard science-fiction novels by *Tony Harmsworth*, the *First Contact* specialist.

Submerge yourself in humankind's cultural and economic dilemma. Try to put your own personal political viewpoint to one side – this story is deliberately intended to make you think about the alternatives. Buy ***FEDERATION*** today.

FEDERATION & EARTH. Book two in the Federation trilogy.

After the dramatic and unexpected turn of events at the end of the first book, Earth is left with several factions trying to resolve the situation. The new president of the USA is trying to secure his hold on power, while a new group who have named themselves FREE AMERICA, is trying to overthrow what it considers an illegitimate regime.

Elsewhere, the new Secretary General of the United Nations is working with the smaller Security Council to try to bring the rest of the world together after the events at the end of the book one. Can the aliens be convinced to provide help or are they just going to watch from orbit?

Take a care. You won't enjoy this story unless you are open to political concepts which could never work on Earth as it is before the trilogy begins i.e. now. If you like speculative fiction, open your mind and enjoy the adventure. This book is like Marmite [look it up], you will either love it or hate it!

MINDSLIP: Those who have read this book say that it is, by far and away, his best work. For some reason, however, it does not sell well mainly because it is difficult to categorise. Is it psychological SF or is it science fiction at all? Whatever the case, if you start it, you won't be able to put it down.

So, what happens in ***MINDSLIP***? Radiation from a nearby supernova, combined with enormous coronal mass ejections from the sun causes the Van Allen Belts to fail in their provision of protection of the Earth. Gamma radiation reaches the surface and every creature on Earth swaps minds! Men to women, children to adults, animals to humans, old to young, and vice versa. How would you handle changing sex or species? Mindslip combines frightening science fiction with psychological anguish.

The change astrophysicist Geoff Arnold experiences is, at first surprising, then fascinating, but quickly becomes challenging, and his wife and children have vanished. He joins the government's catastrophe committee with the brief to find a solution to *MINDSLIP* before it completely destroys society and the economy.

Untold millions die, but billions survive danger, harassment and abuse, and manage to adapt to their change of species, race, sex, and age.

Geoff discovers that the change his wife has experienced is life-threatening. Can he juggle his new life, help save the world and rescue his wife in time?

This stand-alone work is an excellent example of Tony's imagination. Science fiction with elements of soft horror, all in the style of the old masters. A real page-turner.

Many have said that it is reminiscent of John Wyndham's classics — ***Day of the Triffids***; ***The Chrysalids***; ***Trouble with Lichen***; and ***The Midwich Cuckoos***.

Find out for yourself. Become part of the bizarre, yet realistic world of *MINDSLIP* today!

MOONSCAPE: We've known that the moon is dead since Apollo. But what if something lay dormant in the dust, waiting to be found?

In 2028, Astronaut Mark Noble is conducting a survey of a moon crater. An alien entity secretly grabs a ride back to Moonbase on Mark's buggy. Once in the habitat, it begins to infect the crew. They find themselves in a frightening, helter-skelter adventure with only two possible outcomes: losing or saving the Earth.

MOONSCAPE is the first in a series of hard science fiction stories featuring Mark Noble from the pen of Tony Harmsworth, a First Contact specialist who writes in the style of the old masters. If you like fast-paced adventure, fraught with the additional dangers found in space, then Tony's *MOONSCAPE* has been written especially for you.

The second book, *MOONSTRUCK*, is due for release towards the end of 2019.

THE VISITOR: Specialist astronaut Evelyn Slater encounters a small, badly damaged, ancient, alien artefact on the first ever space-junk elimination mission. Where was it from? Who sent it?

International governments impose a security clampdown. Evelyn leads a team of hand-picked scientists who make amazing discoveries within the alien device. Secrecy becomes impossible to maintain. When the news is finally released, she becomes embroiled in international politics, worldwide xenophobic hatred and violence.

This is book one of Tony Harmsworth's First Contact series of novels. If you like realistic near-future stories which compel you to imagine yourself as the protagonist, The Visitor is the book for you.

THE VISITOR might challenge your political and religious convictions – try to put them to one side and explore this story as an imaginative "WHAT IF?"

THE VISITOR is now an exciting audiobook narrated by Marni Penning.

Non-Fiction by Tony Harmsworth

LOCH NESS, NESSIE & ME: Almost everyone, at some point in their lives, has wondered if there was any truth in the stories of monsters in Loch Ness? ***LOCH NESS, NESSIE & ME*** answers all the questions you have ever wanted to ask about the loch and its legendary beast.

In these 400 pages with more than **200 pictures and illustrations**, you will find a geography of Loch Ness; a travel guide to the area; a biography of its mythical inhabitant; and an autobiography of the man who set up the Loch Ness Centre and was integral to commentating the cut and thrust of the research groups including the largest ever expedition — Operation Deepscan.

Explore the environmental and physical attributes of Loch Ness which make certain monster candidates impossible. Find detailed explanations of how pictures were faked and sonar charts, badly interpreted. Learn how Nessie has affected the people and businesses which exist in her wake, and suspend belief over the activities of the monstrous monks of Fort Augustus Abbey.

Tony Harmsworth's involvement at the Loch has lasted over forty years, having created increasingly sceptical exhibitions, dioramas and multi-media shows. This is the first comprehensive book to be penned by someone who lives overlooking the loch. It is essential for anyone interested in Loch Ness and the process of analysing cryptozoological evidence.

Now's the time to discover the truth about this mystery, once and for all. Get your copy today!

SCOTLAND'S BLOODY HISTORY: Ever been confused about Scotland's history – all the relationships between kings and queens, both Scottish and English? Why all the battles, massacres and disputes? *SCOTLAND'S BLOODY HISTORY* simplifies it all.

Discover the history of Scotland from prehistoric man to the current Scottish Nationalist government. Follow the time-line from the stone-age, through the bronze age and the iron age. Find out about the Picts, the Scots, the Vikings and the English. Learn about the election of Scotland's early kings and how Shakespeare maligned one of its finest monarchs.

In simple, chronological order, this book will show you how the animosity between England and Scotland grew into outright warfare including tales of Braveheart and wars of independence.

Tony Harmsworth has taken the bloodiest events of the last three thousand years and used those to clarify the sequence of events. Don't buy this book to learn the boring stuff, this book is packed with action from page one to the final three words which might haunt you over the next decade.

Robert the Bruce, Mary Queen of Scots, the Stewarts and Jacobites. It is all there. Explore *SCOTLAND'S BLOODY HISTORY* now!

Tony's Reader Club

Building a relationship with my readers is the very best thing about being a novelist. In these days of the internet and email, the opportunities to interact with you is unprecedented. I send occasional newsletters which include special offers and information on how the series are developing. You can keep in touch by signing up for my no-spam mailing list. It also gives you the opportunity to assist with future releases by becoming a VIP Beta Reader.

Sign up at my webpage: go to Harmsworth.net, find Moonscape and choose the free book option. I will send you a free copy of the first Mark Noble adventure – *MOONSCAPE*.

If you have questions, don't hesitate to write to me at Tony@Harmsworth.net.

INFORMATION/GLOSSARY

Honorifics:

Yol = male

Ya = female

Yo = hermaphrodite

Ye = budding creatures

Information:

AI – Artificial intelligence

Aconstik net – an electronic network used to destroy orbiting equipment

Afed = Federation currency A̶

Burner phone – a phone which is destroyed after each call so that it cannot be traced.

CEO – Chief Executive Officer, usually of a company

CPO – Chief Petty Officer

CPU – Central processing unit

Dimplert – game similar to snooker and pool

Doctor Strangelove – dark, spoof film about mutual assured destruction

Drindle – low alcohol spirit

Eskorav – FEU rapid-reaction Ship

Esponging – teaching by direct mind control

EUV – Extreme ultraviolet

Federation year = 0.96 x Earth year

FEU – Federation Enforcement Unit

Frame – galaxy-wide digital storage network

Galactic Standard – universal language used within the Federation. Worlds can keep their own languages, but Galactic Standard must be taught to every individual

Grangewood – Free America HQ, Ponte Vedra near Jacksonville

Hidome – FEU ship

Intranet – secure, restricted Internet

Medibot – a specialist robot trained in anatomy and surgery etc. to handle any medical emergency or just the maintaining of beings' health.

Medorin – giant Federation freighter

NGO – non-government organisations

Oridin – capital city of Arlucian, the Federation's capital planet

Orion spur archives are on Delarkon

QE – Quantum Entanglement

RBB is the author

Resolute desk – a gift from Queen Victoria, it is made from the timbers of HMS Resolute and has been used by many presidents of the United States including Jack Edward Spence and John Silvester Slimbridge.

Ronoi – Ambassador Moroforon's ship

Secradarve – sphere which accesses the Frame

Sib – the first thinking Sibernek robot

Shossball – throwing and catching game

Sibernek – large international chip manufacturer

Stamp bomb – an FEU bomb which directs its force downwards over a substantial area

SWAT – Special Weapons and Tactics force

Thorbon – inert gas which suppresses biological activity

UN – United Nations

Federation Characters:

Breganin, Yol Rummy Blin from Daragnen – the author

Bringol – a medibot

Churmbin, Ya Prold – councillor responsible for Earth. Her assistants are Yol Grath and Ye Disteen – they all died in the New York explosion.

Derodin, Yol – navigator on the Eskorav

Destrall, Yol Stirik – captain of the Medorin

Dimorathron, Ye Strighiton – president of the Federation

Distern, Yol Lorel – Federation ambassador to the USA

Esrov, Ya Henedy – Clueb who assists Ambassador Stograther

Gerady, Clueb who assists the president of the Federation

Gerandor, Yol Prestegon – head of finances for the Federation part of the Earth

Indafark, Yol Debert – replacement for Ya Prold Churmbin as councillor responsible for Earth's region

Isfinmaredal, Ya Torendal – head of health for the Federation part of the Earth

Lindron, Ya Lyl – diplomatic assistant died in the New York explosion

Merofort, Yol Slindo from Purrs – powder blue apes – Eloo & Viro, his wives. His children are Daro [Viro's] and Rindo [Eloo's]. Slindo is secretary and assistant to Ambassador Moroforon died in the New York explosion

Mistorn, Ya Heldy from Clueb – small black flying cherub-like individual with photographic memory. Heldy is assistant to Ambassador Moroforon died in the New York explosion

Moroforon, Ya Garincha Dela from Racutaan – tall, slender with lateral jaws. Husband Gerish and sister Telorcha. Died in the New York explosion

Ruud, Yol Ja – diplomatic assistant died in the New York explosion

Serin, Yol Ghal – Federation inspector died in the New York explosion

Sperafin, Ya Istil – captain of the Eskorav

Staz, Captain Yol Braden – captain of the Ronoi

Stograther, Yol Terend – replaced Hareen Trestogeen as ambassador to Earth – from Dihethror – they wear implants to speak as they don't normally use sound on their own world

Trestogeen, Dolodreen – Yol Hareen's niece

Trestogeen, Ambassador Yol Hareen – later ambassador – home Pestoch

Trestogeen, Ya Sloreen – one of Yol Hareen's many sisters

Unsela, Ya Zo – from Terotone – a species with some mind reading and control abilities. Large eight-fingered hands. Body phases in and out of existence.

Vestormoron, Ya Iridold – appointed to assist the USA with its border control

Wukkundi, Commander Ya Dustul – Federation Enforcement Unit

Yeronez, CPO Ya Kro – Ronoi's chief petty officer

Human Characters:

Ahmadi, Salman – Iranian president died in the New York explosion

Alexander, Donald – four-star general Air Force chief replacing General Burko

Andwell, Piers – head of the Secret Service

Armstrong, John – Free America militiaman

Ash, Madelaine – guest at General Braun's granddaughter's birthday party

Avraham, Daniel – president of Israel

Barton, Paul – head of research at Sibernek

Bedan, Jorg – chip designer at Sibernek – one of the 'gang of three'

Beech, Dick – retired four-star army general who leads the Free America militia

Bond, Mike & Helen – President Spence's sister & brother-in-law

Braun, Walter – four-star general – Army Chief – USA

Brown, Matthew – President Slimbridge's economics advisor

Burko, Buck – four-star general – Air Force Chief – USA

Channarong, Anurak – Thailand prime minister died in the New York explosion

Cheng, Lu – Deputy to Che Yang, the president of China

Cheung Da – Chinese president died in the New York explosion

Church, Maureen – UK prime minister who followed Ken Hood

Collins, Jim – assistant to Congressman Charles Mayne

Coran, Jed – chip designer at Sibernek – one of the 'gang of three'

Deirdre – President Slimbridge's secretary

Deloitte, Mark – Online retail guru

Delve, Winston – four-star army general

Derry, Gil – director of the FBI died in the New York explosion

Eden, Charles – White House media consultant, mixed race – white and Asian, forty, balding and short. Died in the New York explosion

Eriksen, Lars – deputy to the secretary general of the UN

Eze, Miriam – Nigerian president died in the New York explosion

Gambon, Drew – major in the Free America militia

Gordon, Douglas – four-star general – Army Chief – USA

Gorman, Malcolm – British defence minister

Grange, Melanie – New Zealand prime minister died in the New York explosion

Greave, Wilson – distribution magnate

Gregg, Brad – Free America militiaman

Hall, Colin – white, sixties, silver hair, once ambassador to the Court of St James

Harrison, Albert – manager for the World Food Programme

Henderson, Mike – colonel in the Free America militia

Hood, Ken – British prime minister died in the New York explosion

Horvat, Lara – secretary general of the UN succeeding Perfect Okafor.

Howell, Mrs Nancy – President Spence's secretary

Hwang Kang-woo – president of South Korea

Ivanov, Dimitri – Russian president died in the New York explosion

Janssen, Stefan – Netherlands prime minister died in the New York explosion

Kass, Burt – assistant to Charles Mayne

Kim, Lung-min – president of North Korea

Lemsford, Barbara – secretary to Charles Mayne

Lymington – mayor of Baltimore

MacNamara, David – stooge used by the White House to give a poor presentation of the benefits of the Federation during the USA referendum debate

Madison, person of unknown gender who writes speeches for President Slimbridge

Mahmood, Ahmed – Egyptian president died in the New York explosion

Mann, Alan – admiral – Navy chief – USA

Martinez, Helena – president of Mexico

Mayne, Charles – Democratic congressman

Mayne, Carol – Charles Mayne's wife

McBride, Harry – Democratic presidential candidate died in the New York explosion

Mendoza, David – director of the FBI

Meunier, Jeanne – French president died in the New York explosion

Mistoba, Juan – Bolivian president died in the New York explosion

Nixon, Robert – Bob – White House chief of staff for President Spence

Okafor, Perfect – secretary general of UN died in the New York explosion

Olov, Marat – new president of Russia

Pattison, Arnold – governor of California

Perkins – one-star army general.

Ramseur, Phillippe – new president of France

Rogers, Dr Melanie – Laboratory manager at Sibernek

Ross, Dr Gillian – AI specialist at Sibernek

Said, Mustafa – president of Iraq died in the New York explosion

Shay, Tanya – well-known USA political journalist

Sillic, Mara – Croatian president died in the New York explosion

Slimbridge, John Silvester – US vice president – became president after the death of President Spence in the New York explosion

Spence, Jack – US president died in the New York explosion

Solberg, Dick – Swedish prime minister died in the New York explosion

Stoddart, Caroline – British delegate to the UN

Stone, Peter – Head of the biggest search engine company

Swinford, Carol – chip designer at Sibernek – one of the 'gang of three'

Talbot, Brian – CEO of Sibernek

Thorpe, Rose – Free America supporter and funder

Tolberg, Anna – Swedish prime minister

Toscano, Maria – Italian president died in the New York explosion

Watson, Ian – commander of the ISS after the USA's isolation

West, Harry – gun shop owner

West, son of Harry – Free America militiaman

Wilson, Paula – Perfect Okafor's biographer/secretary

Wooller, Captain – officer in the Free America militia

Worth, Melinda – head of Social Security in USA

Yamata, Ishi – Japanese prime minister died in the New York explosion

Yang, Che – new president of China

Federation Planets:

Federation comprises 247,213 planets.

Capital planet Arlucian – seat of government – capital city Oridin

Blurel is a planetary system in which a gas giant has moons with vast quantities of emeralds lying on the beaches

Dabrune – strange world with pastel violet oceans and warm coloured vegetation. Dabrunians have tentacles and feelers. It is a transition world close to the galactic centre.

Daragnen – author's planet.

Delarkon – 18 light years from Earth – home to Earth's delegate at the Central Council, Ya Prold Churmbin

Ecisfiip – world with a swirling green atmosphere

Fotpiz – a world which majors on entertainment

Garrstend – world which had trouble joining the Federation two hundred years before the time of this book.

Hmethux – has twice Earth's gravity and exoskeletons are needed to move about

Kasettod – a prehistoric world, protected, but which can be safely visited

Operiom – planet which had a plague which took many years to eradicate

Opwispitt – 3rd planet in the Estrangel system and manufactures most of the Federation's microchips.

Pestoch – almost 95% water – Ambassador Hareen Trestogeen's home world

Rostaren empire was encompassed by the Federation about ten years prior to Earth's first contact. It was almost a thousand worlds and caused a minor recession in the rest of the Federation.

Terotone – a planet whose intelligent species has some mind reading and control abilities

Veroscando – a world which has large quantities of heavy metals like gold and platinum

Made in the USA
Las Vegas, NV
04 March 2023